Shadow Lane
And Other Tales of Dangerous Children

Collection IV

David Dean

Milwaukee Wisconsin USA

Other Books by David Dean

Novels
The Thirteenth Child
The Purple Robe
The German Informant (forthcoming)

Collections
Tomorrow's Dead
The Wisdom of Serpents
Her Terrible Beauty
Shadow Lane

All of David's titles are available
from Genius Book Publishing

Story Credits

All stories in the collection appeared in *Ellery Queen Mystery Magazine*, edited by Janet Hutchings, with the exception of "Reyna," which was published in *Crime Travel*, edited by Barb Goffman and published by Wildside Press LLC.

Shadow Lane
Copyright © 2023 David Dean

All rights reserved. No part of this book may be reproduced by any means without the written permission of the publisher, except for short passages used in critical reviews.

This is a work of fiction. Any resemblance to actual places, events, or persons living or dead is either coincidental or is used fictitiously.

Published by:
Genius Book Publishing
PO Box 250380
Milwaukee, Wisconsin 53225 USA
GeniusBookPublishing.com

ISBN: 978-1-958727-16-4

230916 Digest LH

Contents

Story Credits iii

Introduction vii

Sofee 1

The Devil You Know 30

The Vengeance of Kali 54

Mariel 80

Reyna 108

The Hangman 122

Neighbor 134

Ibrahim's Eyes 166

In a Dark Manner 193

Shadow Lane 226

Introduction

Child protagonists, such as those that are featured in each of these stories, are nothing new to literature. Charles Dickens, Robert Louis Stevenson, Mark Twain, and Harper Lee are just a few of the writers that have presented us with young heroes. Yet most are accompanied, for better or worse, by adults. Very few writers have chosen to craft tales in which children are allowed to pursue their adventures using their own intelligence, motives, and sense of justice in an unfettered way.

Not yet harnessed to the customs, morals, laws, and regulations that (in theory) govern adult behavior, children form their own opinions without regard for such matters. They can be lavish with their love and affection, and savage in their judgments and animosities. And in their black-and-white, good-and-bad thinking, compromise is unthinkable. William Golding provides a glimpse into such a world in his classic novel *Lord of the Flies* where scores of boys stranded on a deserted island build a terrifyingly brutal society free from the interference of grown-ups. Saki's (H. H. Munro) and Graham Greene's memorable characters give further examples of children gone awry. Munro's *The Penance* provides a vivid, and darkly humorous, accounting of "justice" meted out by children, while Greene's *The Basement Room* is a haunting and suspenseful depiction of the psychological effect on a child forced to be an unwilling accomplice to a crime.

The stories contained in *Shadow Lane and Other Tales of Dangerous Children* place the child, or children, firmly in the forefront. You will find in this collection that the young protagonists have mostly been allowed to follow their own instincts and do so with consequences both heroic and tragic. "Mariel" introduces a young girl who will not desist in the pursuit of the slayer of her fearsome dog; in "Neighbor" a teenage boy discovers he has made an enemy of a man who will apparently stop at nothing for revenge, while in the eponymous tale, "Shadow Lane," a girl and her two younger siblings are determined to clear their father as a suspect in their mother's murder.

How can I presume to know the interior lives of children—even imaginary ones? In my defense, I once was one, and have since raised several. The rest results from the subjective lens of memory coupled with an imagination that bends always toward justice, even if it is sometimes of the rough sort.

All of the stories in this collection, but one, were originally published in *Ellery Queen Mystery Magazine* and edited by the remarkable Janet Hutchings. "Reyna" first appeared in *Crime Travel*, published by Wildside Press LLC, and was edited by the talented Barb Goffman.

As for the publishers of this collection—Leya and Steven Booth—I have nothing but praise and gratitude. Their unstinting faith in my work, and their tireless pursuit of excellence in this, and every book, I've had the pleasure of working with them on, has been nothing short of extraordinary.

x

Sofee
(2018)
Third Place in EQMM Readers Awards

Blaise squatted in the damp patch of woods studying the candle he had lit. It was a long white taper and he had found a discarded soda bottle to act as a holder. Though there was little breeze, sometimes the flame guttered and smoked before once more flaring into brilliant life. Brushing a lock of his dark brown hair from one eye, the nine-year old boy waited as the late afternoon darkened toward evening.

Something white glided into the edge of his vision, and turning, he found Sophie had joined him. They often met here after school, though he could never be sure when, or if, she would show up.

Their first meeting had been seven months before, when his mother's latest boyfriend had chased him out of their two-bedroom rental house in a drunken rage. Escaping into the woods that bordered their neighborhood, Blaise had come to the spot he was at now. Weeping, he had not seen, or heard, the seven-year-old girl follow him; had only become aware of her presence when she touched his hand. Startled, he had snatched it back, turning his face from her. When she took his hand a second time, he did not object, and they sat in silence until his tears had ceased.

Blaise had seen Sophie often on their street, wandering without apparent purpose or company, been aware of her in the corridors of their school like a wan, ragged phantom.

Pale with smudges beneath her ice-blue eyes, Sophie squatted next to him now without a word, wrapping her thin arms around her knees. Blaise noticed that her lank, blonde hair was damp with droplets of moisture, her pastel-pink sweatshirt and tights stained and streaked. She coughed.

The two sat side by side watching the dancing flame in silence until Blaise asked, "You want to wear my jacket?"

Sophie shook her head and said in her small voice, "Where'd you get that?" meaning the candle.

"Father Gregory gave it to me at church," Blaise lied.

"Why?"

"It was for me helping out at Mass." Reaching inside his jacket, he removed another candle from an inside pocket and held it out to her. He had stolen both on his way out of the sacristy. "He said you could have one too. It's even been blessed."

This was the second time he had given Sophie a gift—the first had been a plastic tiara that he had stolen from the backpack of one of his classmates. All the girls had them because of some movie everyone had seen.

Taking the candle from him with a slight smile, Sophie looked the gift up and down as if she were unfamiliar with such things. "What do you do with them in church?"

"We blessed throats with them today."

"Why?"

Shrugging, Blaise explained, "Cause it's Saint Blaise's Day and he was like the best saint for blessing throats. It's supposed to be done with candles."

Sophie scrutinized Blaise for a moment, her brows knitting in confusion. "You're named Blaise," she observed.

Feeling his cheeks grow warm, Blaise answered, "Yeah, I know. I'm named after him. It's kinda stupid, I guess. That's why it was such a big deal for me to be the altar server."

Sophie coughed into her hand, then wiped it on the sequined unicorn on the front of her shirt. "Oh," she said.

"Let me show you," Blaise went on, blowing out his candle and removing it from the bottle. Taking Sophie's from her cool fingers he crossed the two like an X, holding each by its end. "It's like this," he explained, placing the scissor-like arrangement to either side of her throat. "Then you say the blessing."

"Okay," Sophie said, holding very still, looking into his face.

Blaise concentrated, trying hard to recall the words the priest had used. "We pray for the *intersection* of Saint Blaise, bishop and martyr, to bless Sophie's throat and… and…" Up close he could see several purplish bruises around her neck, almost hidden beneath her shirt, "… and keep her from being sick… … or anything bad… and… and just, you know, take care of her and don't let anything happen to her, in the name of the Father, the Son, and the Holy Spirit, amen."

Lowering the candles, he added, "That's not exactly right… but it's pretty close." He gave Sophie her candle back.

"Thanks," she whispered.

"You won't get a sore throat now, prob'ly."

He wished he could invite her to stay at his house, but he knew his mother would never agree, even though there was no boyfriend currently living with them—the last had left after noticing a portable electric heater sitting on the edge of the tub as he ran his bath, its coils faintly glowing—it had been late summer.

It bothered Blaise that Sophie would have to go home to whatever awaited her there. It was rumored that her parents cooked meth in the house. Blaise's mom had warned him to never go there, that it was dangerous and unhealthy.

He pointed at the smudges on her skin. "How'd you get those?"

Sophie's face tilted down and she said nothing in answer.

After a few moments, Blaise looked around and realized it had grown almost completely dark. "Well, I have to go home now."

Sophie nodded, then Blaise took her hand and led her out of the woods and onto their street. Releasing her, he watched as she walked away without a word, taking very small steps as she made her way home. She did not look back. Just before turning onto the cracked, uneven pavement of her walkway, Blaise saw her slide the candle up the sleeve of her sweatshirt. Then she was gone.

Hiding his own candle within his jacket, Blaise waited for a few moments longer, studying the tilting mailboxes, the sagging fences, the jumble of cars parked along their street, then set out for his own home.

༄

The following day Sophie did not appear at school. When she had not returned for two more, Blaise went to find her.

Still wearing his backpack from school, he halted on the sidewalk in front of her house. The tiny dwelling was not much different from his—the roof shingles were curling, and a chest-high chain-link fence enclosed the yard. Blaise noticed that black plastic garbage bags had been taped over the windows from inside. One casement was missing a window altogether and had been boarded over with a sheet of plywood. Swallowing hard, he pushed open a gate that hung by a single hinge and went through.

He did not see the blunt-faced, big-headed dog until it came charging around the corner of the house snarling and grunting, its pink and black mouth thrown wide, fangs bared. Without time to cry out, he back-pedaled, tripping over his own feet in his terror. Reaching the end of a long chain at the same moment, the slavering canine, with a surprised yelp of pain, was snatched back to land with a thud on its slat-ribbed side.

Scrambling back to his feet, Blaise saw the front door fly open and was confronted by a tall, shirtless man with ribs as prominent as his beast's, his long patchy hair swept back from his cadaverous face with what appeared to be a handful of petroleum jelly. "Who the hell are you?" he asked Blaise, "and what are you doing on my property?" He held up one hand to shield his eyes from the weak, wintry daylight.

There was no part of this man that was not decorated with a colorful swirl of intertwining images, everything from motorcycles to guns, naked women to fire-breathing dragons, gravestones to angels. Blaise didn't know where to look first to make sense of it.

"You better not run," the man warned, flipping a cigarette butt onto the wiry grass. He nodded at the dog, now back on all fours, barking and straining at the chain. "I cut him loose, you won't get ten feet from here."

Blaise shook the hair from his eyes and forced himself to speak. "I need to see Sophie. She hasn't been to school… and I brought her homework—her teacher told me to." This last part wasn't true, but Blaise thought it might add weight to his presence there.

A short blonde woman materialized out of the darkness of the foyer behind the man, peeking around him at their visitor. "Who is that kid?" she asked him in a deep, raspy voice that seemed too heavy for her slight frame. Like the man she sported a number of illustrations, as well as piercings through her sparse eyebrows, ears, nostrils, and lips.

"I'm Blaise. I go to school with Sophie."

"She's sick," the woman replied, still staying out of the light.

"Can I see her?"

"No, you can't see her," the man answered. "She can't do no homework for Christ's sake. Her mother just told you she was sick." The man's lips appeared to stick together making a smacking sound each time they parted. His pupils were so large that Blaise thought he looked like a marmoset at the zoo.

"Just leave it with us," he heard the woman croak.

Thinking hard, Blaise countered, "I'm supposed to have her sign that she got it. The principal says so."

"Oh bullshit," the man spat out, "get your scrawny ass down the road before I lose my patience. Nobody sent you here. You're just that little punk that she's been sneaking off to see, ain't you?" He took a step out onto the porch. "What do you two do out there in those woods, anyway? What—you think I don't know about that—I've got eyes everywhere." He came down two steps. "Have you kissed her, yet, Studly Doo-right—what else you done?"

When he stepped off onto the muddy lawn Blaise took off running, his short legs pumping, his lungs sucking oxygen.

Two houses away, he glanced back over his shoulder and saw that the man had not followed, heard his braying laughter.

Blaise stopped.

Licking his lips, he raised one small fist above his head, then allowed its middle finger to spring up. "Screw you, crank-head!" he sang out as loud as he was able.

His laughter breaking off in the middle, the man leapt toward the dog and its collar.

This time Blaise didn't stop running until he was home.

☙

On Friday Blaise approached the school office with almost as much trepidation as he had Sophie's house. Though familiar with the administration personnel, it was not a welcome relationship. In this place he had few secrets and even less leverage.

Mrs. Reeves snorted when she noticed Blaise standing at the counter, reminding him of water buffaloes, huge, skittish beasts he had seen on TV programs. Her great winged hairdo did not lessen this impression.

After rearranging a stack of mail to her satisfaction, she finally turned her attention to Blaise. "Did Mrs. Chamberlain send for you again?" she asked, referring to the principal of the school.

Blaise shook his head, his thick hair swinging across his eyes.

"Who did then?"

"Nobody..."

This gave her pause. "Then why are you here? Are you sick? You should go to the nurse if you're sick."

"I'm not sick—Sophie is." Blaise felt his voice catch at her name. He took a deep, shaky breath. "I was just wondering when she's coming back."

"I see," the water buffalo answered, drawing in her horns a little. "Well, Blaise, I'm not sure that's something I can tell you. You see, we're not allowed to give out medical information on students, providing that we even know it in the first place. I wish I…"

"Her name is Sophie…" Blaise repeated without hope.

"Sophie… *what*… sweetheart—I'd have to have her last name to even begin…"

"Caldwell…" the admissions secretary called out through the open door of her office. "He's talking about Sophie Caldwell. Her mother withdrew her from school two days ago. She's gone to live upstate with her natural father."

"Well… I guess that's that then," Mrs. Reeves said, regarding the top of Blaise's head for a moment before adding, "At least you know she's not sick anymore, Blaise."

"She wouldn't go…" Blaise spoke to his feet, but loud enough to be heard.

"I beg your pardon," Mrs. Reeves began.

"She wouldn't go without telling me," he went on, looking up now at Mrs. R and the admissions officer who had just stepped out to see if she could help. "Sophie would've said goodbye."

"I'm sorry, young man, but I've got the paperwork in my office," the admissions lady assured him. "It was all kind of sudden, so maybe she just didn't have time to say good—"

"That's bullshit," Blaise announced with firmness, his face set and tough, an intimation of what he might someday be.

"Blaise O'Connor!" the water buffalo snorted, her horns lowering once more. "You go right into Mrs. Chamberlain's office and tell her what you said! Do not turn your back on me, young man! If you go out that door…"

Never looking back, Blaise flew through the hallways and out the main entrance, mounting his second-hand bike on the fly and standing on the pedals. Though he knew he had no hope of escaping the school's retribution, he was content to postpone it. He needed time, though for what exactly, he didn't know.

Bumping and jolting his way along the root-filled trail, Blaise made his way through the band of woods that ran through his neighborhood. Here and there, candy wrappers and cigarette butts festooned the path along with crushed beer cans and condom wrappers. Skirting the local cemetery he spotted the flickering of candles, their flames dancing inside red jars that had been left on some of the gravestones.

Emerging onto his own street at the same spot he had last seen Sophie, he halted to ensure that no police cars, or other agents of adult authority, were present. Satisfied, he thrust a pedal downward and launched himself ahead, swerving around the garbage cans that had been placed out at the curb.

Jumping his wobbly steed up onto the sidewalk as he neared Sophie's house, he spotted a bicycle leaning against the cans out front. He slowed to a stop to examine it. It was a small pink bicycle with a bell on its loose handlebars, the grips sporting tattered, plastic ribbons—Sophie's bike.

Whatever plan that had been formulating in Blaise's mind evaporated like a waking dream.

Then the dog spotted him.

Bumping back out into the street, Blaise made a clumsy U-turn as the dog announced his presence. Barking ferociously and flinging itself against its restraints again and again, it seemed determined to either reach Blaise or kill itself in the effort.

Moments later, Blaise attained the shelter and concealment of the woods once more, the demon hound's ragged barking grown faint. Panting with exertion, he hung over his handlebars trying to understand what he had just seen. He couldn't imagine Sophie leaving her bicycle behind. Always a late starter, she had only recently shed her training wheels. If she really had been sent to be with her dad, why hadn't they sent the bike with her instead of throwing it out with the garbage?

He knew now that he had to get inside Sophie's house.

☙

Even with a week of in-school suspension as a result of his behavior on Friday, Blaise found time to prepare his plan. Each evening, after his mom had gone to bed, he eased himself out his bedroom window carrying whatever packaged meat he had succeeded in shoplifting from the supermarket on the way home. It wasn't hard. All he had to do was a find a woman alone who was about his mother's age and follow behind her, stopping along the way to look at the kinds of products kids liked, such as sugary breakfast cereals and packaged doughnuts.

To the store clerks it appeared he was simply lagging behind his mom, something they were accustomed to seeing. If anyone was actively monitoring the security cameras it would look much the same. The only dicey part was the actual snatching of the packaged meats and concealing them in almost the same motion, but Blaise was both practiced and bold. And his luck had held.

When he rolled up to Sophie's house, the dog was looking for him.

The first night Blaise had simply flung the meat within reach of the baying creature and quickly pedaled off again into the darkness. The second night, the dog ceased barking when he saw Blaise withdraw the package from his jacket, his eyes glittering in the moonlight, then fell upon the offering as if he had not eaten since the boy's previous visit. The third night he was simply waiting, staring into the direction he had seen Blaise arrive before, rising up to place his forepaws on the fence in anticipation of his nightly treat. Though he began to growl as Blaise dismounted the bike and drew closer, he didn't bark, scarfing the sliced bologna with a huffing noise, his terrible teeth mere inches from the boy's fingers.

Tonight, Blaise risked touching his round wrinkled head for the briefest of moments before giving him his meal. The dog allowed it with only the smallest of rumbles from somewhere deep within him. When he was done with the meat, he looked up to see that Blaise was still there and his whip-like tail sliced back and forth.

Blaise held his hand over the fence and waited. Lifting himself up onto his hind legs, the dog sniffed his benefactor's fingers, his flat snout dripping and cold. For several seconds the brute danced around the proffered hand, taking careful draughts beneath the pale light of the moon. Then, satisfied at last, he licked Blaise's palm.

Smiling at the animal, Blaise whispered, "Good boy, Tony." He didn't know why he named the dog Tony, except that it was the name he wished he had been given. "You're a good boy." Tony's tail whipped the cold air with increasing velocity as Blaise stroked the dog's scarred, concave skull.

From within the house there came the bass pulse of rock music being played at great volume. Stars of light leaked out from tears in the ad hoc window coverings and seams where the cheap tape had fallen away. Seeping through the rotten window frames was a poisonous stench, part hospital disinfectant, part paint remover, a pong both nauseating and euphoric. Within, Blaise heard a male voice laughing, then that laughter dissolve into ragged coughing.

Wrinkling his nose in distaste, Blaise noted that the tiny house was completely lit but for the far rear corner. This was the room that corresponded to his own bedroom at home; the room that he believed must be Sophie's. "Tomorrow, boy," he promised Tony with a final pat on his furrowed skull.

Glancing over his shoulder as he rode down the moonlit street, he could see the silhouette of the dog watching his departure with concern.

℘

When Blaise arrived the following night he found Tony busy digging, his broad forepaws tossing dirt this way and that, his chain stretched to its limit in the shadowy backyard. The house, like the other nights, pulsed with bass, glowing like a jack-o-lantern around its windows and through its cracks and seams, the evil smell a pall of dread.

Approaching the fence, Blaise whistled softly causing the dog's head to come up with a snort, his wet nose caked with earth, his eyes fierce with alarm. When he saw who it was he gave up his solitary occupation and trotted to the fence, eager for his nightly feeding.

Blaise fed him by the slice, taking time between each offering to stroke the dog's big head. When there were only a few pieces left, Blaise let the dog gobble up the rest in a single gulp, then petted him once more. "Good boy, Tony," he whispered, before circumnavigating the fenced yard to arrive at the opposite corner. The dog walked along with him as far as his tether would allow, following the boy's progress with interest.

Removing his jacket, Blaise laid it across the wire prongs that lined the top of the fence. Then, with one more glance at the dog, he heaved himself atop it and over, landing on his sneakered feet. Tony was silent, the chain straining, only the side-to-side motion of his hindquarters revealing his delight with Blaise's company.

Blaise breathed out, his exhalation a silvery mist. Removing the screwdriver from the back pocket of his jeans, he moved toward Sophie's darkened window, noticing that unlike the other windows in the house it was uncovered. As he neared, he could also see a cinderblock standing on end beneath the window and instantly grasped its significance—like him, Sophie liked to come and go as she pleased. It would make his task both faster and easier.

Stepping up onto it, he placed his face against the cold glass, attempting to peer in but could see little other than the suggestion of a dresser and a bed in the darkness. When he attempted to raise the sash it slid upwards with bumps and shudders and he returned the unnecessary screwdriver to his pocket. Framed in the now open window, the thudding music grew in volume and the man and woman's hoarse, drunken voices surfaced through the sound, their shouted words disjointed and incomprehensible. Like the time he had huffed gasoline, the chemical stench rocked Blaise's senses.

Stretching his pullover shirt to cover his mouth and nose, he slid over the sill and into the room. When nothing resulted from this, he whispered, "Sophie, are you in here?" At the same moment, he risked switching on the tiny LED light he had removed from his mom's keychain and swept it around the room. The brilliant beam revealed brief black and white glimpses of a rumpled, unmade bed, and a small dresser with a cracked mirror and a mismatched chair in front of it. A hairbrush lay on this last item, strands of fine blonde hair caught within its bristles. Coming to an open closet, Blaise saw several of Sophie's Goodwill outfits hanging haphazardly within, an equal number lying in a pile on the dusty floor beneath.

Blaise knew it was unlikely she would have left behind her clothes and her hairbrush, but not impossible—her dad may have promised to buy all new things for her.

But he did know what she would *not* have left behind.

Like his own room, he could see that Sophie had little furniture within which to hide anything, but he searched anyway, coming to the bed last. Dropping onto his belly he shone the light beneath. Besides the tiny dust balls set into motion by his activity, there was only a single object—a cardboard shoebox. Retrieving this, he placed the flashlight between his lips and removed the cover. When he saw what lay within, he stood absolutely still, feeling his heart slow, growing heavy as if it had been replaced with lead. His vision swam, then cleared once more. Slipping the lid back on with thick, clumsy fingers, he set the box down on Sophie's rumpled bed, feeling a righteous fury growing inside him.

Looking around the lonely room, Blaise spotted a broken crayon lying on the dresser. Picking it up, he stalked to the hall door and placed an ear against it.

Besides the music and the accusatory conversation that erupted from time to time there was nothing else. All the activity appeared concentrated at the front of the little house. Cracking the door open, he peered out into the hallway. Seeing that it was empty, he opened the door all the way into the room and began to write in large block letters on its grimy, white surface. The voices rose and fell, approached and withdrew. Blaise kept at it.

When he was done, he stepped back to view his handiwork. It read: WHERE IS SOFEE BASTERDS? Satisfied with his handiwork, he eased the door shut once more, leaving the couple to find his message when they next passed down the hall. Snatching up the shoe box, he climbed back out the window.

Seeing Blaise emerge, Tony began to make small leaps, his tongue dangling from his open mouth, his tail slashing back and forth. Ignoring him, the boy slipped back over the fence and retrieved his bike. Hurrying down the midnight street, he clasped the box under his arm, breathing through his mouth and pedaling hard.

Reaching the spot in the woods where he and Sophie had met, Blaise stopped and jumped off his bike, letting it fall to the ground with a crash. Sitting down hard on the damp earth, he opened the shoebox once again, illuminating the objects it contained with the penlight. There in the harsh glare of its beam lay a plastic tiara studded with fake jewels, next to that a white candle.

Blaise lowered his head and wept.

⁂

The voices were back, rising and falling in the near distance, anger, guilt, and fear informing their cadence and flow. Blaise struggled to open his eyes, fearful he had fallen asleep in Sophie's room and was about to be discovered. A third voice also entered into the fray, defensive and familiar—a woman's voice—Blaise's mom's voice. His eyelids fluttered like butterflies caught in a big fist, then flew open.

The voices were in his house—the couple was here—his mom was alone with them.

Leaping from his bed in his T-shirt and sweatpants, Blaise threw open his door and rushed toward the living room, sliding in on stockinged feet. His sudden appearance halted the argument mid-sentence, his mother's curly head swiveling to catch his arrival. The tattooed man and the pierced woman stood side by side looking at him.

"That's him," the man accused Blaise, pointing at him with a long finger capped by a dirty, broken nail. "He was snoopin' around our house just the other day and I had to chase him off. Now he broke in and wrote crap on our walls. That goddamn kid ain't right."

"Don't you call my son names," Blaise's short, feisty mother fired back. "I won't stand for that in my own home!" She turned to Blaise. "Is what they're sayin' true, Blaise? Did you go to their house last night?"

Staring back at the couple, Blaise noticed that both of them were missing teeth and patches of hair, like dogs with mange. "I was looking for Sophie," Blaise answered, his chin tucked in.

"She lives with her dad now," Sophie's mom croaked.

"That's bullshit."

"Blaise," his mother cautioned, "watch how you talk!"

"That's where she is," Sophie's mom insisted in her hoarse monotone. "She won't be comin' back here no more." She lit a cigarette with a shaky hand.

"At least you were man enough to admit it," the boyfriend said, his voice grown reasonable, calm. "I didn't want to have to call the police. A warning will do this time."

"Blaise, honey," his mom began, "what in the world am I gonna do with you…"

"Go ahead and call the police," Blaise challenged. "I dare ya."

"You little sonofabitch," the man fired back. "I oughta rip you a…"

"That's enough!" Blaise's mom shouted. "I want you two off my property right now! Who the hell do you people think you are comin' in here threatening me and my son?" Turning to the woman, she snapped, "And you! Who gave you permission to smoke in my house, you nasty skank?" Like a conjuring trick, a cell phone appeared in her pudgy hand. "I've got the police on speed dial. Whadda ya say we just discuss this whole thing with them right now?"

Sophie's mom retreated to the door, opening it and stepping out onto the porch, the cigarette still going. The man stood his ground, his sore-looking marmoset eyes sliding over Blaise and his mom. "You don't want me for an enemy," he warned them. "You don't want that."

"I do," Blaise snapped, taking a stance next to his mother and staring back, shoulders squared.

"You goin'… or not…?" Blaise's mom asked, her finger hovered over the phone keys.

The man backed out the door as Sophie's mom hurried to the jacked-up truck they had arrived in.

"I *know* what to do," the man assured Blaise. "*You* know that I do." He left the door standing open and sauntered down the walkway to the truck. A moment later, he fired up the engine and roared off down the street.

Blaise turned to his mom just in time to have her palm glance off his cheek. Stunned, all he could do was stare at her, seeing the tears standing in her eyes, her face gone pale. "Blaise," she cried, "what is the matter with you? Those people might've killed you last night! Can't you see that, honey?"

Dropping to her knees, she seized her son's shoulders and shook him. "You're all that I've got, Blaise!" She pulled him to her bosom, pleading, "Please, honey, don't do crazy things like that, okay? Not anymore. Promise me?"

Choking back his own tears, Blaise lied as he had done often enough before, "Okay, Ma, I won't. I promise."

☙

"So you think Sophie's mother and boyfriend have done something… *bad*… to her?"

Mister Allard, the school resource officer, sat across from Blaise. On his desk was a scale-model miniature of a police car that he drove a few inches with his finger. Even though he was wearing khaki slacks and a pull-over collared shirt instead of a uniform, and Blaise thought he had a likeable-enough face, he was still uncomfortable talking with a police officer.

He nodded a little in answer to his question.

"Why do you think that?"

"Her clothes are still there," Blaise said without explaining how he knew this.

Mister Allard studied him for a moment but didn't ask the obvious. "Well," he said after a bit, "maybe she didn't want them. Her dad might be buying her new ones. Have you thought of that?"

"She left other things behind too…"

"Like what?"

Shrugging, Blaise looked at the linoleum. "Just some stuff… stuff I gave her…"

Mister Allard put his feet up on his desk, pulled a nerf football from a drawer and tossed it to Blaise. "Was Sophie your girlfriend?" He had heard the story of Blaise's visit to the office from Mrs. Reeves.

Feeling his face growing warm, Blaise stared hard at the ball, unable to find words that adequately expressed his feelings about Sophie. He shrugged once more.

"So you don't think she would have left those things behind then?"

Blaise shook his head a little, his long bangs sweeping across one eye.

"Anything else you noticed?"

Chewing his bottom lip, Blaise thought this over, then added, "They make drugs there."

Mister Allard sat up a little. "Yeah? How do you know?"

"Everybody on our street knows."

Mister Allard appeared to give this some thought. "I'll tell you what I will do, Blaise. I'll call Sophie's dad and ask to speak with her. If she's there, you can relax and know that she's all right. If not… well… we'll cross that bridge if we get to it."

"Okay," Blaise agreed, sliding down from his chair. He tossed the ball back to the officer. "But she won't be there."

"In the meantime, Blaise, you stay away from Sophie's house, okay? I don't want you getting into any trouble."

"Okay," Blaise agreed once more.

☙

When Blaise returned to Sophie's that night, he noticed right away that the chemical miasma was no longer present, the music was lower in volume and, of more immediate concern, Tony was not waiting at the fence. His heart sank with fear that the wicked couple, angry that Tony had allowed Blaise's earlier trespass, had gotten rid of the dog.

Hurrying along the fence, Blaise made his way around to the backyard, his breath making frantic little puffs of mist. Risking all, he switched on the penlight and swept its beam across the churned lawn. Tony's post and chain were no longer where they had been.

The spot Blaise had last seen him digging appeared raked over, the furrows glinting with moist, tiny seeds.

Swinging the beam over to the side of the yard beneath Sophie's window, Blaise spotted Tony watching him, his dark eyes anxious, his lean body quivering. His chain had been reduced to only a few feet of movement. In the silence, Blaise could just hear the dog's soft, pitiful whine. He switched off the light.

"Tony," he whispered, hurrying on now to the far side of the fencing and closer to the dog. "It's okay, boy. I'm here. I brought your dinner."

The dog remained immobile but for his shivering. Blaise noticed a hind leg kept a few inches off the ground. A couple of fresh cuts glistened on the dog's blunt head.

Pulling his jacket off, Blaise prepared to throw it on the fence and clamber over… then froze.

Behind the darkened glass of Sophie's window he saw a movement. Not so much a movement as a slight change in the density of the darkness behind the glass.

Tony continued to whine.

It's a trap, Blaise thought with a catch of his breath. They were trying to lure him into the yard, perhaps into the house itself.

Taking several steps back, he felt his anger growing even faster than his fear—the hellish couple had not only taken his only friend but had hurt Tony and were using him as bait.

In defiance, Blaise launched the meat over the fence to Tony, and with a heart smoldering like bellowed coals, turned and fled the scene.

"The number on the transfer form was out of service," Mr. Allard explained to Blaise, "so I went by and spoke with Sophie's mom about it. She said it was the only number she had for Mr. Caldwell."

Man and boy stood at the edge of the playground, the other children throwing them curious glances from time to time as they played in the late-winter sun.

"Told you," Blaise replied. Then was struck by a thought. "You went inside?"

Nodding, Mr. Allard replied, "Yeah, she invited me in."

"So you searched the house?"

"Well, no, we just talked for a few minutes in the living room. I didn't have any cause to search the house—it's not that easy, kiddo. Besides, everything seemed okay—I mean the place is a dump, I'll grant you that, but otherwise I didn't see anything wrong there."

"No bad smells?"

"No, Blaise… nothing besides air freshener, which judging from the housekeeping, they needed."

Blaise considered how foolish he had been to write that message on Sophie's door. He had accomplished nothing but to give the couple a warning of their vulnerabilities, allow them time to plan.

"I've tried to find a telephone number for Mr. Caldwell through four-one-one and the internet but so far I'm coming up with nothing." Mr. Allard could see the disappointment and frustration in Blaise's stubborn posture, his closed, tough face.

"Blaise… I would do more if I could. It's just that there are rules you have to go by as a police officer. It's not like on TV and in the movies. For me to search someone's house I have to have PC…"

Blaise glanced up.

"… probable cause," Mister Allard clarified. "In other words, we can't just search people's homes based on someone's impression of them, or neighborhood gossip. It doesn't work that way."

"What *do* you need then?"

"We need evidence of a crime… or at least something more than mere suspicion. Sometimes we get those through a reliable informant… not a child though." Mr. Allard winked at Blaise, "the courts don't normally go along with the use of underage informants. Sorry, kiddo."

Blaise shrugged his unwilling acceptance of adult rules.

"What other ways?" he asked after a while.

It was Mr. Allard's turn to shrug. "Well… I guess… emergency circumstances sometimes get you there. Like if a police officer hears someone screaming inside a house, he doesn't have to get a search warrant, he can just go right in because he has reason to believe someone's life may be in danger."

"Oh…"

"But that doesn't do us much good here."

The school bell began to ring signifying the end of recess.

"I hafta go," Blaise said in a tired voice.

Mr. Allard watched as the boy shuffled toward the school, the other children shouting and screaming around him—a sad, solitary figure with a defiant set to his shoulders. When he reached the entrance, Blaise turned and looked back at him for a moment, his face solemn and thoughtful. Then, with an unsmiling wave, he disappeared inside.

☙

Blaise caught the alarm almost as soon as it began to sound. Having set his clock for four a.m., he was betting that even zombies like Sophie's mom and boyfriend would be asleep by now.

He swung out of bed already clothed in his darkest hoodie and black jeans. Slipping his feet into sneakers, he listened for any sign that his mother had been disturbed. There was nothing. Easing open the window, he climbed out, being careful to close it behind him.

Having left his bike leaning against the back of the house, he walked it out to the street carrying the two items he had hidden behind some shrubs earlier. Though it was awkward, he managed to navigate his way without dropping anything or making any noise.

As he had hoped, Sophie's house was completely dark, not a single light showing, no music blaring. Just to be certain, he remained in the shadows of the cars parked along the street to watch.

When the chill of the early morning began to seep through his light clothing, he set the items down, then propped his bike against a car, its front wheel pointing toward home in readiness. Satisfied, he picked up the things he had brought and made his way along the fence to the backyard, stopping there to study the house once more.

Tony was still staked beneath Sophie's window. Blaise could make out that the dog was staring at him from across the yard. Not daring to call out, even in a whisper, he raised a hand in salute. Tony wagged his tail in recognition. Blaise could feel his heart thumping.

Throwing his jacket on top of the fence, Blaise transferred first one item, then the next, to the other side. Taking a steadying breath, he followed, being as careful as he could not to rattle the chain link fencing. Once on the other side, he picked up the first article, a slate paver he had removed from someone's garden, and worked it upright into the soft raked soil near where the grass seeds lay awaiting warmer weather. That done, he picked up the next thing he had brought and walked toward the house, doing his best to stay out of the window's line of sight.

Reaching the back wall, he opened the container of gasoline and began to pour its contents along the base of the house. Stolen from a neighbor's shed, the plastic canister held only two gallons so Blaise had to be frugal. It took him five sweat-soaked minutes to circumnavigate the small residence and arrive back to where Tony awaited him. He glanced at the dark window, then continued quickly beneath it.

Stopping only long enough to pat the dog's head reassuringly for a few moments, Blaise continued the trail of gasoline from the base of the house in a straight line to the patch where Tony liked to dig. Using the last of it, he doused the area as best he could. When he was done, he left the empty container where it was and hurried back to Tony.

Managing to get the dog's collar off despite cold, clumsy fingers and Tony's face licking, Blaise dared whisper, "Good boy, Tony… you're a good boy."

Once released, the happy dog began to run back and forth in the yard favoring the injured hind leg. Delighted with freedom, he began to bark. With a scared glance at the window, Blaise ran to the gate, and disregarding the possible noise, threw it open, the screech of its unoiled hinge sounding like a scream in the silence.

With his heart pounding now, he ran back to the nearest wall, fumbling to retrieve a wooden match from the box he carried. A light came on in the kitchen, its door mere feet from where he squatted. Tony continued to dash this way and that, barking with abandon now.

His fingers so numb that he could not separate one match from the next, Blaise withdrew a handful and raked the entire bunch against the striker. Two caught, but the rest erupted in a chain reaction that scorched his fingers causing him to drop them all onto the damp grass.

One managed to fall onto the gas trail he had drawn and Blaise heard a small whoosh of sound, like a drawn breath. Then, suddenly, a blue flame went racing in two directions at once. When one reached the trail leading away from the house there began a third. Blaise turned for the open gate. Flying through, he was dimly aware of the kitchen door being snatched open behind him.

Reaching the street with Tony at his heels, he heard the roar of the third flame arriving at its goal, saw the sidewalk and the cars parked along it appear in an orange glow, as if the sun had risen in a single moment. Beneath this concussive breath of sound, a man's voice cried out, "Fire, goddamnit, fire! We're on fire!"

Boy and dog raced for home.

༄

A short while later, Blaise stumbled out of his bedroom making a show of rubbing his eyes to ask his mom, "What's going on? What are all those sirens for?"

"There's a fire," she answered in a worried voice, peeking out the living room window at the glimmering red-tinted sky in the distance. "I'm not sure, but I think it might be Sophie's house."

Blaise managed what he thought to be a surprised expression. "Really…? Can I go see?"

"*No*, you may not. There's too much going on right now. You could get run over in the dark."

Blaise could see the glow through the open blinds, could feel the thumping of his heart still.

"It was prob'ly all those drugs they cook," he offered.

Mom turned and studied him for a moment, as if she were thinking of something altogether different. "Blaise…" she began, then stopped with a slight shake of her head.

"Can I go later then…?" he asked.

"If the fire trucks are gone, you can ride by on your way to school," she said, then added, "Did you hear a dog barking earlier? It sounded so close to the house."

Turning away, Blaise answered, "No, Ma, I didn't hear anything." He had yet to think up a convincing explanation for the dog in their backyard.

&

Riding as slowly as he could, Blaise approached the house in the new light of day, the air heavy with the stench of charred materials, black, wispy tendrils of smoke still rising above the trees.

Coming abreast of the residence, Blaise locked up his brakes and came to a complete halt. His mouth opened.

The house still stood.

Though scorched all along its cinderblock foundations, only one corner of the roof had caught and burned; the opening blackened and sodden with water. A single firetruck remained on the scene, its crew joking and laughing as they cast a light spray of water on various points that appeared to smolder.

It was the scene of the fire in the backyard that was drawing the most attention. There, Blaise could see several uniformed police officers, as well as three men in plain clothes who he suspected were cops as well. They were all staring at the patch of burned earth and the makeshift marker that Blaise had left there.

One of the men shuffled closer to the marker, being careful to avoid the charred soil. Blaise recognized Mr. Allard.

At the same moment, he became aware of muffled voices and cries, a steady litany of barely audible cursing. Turning toward the source, he saw the tattooed man seated in the back of a patrol car, his long, ugly face pressed against the smeared glass of the rear window, the veins in his forehead and throat distended with rage. He was looking right at Blaise, his mouth working and spewing invectives. In another police car parked just behind the first, Sophie's mom sat weeping and screeching. Blaise could see that they both had their hands cuffed behind their backs.

Just as he had done on their first meeting, Blaise raised his middle finger in salute, but this time added a grim smile for good measure.

When he looked away again, he saw that Mr. Allard was looking right at him. Lowering his arm, Blaise stood on his pedals and made for school.

☙

Mr. Allard caught up to him just after lunch, summoning him to his office. Unlike before, he didn't ask Blaise to sit. Blaise studied the items on Mr. Allard's desk.

"How do you spell your first name?" Mr. Allard asked.

Confused, Blaise looked up, then down again. "B-l-a-i-s-e," he said.

"Oh," the officer said after a moment, "I thought it might be B-l-a-z-e… as in fire—like the one at Sophie's house this morning."

Blaise refrained from looking back up, chewing instead on his lower lip.

"Arson is an easy crime to determine," Mr. Allard continued. "There's always a fire, and that fire usually involves an accelerant… such as gasoline. The accelerant is pretty easy to locate and identify, as well." Allard stopped speaking to let this sink in.

Blaise nodded a little, as if a lesson in arson investigation was the reason for his having been summoned.

"However… it can be extremely difficult to prove who, exactly, committed arson. Often the evidence needed is destroyed in the fire… such as fingerprints on the accelerant container. Another problem can be a lack of eyewitnesses, or at least witnesses that have any credibility—such as Sophie's mom and her boyfriend."

This time Blaise did look up. Mr. Allard locked eyes with him before going on.

"They must have dismantled their little meth lab before my visit the other day—possibly they were worried that someone was on to them. I'm not sure who. Like the brainiacs they are, they had stored all that nasty stuff in a closet instead of getting rid of it. The firemen discovered it when they were checking the house for occupants. They had seen such things before and called us—the police, I mean. If the fire had reached the interior, Blaise, that entire building would probably have blown up and contaminated the whole neighborhood."

Blaise tried to look away but couldn't.

"It's lucky for… well, it's just lucky that didn't happen, don't you think?"

"Yeah… yes, sir," the boy answered softly.

"There's something else, though, Blaise…" Mr. Allard continued. "Whoever set the fire also left a marker, almost like a gravestone, on the burned spot in the backyard. That person had written in white chalk, 'Sofee is here,' with an arrow drawn beneath pointing downward." He almost smiled. "I guess whoever did that figured us dumb cops needed some help. So, since I hadn't been able to reach her dad or determine her whereabouts, I asked for a cadaver dog to be brought to the scene."

"What's that?" Blaise asked, his voice grown smaller still.

"It's a dog trained to find buried, or hidden, bodies."

"Did he?"

"Yeah… he did."

"It was Sophie?"

"Yeah," Mr. Allard nodded, "we're pretty sure it's her."

"Oh…" Blaise said after a while.

"Sophie's mom and her boyfriend are going to prison for the rest of their lives, I promise you that."

Blaise felt a tear escape and slide down one cheek. "Good…" he whispered, "… I'm glad."

༄

The night after Sophie's funeral, Blaise returned to the cemetery accompanied by Tony. No marker had been provided for her small grave other than a metal plaque that lay flush with the earth. On it was engraved her name and the dates of her birth and death.

Having left his bike in the woods that bordered the graveyard, Blaise set the shoebox down and opened it. Removing the plastic tiara, he laid it atop the name plate, then retrieved the two candles remaining inside. Using empty soda bottles as holders, he lit each one, then set them side by side on the grave.

Satisfied with the arrangement, Blaise threw his arm around Tony's neck, and boy and dog kept watch over Sophie through the long, dark night.

The Devil You Know
(2013)

The city bus ground to a halt at sixteen-year-old Sonia York's stop and with a hiss of compressed air knelt and flung open its doors. She stepped out clutching her books to her chest and feeling as if she had a bullseye painted on her forehead. Scanning the street she began to walk rapidly towards home, allowing her tumult of dark wavy hair to shield her face. She had never ducked out of school before, and it seemed certain to her that the police must have been alerted by now. Her pace increased, her boot heels clacking loudly on the sidewalk.

Sonia risked a glance up but saw no curtains parted, no anxious busybodies at their phones, no police cruisers edging along the curb. There was only a block left to traverse and she was beginning to perspire.

She wasn't normally a rule-breaker, she didn't look for trouble. Out of respect for her grandmother, who had been her guardian for the last four years, she tried to do well at school and behave. But Rachel's announcement that they would move, yet again, just as she was making some real friends at school, just as a few boys were showing interest, had ignited a small hot flame in her. Sonia scuffed a boot on the cracked, weedy pavement, then tried on a lopsided go-to-hell smile for anyone that might be looking, but no one was.

Or maybe, her thoughts went on as the smile slipped away, it was the result of her period which had just started, or the sudden onset of glorious spring after a long dreary winter of low, leaden skies, and damp clinging winds. She just didn't know. But, when she had seen the fire exit propped open as the janitor mopped up some stinking mess a fellow student had barfed up, she had simply walked out the beckoning door. The custodian had never once turned around and everyone else had simply rushed by trying to make class before the bell. Sonia smiled at her own nerve. She imagined that it was the kind of thing her mother would've done when she was a girl.

Rachel's car was not in the driveway of their small rented house, and that was a relief. Not that she had expected her to be home, as her grandmother worked long days in a box store warehouse and was often not home till after dark. She pushed the key at the lock, missing twice before at last driving it home. Her lips felt chapped from nervous licking.

The door gave way and she dodged quickly inside to shut it behind her, her books still clasped to her chest, her breathing loud in the darkened foyer.

Tossing her keys onto the wobbly side table, Sonia shuffled down the hall towards her bedroom at the back of the house. To her eye, everything seemed to have an unfamiliar look. The coats hanging on the wall pegs, the clock notching moments of time from the kitchen, all things she took for granted each day, seemed imbued with expectancy. It was as if her arrival had caught them all by surprise, had interrupted something.

Allowing her books to cascade onto the mattress and box spring that served as her bed, Sonia collapsed next to them with a sigh. Her room was dim, as Rachel was fiercely private and insisted that Sonia keep all curtains drawn and blinds shuttered. She pulled off her boots and let them fall, thump, thump, to the cheaply carpeted floor, and lay back once more. After a long silent moment she stretched her slender frame until she heard the tiny cracks and pops of her bones and joints. Then, feeling at last safe, she began to laugh softly at her success. The silent rancher, devoid of all but the most essential furniture, echoed the sound with an ugly chuckle.

She knew the school would eventually discover her absence and contact her grandmother, but she knew also that Rachel, as her grandmother insisted upon being called, would confirm that she was home and let it go at that. Sonia would have to accept whatever punishment the school meted out as Rachel would not intervene. She allowed Sonia her own life but offered little else. She didn't attend parent-teacher conferences and had no interest in meeting any of Sonia's few friends. As it was Rachel's custom to move every few years, it made little difference. She believed that her granddaughter had to stand on her own… that all women should.

Though Sonia had been in the care of her grandmother for some time, they did not share a true closeness. Sonia was well aware that she lacked that certain 'something' Rachel carried before her like a sword and buckler, that aloneness that marked her whole bearing and stamped her weary features with a smoldering defiance. When Sonia thought of Rachel, she pictured her as one of the Valkyries of Norse myths, or the Amazon warriors of Greek legend—a giantess.

Sonia knew she was not like that and feared it meant that she would follow in her mother's weak and faltering footsteps. In the dozens of photos she had managed to hold on to, her mother featured in nearly all—a tall, lithe, blonde, smiling and laughing. In a few, Sonia also appeared in the arms of her pretty mother, or standing next to her, at what must have been outings to county fairs, the beach, visits to long-forgotten parks in a dozen different towns. But just as often she was sitting on the knee of yet another of her mother's boyfriends, none of whom remained for long; one of whom must have been her father. Sonia was seldom smiling in these pictures.

Rolling to the edge of her mattress, she pulled the photo album from the plastic milk crate that served as her night table. Throwing it open she perused the pictures for perhaps the thousandth time: several of the men were dark-haired and neatly built, but beyond that she could discern no further clues as to her progenitor. She didn't remember the name of a single one. Closing the book, she sighed once more. The headiness of a stolen holiday threatened to escape her.

Jumping up, Sonia walked toward the kitchen, turning on lights as she went. She thought she might go around opening the blinds, as well. It was too beautiful a day to be in darkness. But what if Rachel came home early? She would be angry.

Sonia opened the fridge and selected an individually packaged fruit juice carton and skewered it with the drinking straw provided. Sucking on it, she pulled her cell phone from the front pocket of her favorite jeans, which she knew exhibited her derrière perfectly (after trying on some thirteen pairs), then remembered that everyone she knew to call was still in school. Her battery display was showing a single bar, which even as she watched, winked out with a frightened peep. Setting the useless phone on the counter next to her juice, she opened the blinds at the window above the sink.

A grey car flashed into the view framed by the window and ran head-on into a telephone pole halfway down the block. Simultaneous with the crunch of metal she heard a loud, but muffled, pop, then the lights went out in the house.

Stunned, Sonia stood staring, as two youngish-looking men tumbled out both driver and passenger doors and onto the verge where they crawled around in the weeds for several moments like senseless insects before finding their feet. Then, stiffly at first, they began to stumble off in the same direction, becoming more agile and quick with each step. Before they left the small frame of Sonia's view they were sprinting like gazelles into the nearby wood line that separated her neighborhood from a series of strip malls and busy avenues to the east.

Sirens wailing, several police cars arrived within moments of the crash, the officers flinging open their doors and dashing off after the fleeing men, the entire spectacle unfolding within mere moments, its climax continuing beyond her limited view. She became aware that her mouth was open and shut it.

Sonia wished desperately that there was someone with whom she could call and share this amazing event. With a squeak of excitement, she thought of her computer perched on her small, scarred desk, and her Facebook page, and hurried back to her room. After stabbing at the mouse several times with a lacquered nail, it dawned on her that there was no power. As she did not have an iPad or laptop, she was no longer in communication with the greater world, or even her very small one. Slamming her fist down, she shouted, "Shit!"

This communication was answered by the ringing of the doorbell.

Sonia gasped, placing a hand over her mouth, and thought, *Did I lock the door behind me?*

It couldn't be the men who fled the police, her thoughts ran on, *they wouldn't dare come back here.*

The small house resounded with the blows on the front door and Sonia bolted to her feet. *Maybe they would,* it occurred to her. *Maybe she was about to be taken as a hostage by two desperate outlaws.* This sounded vaguely exciting until she remembered that she was playing hooky from school and that it was more likely a truant officer… whatever that was exactly.

Approaching the front door with her heart hammering, she could make out an unmistakably male silhouette through the frosted glass, one with broad shoulders and a head of short curly hair. Reaching for the door handle as if in a dream, she saw it turn of its own volition. With a squeak, she fell back as the door slid open a few inches and a young man peeked around the corner at her.

"I'm sorry, miss," he stuttered. "I didn't think that anyone was at home."

All Sonia could think to say was, "Who are you?"

He blushed, and Sonia suddenly realized that her intruder was very cute.

Pushing the door open a few more inches so that she could see his badge and uniform, he explained, "The police, miss… I'm with the police. I'm sorry I frightened you."

"Come in," she managed.

Her policeman, as Sonia immediately began to think of him, was clad in a short leather jacket over his standard-issue blue shirt. He had curly, black hair, and arched eyebrows. The kind of eyebrows women tortured themselves over, she thought, even as a smile began to play on her lips. His eyes were large and dark, mesmerizing, while his skin was pale and smooth. But there was nothing feminine about him, she thought, the smile growing to idiotic proportions as he stepped into the foyer: his shoulders *were* broad and he was slim and wiry looking, very athletic, she'd bet. She felt her cheeks growing warm and raised a hand to one without thinking.

"We're checking the houses in the neighborhood," he went on. "You may have seen that there was a police pursuit of some burglars that ended in a crash right up the street. They got away… for now, but we're just ensuring that they didn't rip off any other houses in the neighborhood, and that everything is okay."

Sonia watched his mouth.

"Everything *is* okay…?" he repeated.

Sonia managed to stop smiling and respond, "Sure, everything is… okay."

He smiled back at her, then took a step toward the door.

"Except, we don't have any power and my phone isn't charged so I'm a little nervous…"

Her policeman raised his marvelous eyebrows.

"… about what to do if they come back… we don't have a house phone…" she blathered on, trying to hold him back from leaving.

He looked hard at her face. "Are you home sick from school?"

Sonia felt her cheeks grow warmer still. "Yes…" she blurted, "I think I might have the flu." Even to her it sounded untrue.

"I see…" He seemed unconvinced, as well. "And you're by yourself?"

She nodded once more.

"Do you want to use my phone to call your mom and have her come home?" He fished his cell phone from a holder on his gun belt.

"No…" Sonia blurted. "I… she can't afford to miss any work, and besides she's my grandma… I live with my grandma… my mom's gone."

"Oh… okay." The handsome officer looked troubled. "Well, then, you just make sure and lock up after me, alright?"

Sonia nodded dutifully, feeling as if she were falling into his eyes.

"Okay," he said, while backing out the front door.

"What's your name?" she asked, hating herself.

His smile returned, "Jason… Patrolman Jason Gorgasali."

"*Gor-ga-sali,*" she repeated. "That's different… what kind of name is that?"

"Georgian," he answered.

"Oh… I see. But you don't have a Southern accent."

"No," he agreed. "I meant as in the Republic of Georgia. I'm first generation, but I was born and raised right here in this town. Probably went to your high school." The smile crept back. "I played hooky sometimes too."

Sonia had never felt quite so stupid.

Jason glanced over his shoulder, then back at her. "Well… gotta go," he said. "It was nice meeting you…?"

"Sonia… Sonia York." He had asked her name… sort of… and Sonia felt like dancing around the room.

"Pretty name," he added as he closed the door and stepped off the porch to return to his patrol car.

Sonia stood without moving for several moments, then squealed loudly and threw up her hands and began to do a jig.

The door opened and her policeman peered in. She froze in humiliation.

"Lock the door," he commanded, then shut it once more.

Sonia, her face aflame, turned the deadbolt and fled for her room once more.

☙

The only thing worse than having met Officer Jason Gorgasali and then having him go away, was not being able to tell anyone about him. Sonia wondered if he had one of those playing cards with his picture on it that some police departments handed out. Would it be too slutty of her to call headquarters and ask for one, she wondered. Then she remembered her phone was dead.

Leaping to her feet, Sonia huffed and stamped in frustration, scanning the room for something that might provide some entertainment. Her few celebrity and teen fashion magazines had been read cover to cover several times over and lay strewn about the floor.

With a sigh for the stolen day that was running through her fingers, she drifted from her narrow room and down the hall. Arriving at Rachel's closed door, she halted before it. She was forbidden to enter this room without her grandmother's permission and presence.

Like a sleepwalker she watched her hand rise and come to rest on the doorknob. After a few moments, she tested it.

It was locked. Her hand fell away to her side. Even as she turned to walk the short distance to the living room and their single television, she remembered again that there was no power. It was this final thing that galvanized her.

Striding purposefully to her room, Sonia retrieved a metal nail file and returned to the door. *We are two grown women,* she thought, *we share a house together and I am not allowed to keep a locked room, so why should she? Besides, she may have some magazines herself; some issues of Cosmo or People.* Even as she thought this, Sonia knew it to be ridiculous—Rachel cared nothing for fashion, as evidenced by her careless, sloppy appearance, and as for celebrities, she found them contemptible. "Media whores," she had once called them when Sonia had been gushing over some teen heartthrob or other.

Sonia had seen Rachel jimmy a door years before, not long after her mother abandoned her. Having locked her grandmother out of the house during a tantrum over something she no longer remembered, Rachel, with the use of a pocketknife, had regained entry in mere moments. Sonia had watched the whole thing from a window. She had been sure that she would receive a beating, but Rachel, her face scarlet with rage and her breathing ragged, had held back. Even as she raised a clawed raw hand to strike, Sonia had seen something in her grandmother's eyes—evidence of a terrible and implacable willpower.

The blow never fell. Yet, when Sonia recalled the moment, she almost wished that it had, as she had lived in fearful dread of it since. There was an awful power in that upraised hand.

Even so, enough was enough, Sonia fumed; it was ridiculous to be afraid of one's own grandmother. The door popped open with a soft metallic click and swung inward on its ill-fitting hinges.

Rachel's room was scarcely larger than Sonia's own and, not surprisingly, just as shrouded. The faint light that seeped through the blinds gave the room a grey, smoky quality. Rachel's mattress lay beneath a window, narrow and unmade, a twisted nest of unclean sheets. A backpack rested against the wall next to it. Like Sonia, she utilized a stack of plastic milk crates as storage for clothes and a few books. Their bright oranges and blues were the only colors in the room. With equal parts curiosity and dread, Sonia pushed forward into the room.

A closet stood a little open just beyond the bed, darkness spilling from it. If possible, her grandmother's room was even sparser than her own, she thought. There weren't even posters tacked to the wall. As her vision adjusted and the room grew in detail, she could see, with a pang of unexpected sadness, that neither were there any photos of Sonia or her mother hung upon the walls or propped up on the crates.

Her grandmother's room was more barren than a monk's, Sonia imagined, though she had never seen a monk's cell or even been to a church. Rachel was vehement on that subject—religion was merely a means of enslavement, a yoke especially devised to control women and minorities, she had assured Sonia one summer Sunday as they had passed a church on their way to the park. Sonia had made the mistake of commenting favorably on the sounds of the choir within.

Why does she live like this? Sonia asked herself as the awful barrenness bore down on her. Then, *Why do we live like this?*

As she stood in the perpetual twilight of her grandmother's purgatory, the enforced shabbiness of their lives unfolded before her with a clarity that she had never before experienced.

Striding to the beckoning closet, she threw the door open wide. The interior was a miniature of the bedroom minus the single mattress, dusty and dim, empty and without purpose. A few wadded pieces of paper lay balled up in one filthy corner. She spun back to the room at large, then marched over to the rat's nest of a bed.

Dropping to her knees she slid her hands beneath the mattress and ran them the length of one side then the other. She found nothing, no hidden letters explaining their ceaseless migrations, no evidence of any past whatsoever.

Sonia saw that her palms had come away grimy from their task, and she made a face. Reluctantly, she wiped them on her precious jeans and turned to the rucksack. One outer pocket revealed a small toiletry kit with toothbrush and paste, a comb, a brush, a pair of tweezers and other items for the motel traveler. Another contained a well-stocked first-aid kit that even provided a curved stitching needle and filament. The words, U.S. Army, had nearly faded from it altogether.

Sonia regarded this piece of intelligence in bewilderment. Had her grandmother been an army nurse, or medic of some kind? If so, why had she never mentioned it? Yet none of this explained their gypsy lives together.

The top flap of the ruck was thrown back revealing some clothes, and with pursed lips she cautiously, and carefully, removed nondescript work shirts and worn, faded jeans, until she reached the bottom. With the removal of the last pair of rolled khaki pants the sack collapsed in on itself, empty and useless.

Why did Rachel keep a packed rucksack next to her bed? Sonia wondered. *Was she planning to run off somewhere?* A bolt of fear and sadness at such a prospect shot through her, making the pit of her stomach feel light and empty. It had never occurred to her that she might actually harbor some affection for Rachel, that she might love her a little.

She began to reverse the unpacking of the clothes, returning the faded, worn garments in the order that she had removed them. When she was satisfied with her work, she went to throw the top flap over the rucksack, only just remembering that it had been opened, not closed, when she had entered the room. As she handled it once more, it became apparent to Sonia that the flap itself contained a compartment, as she could feel a thickness within it, a flat *something* that slid between her thumb and fingers as she kneaded the material.

Examining the underside, Sonia found a pocket closed with Velcro, a small tab, like a green tongue, protruding from it. Without further thought she pulled it down and was rewarded with a gaping mouth lined with plastic for waterproofing. Peering within, she could discern something flat, and this she removed, drawing it out with her highly polished nails. She found that she was in possession of an envelope.

Carrying it over to the window, she unshuttered the blinds a little in order to study this secret find. The rays of sunlight sliced the gloom into bars of gold dancing with motes of suspended dust. In the improved lighting Sonia could see that there was nothing written on the outside of the envelope, only that it was smudged and yellowish. She examined the flap next. It was not sealed. Drawing a deep breath, she exhaled slowly, feeling a growing sensation that she was about to cross some great divide, some chasm from which she might not be able to return.

Squatting, Sonia dumped the contents onto the bare floorboards, yellowed newspaper clippings drifting like ancient leaves into a heap before her, then began to separate and examine them. One thing was apparent to her right away, Rachel had not been much of an archivist. Most of the clippings had had the dates and the newspapers' names removed by her careless scissoring. Rachel was just as careless when she cut her own hair, Sonia thought. In all their years together, Sonia could not remember Rachel ever wearing her hair in anything but a ragged, over-long pageboy.

Most of the articles featured grainy photographs of the same small house. In fact, Sonia thought, leaning close to the page for detail, not unlike the succession of run-down bungalows that she and Rachel had occupied for the past several years. The tiny white house of the photograph had a sagging chain-link fence around it, and what appeared to be a discarded bike missing a front wheel in the weedy front yard.

Next to this was another photo of apparently the same residence, but this time it was in flames. The caption for this article proclaimed in large, bold print, "**Shootout in Compton,**" while beneath it in smaller type, "Five Dead—Hostages Rescued."

Another clipping contained almost identical pictures but ran the headline, "**People's Liberation Army Wiped Out.**" This article also ran photos of the five killed, self-styled "freedom fighters" and urban guerillas according to their manifestos. The two men, one black, one white, bore the unmistakable stamp of the seventies upon them. The black man, identified as Field Marshal Dante, sported a small afro, while the white guy had shoulder length hair and a large mustache. Both wore jaunty, military style berets. They looked very young, as did the three women in the remaining pictures.

Like their male counterparts two sported berets and stared defiantly into the lens of the camera, their faces plain and unadorned. The third woman's features were nearly concealed beneath a floppy, Viet Nam style forage hat, the upper half of her face cast in shadow, the lower revealing a strong, cleft chin. In all the pictures automatic weapons were brandished, while behind each of the posed subjects hung a red flag with the image of a black rampant lion as a dramatic backdrop.

Sonia was shocked by the raw hatred on the faces of the women. The men's expressions, while determined, seemed less genuine to her, as if they were not fully resolved to the fiery end that they must have known they were courting.

A third article, this one with a banner still attached announcing that it was the San Francisco Chronicle and bearing a date of February 7th, 1975, carried an article on a daring daylight bank robbery and the taking of hostages. Two men, one a guard, the other a customer, a young soldier, had been shot to death by the armed gang, a gang identifying themselves as the People's Liberation Army. They were already being sought by the FBI for numerous bombings of government buildings and the assassination of a city councilman. Apparently the bank shooting began when an alarm was set off.

Photos taken by the security cameras revealed the revolutionaries arrayed throughout the bank, their automatic rifles leveled at the cowering tellers and customers within. The three women appeared to be controlling the captives and gathering the money, while the black man remained closest to the front entrance, and presumably, escape. Sonia did not see the white guy with the Pancho Villa mustache and presumed he was outside in the getaway car that witnesses reported idling near the door.

Several customers within the bank reported the abduction of a young woman with a small child—a girl. It was unclear as to whether they had been in the company of the murdered soldier. The police were making inquiries at the nearby Presidio to determine if the soldier was married and a father. His name was withheld pending notification of relatives.

Sonia felt a surge of sympathy for this unknown young man. What kind of people gun down unarmed customers in a bank? Then she remembered the first articles, which were obviously the later ones, and their mention of the hostages saved. Was it the young woman and her little girl?

The papers were so brittle that Sonia had to be very careful handling them; the edges crumbled with the slightest pressure. She strained to read the faded print. It appeared that it *was* the same woman and child from the bank, and that they were, indeed, the wife and daughter of the slain serviceman identified as PFC Travis Wheeler. The woman's name was Sherry, her daughter Melissa. The young mother had seized her chance and fled the burning building with her daughter in her arms, even as she risked both their lives in the withering crossfire of the exchange. The police spokesman commended her courage. Halfway down the page was a flash photo of a rangy-looking woman, filthy with grime and soot. She was holding a terrified little girl who stared into the camera with an open, screaming mouth.

Sonia felt the room grow dark and light in turns and then begin to spin ever so slowly. She recognized her mother from the few childhood photos of her she possessed. The woman holding her was Rachel—in spite of the years, she was unmistakable.

She looked again at the names… Sherry… Melissa… Wheeler.

But her grandmother's name was Rachel… her mother's name Sandi; their last name York… as for Wheeler… she had never heard of it before.

Even so, there was no mistaking her mother and grandmother in the photo, they *were* the mother and child kidnapped from the bank, Sonia was certain of it—this was the reason for Rachel keeping the clippings.

Suddenly, the sad, bumpy itinerary of her own life began to make sense; she began to understand the trauma that had spawned her family's tumultuous history, and to feel the first beginnings of sympathy for her restless, lost mother; her distant, angry grandmother.

The People's Liberation Army had *liberated* her family of their chance for happiness and normalcy with their psychotic self-importance, their tired propaganda, their bullets. She hated them even though she knew that they were all dead. *They* were the reason her mother had run away, leaving her with her grandmother, and the reason that even now she was grubbing about in the grime and dirt of Rachel's bedroom for some explanation of who she might really be. It was all so unfair… something that happened so long ago, long before she was even born.

Sonia felt her eyes grow hot and her vision begin to blur. Raking a sleeve across them, it came away streaked with moisture. "Bastards," she whispered to the empty room. She began to gather the brittle yellow clippings and slide them back into the envelope. The sun of the brilliant day had dropped low in the sky and the light was fading fast. She hurried to complete her task and return the articles to Rachel's backpack.

As she sealed the Velcro of the waterproof compartment a husky, familiar voice asked, "You finished now?"

Sonia squealed and leapt to her feet. Rachel stood in the doorframe, her long arms hanging loosely at her sides, her grey complexion stained with a crimson tint, like a sunset hidden behind a storm cloud. Her bleak eyes swept the room from one end to the next.

"What?" Sonia answered back, confused and suddenly frightened.

Her grandmother nodded curtly at the rucksack that Sonia stood over. "Interesting reading, isn't it?"

"What?" Sonia repeated, unable to think of a good enough lie.

Rachel walked a few steps into the room. "Don't even try it on, little girl, I've been standing here for five minutes. Well…?"

"Yes," she managed, at last. "It was interesting… you could have told me, Rachel. I should have been told." Sonia felt her courage returning after the shock of discovery. "I've been affected by what happened to you and mom too, you know. Maybe if I had known, it would have helped me understand Mom better… you, too…maybe."

Rachel stared at her granddaughter, her expression blank. "You think so?" she said at last, then added, "Maybe… but, you're not supposed to be in here, are you?"

Sonia stood firm and said nothing. It was time she was treated like an adult.

Rachel smirked, then turning to the door, said, "Come on, let's make some coffee. We'll talk."

She walked ahead as Sonia followed to the kitchen.

"Sit," she commanded and began to measure coffee into a filter. Sonia did as she was bid and waited. She wasn't normally allowed to drink coffee after breakfast, as Rachel insisted she was too high strung as she was. This exception seemed to mark the beginning of a new era between her grandmother and her, an evolving of their relationship into that of two mature women.

"Cream and sugar, as usual?" Rachel inquired.

"Yes, please… but I would prefer honey."

"Oh would you? Well, we're out… sugar will have to do." Turning away, she ladled a few spoonfuls from a glass jar into a mug. "So you read everything… all the articles?"

Sonia squirmed at the reminder of her trespass. "Yes, I did. At first, I couldn't understand why you had cut out those articles and kept them, but when I saw the picture at the shootout of the little girl and her mom… then I knew… I understood."

Plopping the brimming mug onto the bare tabletop, Rachel spilled some over the sides, then retrieving her own cup from the counter, pulled back a chair, and joined Sonia. "Understood *what*… exactly?"

"Well," Sonia resumed, taking a sip of the hot liquid, "you're the young woman in the bank… the little girl is mom." She blew on the coffee before taking another sip. She felt confused by Rachel's questioning—this didn't *feel* like family bonding. "The only thing is… why do we move so much… wasn't that whole gang killed by the police… are you afraid that there might be others that are looking for revenge?" This last had just occurred to Sonia and seemed a very exciting prospect, lending a certain style and romance to their Spartan lives.

Rachel's smirk grew wider.

"Is that it?" Sonia insisted through lips that felt numb and swollen. "Are we being hunted?" Rachel's face wavered like a desert mirage and Sonia shook her head to clear her vision. She took another sip of the sweetened liquid.

"No," Rachel answered. "They're all dead… including your grandmother, actually. I killed *her* myself."

Sonia felt as if she was being pelted with words as soft and palpable as marshmallows, their meanings arriving seconds later like echoes. "What…?" she heard herself ask.

"When the house caught fire, there was only one of my comrades still alive. We were surrounded, and the ammo and bomb making materials were bound to go up soon… the fight was over, but General Dante didn't accept that. He was never as smart as he wanted us to think. He said, 'We've still got the woman and the little girl! We can bargain our way out.'"

"That's when it hit me, when I knew what had to be done—I shot him right between the eyes before he could utter another stupid word."

Sonia felt herself slumping forward in her chair but struggled to keep her eyes open, and not succumb to this waking nightmare.

"Then I shot your grandmother. She was roughly the same weight and build as me… blonde hair, too. You saw the photos the papers had," she addressed Rachel. "That hat I wore the day we took the pictures hid my face. Field Marshal Dante was furious over how it turned out; he wanted all our faces in the public's eye." Rachel winked at Sonia. "He knew then we'd remain loyal… after all, what choice would we have had? But, by then, the papers already had them, and we were on the move again. We always wore disguises whenever we were outside the safehouse," she explained.

Rachel continued as if she were relating her day at work, "I knew her husband was dead… we had killed him during the hold-up—a fascist in uniform… who could resist?"

Sonia heard the woman's chuckle as the low rumble of distant thunder. "Wait…" she mumbled. "Not my grandma…?"

"Try to keep up—I shot her in the head, then changed clothes with her, stuck my rifle into her hands. Your mother was just a little girl, not much more than four, I think. She was screaming bloody murder, though I could hardly hear her over the gunfire.

"I waved a piece of torn sheeting out the front window a few times, snatched up the girl and ran out. I half expected to be cut down, but I think seeing your mom in my arms made all the difference. It gave those pigs that moment of hesitation I needed. I sprinted across the lawn and into the middle of them like a jack rabbit. The cops all seem stunned. They thought Sherry and Melissa were already dead.

"Suddenly, they were all cheering and hugging me and your mom, congratulating themselves like the smug pigs they were. None of them knew what the real Sherry Wheeler looked like… my gamble had paid off. I had counted on the bank photos of her being too blurry and she had already told me that she didn't have any family, and that her husband's lived in Texas.

"Even so," the woman went on, "I got us out of there as soon as the Feds finished questioning me about who all was inside the house—the bodies were burned beyond recognition, you know. I identified everyone in the photos, of course, and they were thrilled, I can tell you… gloating over their victory. Then, your mother and me hit the road and kept going. I couldn't afford for the Wheeler family to show up; that would have blown everything—it turned out they were cashed-up, and every few years their private detectives came nosing around our latest digs, so we kept moving. Plus, I could never be sure when the FBI might get wise to what I had done. They had no reason to question my identification, but who knows when something might change that. These things never really die, you know… just the people in them."

Sonia felt drool running down her chin as she tried hard to frame words with her useless lips, "You… killed… my… grandma?"

The older woman looked at her with contempt. "You were never very bright… you took after your mother that way… nosy, but stupid."

"Mom…?" Sonia felt herself swaying dangerously in the chair.

"Yeah, somewhere along the way, she started to remember. You'd think somebody with an appetite for drugs and booze like your mom would've had trouble remembering her own name. When she showed up with you to live here, it all started to come back to her. I couldn't allow that… I won't be blackmailed by a reactionary little druggie. I've got enough to worry about without that.

"Melissa… *Sandi*… made good cover; no one suspects a mother of being a danger to the state... or a grandmom, for that matter" she added. "But that's all over now. The moment I saw you reading those articles I knew that you'd start talking, bringing attention to us—you should've stuck with the devil you know."

Sonia wanted to jump up from her chair and run but found she could only sit there and cry. "I… won't… tell…" she blubbered, snot running down from her nose. "I… promise…"

"No, you won't," Rachel agreed, her thin, corded arm lashing out across the table, the long-awaited blow crashing into Sonia's jaw. Falling backwards onto the kitchen floor, her arms and legs flopping like a ragdoll's, Sonia's head struck the floor and bounced with the impact. As she lost consciousness, she saw Rachel's face grow large in her fading vision, the cleft in her chin a canyon.

A sensation of weightlessness followed, and Sonia could feel herself rising towards the heavens, floating towards something warm and welcoming. After a while this motion faded, and she rested without light or thought in a silent, dark void. She was content with this and wished nothing more than to remain in this state forever, but the acrid smell of smoke was irritating and she heard someone whine in discomfort. After that, a pounding began in her tender skull… a pulse that grew louder and louder, seeming to emanate from the spot where her head had struck the floor. The whining grew louder still.

It was only when she sensed the sun, impossibly rising within the walls of her home, that she began to fidget, the light stabbing through her eyelids, the heat searing her skin as if she were laid out on a skillet. Her false grandmother was really a witch, her returning consciousness warned her; a witch that even now was cooking her alive!

The pounding stopped, and Sonia was relieved, though the silence was flawed and imperfect, containing within it a small, distant voice repeating something over and over. The light, however, was something that was unrelenting and inescapable, as the sun swung so low over her that she now began to smell the unmistakable odor of singeing hair. The tears that slid down her cheeks sizzled like bacon fat.

The voice grew louder and she realized that it was her own name that was being repeated. She wanted to turn her head toward the sound and answer, but it was no use, her lips had melted together. A thunderclap of colliding planets followed by a great, hot breath swept over her, and Sonia felt herself seized and roughly handled—an angel, it seemed, had arrived with the beating of great wings. Soundlessly now, he carried her forth into the cold, dark places that lie between the stars and laid her down.

At last, in the twilight of flames and constellations, shouts and sirens, she managed to open her eyes to painful slits. Leaning over her, his face sooty with smoke was Jason Gorgasali… her policeman—he had come back to check on her.

☙

The newspapers trumpeted that the last surviving member of the People's Liberation Army had vanished once more, leaving behind yet another burning house. This time, however, she had been robbed of her victim, as well as her anonymity—thanks to Sonia the police knew exactly who they were looking for now… who Rachel really was.

Sonia's ordeal made her a seven-day wonder, which she thoroughly enjoyed, happy to be interviewed by any and all media "whores." A nurse in the hospital had shown her a few make-up tricks that her magazines had neglected, creating just the right touch of sexy maturity without too much sluttiness; her singed hair hidden beneath an expensive donated wig. Jason had saved her from the worst effects of the fire, and she was well pleased with both her policeman and her appearance on the television screen.

When Sonia referred to Officer Gorgasali during an interview as, "her angel," the press made the most of it, and he was nearly forced into hiding; mostly from his fellow officers, who henceforth called him 'Angel' Gorgasali, or the 'Archangel Jason'.

His community policing photocards, meanwhile, became very hot trading items amongst the girls at Sonia's high school.

As for the Wheelers of Texas, having already lost three family members to the People's Liberation Army, they quickly reached out to claim the last of their battered tribe. So, even though it broke her heart a little to say goodbye to her policeman, Sonia was at last headed for her own true home.

The Vengeance of Kali
(2010)

Kieran sat on his bike at the edge of the wood line and watched the new people transfer their furnishings from the van to the house. He had been doing so for half an hour and not been noticed. This did not surprise him. It was in his character, in fact integral to his lifestyle, that he not be seen or remarked upon. Living in his older brother's long shadow, and dwelling at the lower tier of his neighborhood age group, had taught him the art of near invisibility. Even his red hair failed to excite notice so practiced was he at living in the shadows.

The people that he watched from astride his travel-worn, stripped-down bike, however, could expect nothing but scrutiny. The strange reddish hue of their dark skins and the exotic chirping of their outlandish language guaranteed it in Kieran's neighborhood, and he found it difficult to take his eyes from them. In fact, he could not have been more astounded at their manifestation had they been deposited there by a spacecraft, as opposed to the Mercedes SUVs and other expensive cars they had arrived in just minutes before the moving van.

Moments before their remarkable landfall, Kieran had been coursing along on the narrow bike paths that bisected the few remaining woods of his neighborhood, traveling unseen from one street to the next as he studied the backyards of the houses within a several block radius. It was from these observations that he would sometimes schedule return visits under cover of darkness to select and remove objects that he coveted—his bike being an example, hence its stripped-down conversion to avoid identification.

Other thefts lacked such obvious value, but spoke to some inarticulate need, such as his surprising and difficult appropriation of a backyard soccer net. The actual removal of this unwieldy object had been extremely difficult and fraught with the peril of discovery, yet he had accomplished it in the dark of night and somehow dragged it the two blocks to his home, without arousing victim or witness.

Kieran had failed to secure a soccer ball and did not know how the game was played, so the net was left to collect only leaves and debris—a monument, perhaps, to something he could not yet articulate. But on this long Sunday afternoon in early autumn no such thoughts occupied his mind, for he had chanced upon the interlopers just as they began their disembarkation.

With cries like strange birds they greeted one another as their caravan of luxury cars disgorged them onto the newly asphalted drive. The men were all quite thin and small, sporting thick mustaches; their clothing running the gamut from somber suits to brightly colored and zippered warm-up togs. The women were even more arresting, with long, black hair that glistened in the warm sun, while their bodies, draped in diaphanous materials dyed outlandish pinks, purples, and greens, glimmered beneath the soft September sky.

Each person stopped short of embracing the other, instead bringing their hands together as if in prayer and bowing their heads. Once this had been accomplished, it appeared they were free to hug, shake hands, or kiss. Kieran watched entranced, thinking of the dragonflies he sometimes observed over the lichen-covered bird bath in his backyard, hovering and circling close to one another before dipping in the humid air and racing off.

Suddenly, one of the older men pointed in Kieran's direction and without any unnecessary movement the boy withdrew several feet further into the shadows beneath the canopy of dry, coloring leaves. It was as if he had simply faded out of the picture—a minute, but possibly distracting figure in the landscape removed with cloth and turpentine.

Yet, he needn't have feared, for the gaze of all rose to the treetops and halted, the faces of the men closing in consternation, even as the women's pursed in distaste and their large, dark eyes widened in horror. There followed a silence that was, in turn, replaced by a hubbub in the foreign tongue of the newcomers. Several more of them began pointing at the treetops and exclaiming in alarmed tones.

Kieran had no need of a translator to divine the cause of their clamor; he was very familiar with the troop of undertakers that roosted opposite their home site and even now, flapped their ragged wings, and sidled uneasily on their branches under the hostile gaze of their new neighbors. Kieran could not recall a time when they had not dwelt there.

As a small boy, he could remember lying on his back in the adjoining field, now long given over to lots for upscale homes, and watching the great birds rustle and flap amongst the branches of the largest trees. On such mornings, clear and dappled with sun, they emerged from the boreal gloom as dark, shapeless shadows perched singly or in discontented, peevish clusters, shoving and pecking their fellow tribe members.

As the sun's rays began to pierce their enclave, wings would be thrown wide to absorb the warmth and dry the damp from their feathers; these violent, inconsiderate actions often dislodging a fellow vulture and forcing him to flap wildly as he sought to obtain the next available perch and avoid crashing into the earth.

After a period of this, at what always appeared to be an agreed upon moment, though Kieran had never heard the carrion eaters utter a single sound, first one, followed by another, then another, would fall forth from the limbs they had been so unwilling to leave but moments before, extending their great wings and beginning their ungainly climb into the morning sky.

At these moments, Kieran thought there could not be a clumsier, less flightworthy bird, yet once they clambered onto that first thermal that would raise them into the heavens on its column of superheated air, they attained the grace of angels. They were no longer the clown princes of the bird world, but an aerial ballet troupe wheeling across the heavens in follow-the-leader acrobatics. It seemed to Kieran that they could glide for hours without a single beat of the wing; without the least effort at staying aloft. It was only when they returned to their roost each evening that he was reminded again of what ugly creatures they really were, with their ragged cloaks of dusty wings and their raw, blood-dipped heads— their forlornly comic return heralded by the crash of branches, the scattering of leaves, and a rain of sad, dirty feathers.

Kieran watched as the oldest of the men, the same one who had first noticed the turkey vultures, hurried over to the rear door of one of the Mercedes. Even from across the street, Kieran could recognize the body language of deference, as the man opened the door, made the obligatory prayer gesture, and offered his arm to whomever was within.

Kieran stared in wonder as the tiny figure, wrapped in gold and white cloth, was deposited onto the smooth, oily-looking drive and the entire company went silent, brought their hands together as one, and bowed. The ancient woman, who appeared no larger than a child to the eleven-year-old Kieran, returned the gesture, then spoke, her tiny voice carried away in the light breeze. The newcomers smiled without showing their teeth, their heads still inclined. Kieran sensed that they were uncomfortable about something—that they were awaiting the old woman's judgment.

The older gentleman who stood clutching her elbow (Kieran couldn't help but think of him as a gentleman due to his age and the fact that he wore a suit) spoke then and pointed again to the trees, though this time it appeared to be for the old woman's benefit. His gesture was at once reluctant and dismissive. Then he and the rest returned once more to silence.

Kieran had already guessed that this ancient woman was the matriarch of the clan and the rest her children, grandchildren, and possibly great-grandchildren. He awaited her judgment with interest—if she disapproved of the vultures, would they simply return to their cars and leave?

She stood within the circle of her large family and tilted her head up to the treetops, shading her eyes with one hand as she steadied herself on her eldest son's arm with the other. Her hair, uncovered like the younger women, fell down her back as a great rope of grey, bound by gold ribbon.

All eyes, including Kieran's, followed her gaze to settle on the unattractive birds who shuffled uneasily on their whitened limbs. Several, unable to bear the tension, launched themselves in muffled explosions of discomfort to cant this way and that between the trees as they sought the anonymity of the deeper forest. The old woman continued to study them.

Kieran's interest returned to her and there he found her eldest regarding her with concern and it dawned on the boy that this gentleman had failed to notice the birds prior to this day, and that this failure might have actual consequences—it was up to the old lady to pronounce judgment.

Suddenly, she brought her palms together and held them aloft as if greeting the vultures and smiled. She spoke several words to the assembled family and laughed, then pointed to the great birds and spoke once more. Now everyone joined in on the joke, if that was what it was, and Kieran could see, even at a distance, relief flood the features of the eldest son; the lines of consternation smoothed out by hilarity and laughter. This time when they smiled, the entire family revealed brilliant teeth and uplifted faces. They would stay—and with that, the eldest escorted her toward the front door and possession, as the older sons and all the women followed in train, leaving only the younger men to resume the job of unpacking the van.

As the front door closed behind the procession, Kieran was left in the shadow of the wood, his curiosity replaced by a strange longing that felt like a fragile egg within his bony chest. After several long moments of watching for something more, he lifted the bike between his legs and walked it in a semi-circle to face the way he had come, then, like his feathered companions, flew back into the woods, bumping and careening his way into the darkness.

☙

When Kieran arrived home, his mother stood at the kitchen sink, still wrapped in her housecoat, coffee in one hand and first cigarette of the day in the other, watching the sun sink beneath the western tree line. Her mass of springy red hair floated about her shoulders in an unkempt nimbus highlighted by the fading light from the window. Though she looked tired and dark beneath the eyes, her smile upon seeing him lent her face a plucky, good-natured attractiveness that might be confused with beauty in a younger woman. Kieran sometimes thought that she was beautiful.

She reached out expertly with the hand holding her smoke, and without so much as spilling her ash, caught his long hair as he tried to slip by, leant over and planted a large, moist kiss on his reluctant cheek. In that brief instance, Kieran was treated to an unwanted glimpse of her ample cleavage, barely contained within the loose confines of her gown.

As she straightened up and caught the focus of his gaze, she popped the cigarette back into her mouth and ran a finger down his short, straight nose, "Boys," she said wistfully and smiled, "always grow up to be men and men can never get over…" She caught herself and stopped. "All girls have these, you know," she arched an eyebrow at her son. "They're no big deal, believe me."

"I *know* that," Kieran mumbled as he tried to slip by once more.

"I've got to work tonight… you *know* that too, right," she continued, turning to place her cup in the sink, still smiling.

"Yessss," he hissed in exasperation and embarrassment. Kieran's mom worked rotating twelve hour shifts as a dispatcher at the police department, and he was well acquainted with her schedule—it was while she was on night shifts that he was able to do *his* best work. Kevin, his sixteen-year-old brother, was supposed to watch him during these absences, but seldom did and made little pretense of the matter.

"You smell like pine," his mom said. "Where've you been?"

"Nowhere," he replied automatically. "Did you know some foreigners are moving in on Palomino Drive?"

"Foreigners," she repeated. "What makes you say that?"

"You should see them," he answered.

"There are some barbeque ribs from that take-out you like in the fridge," she pronounced, suddenly aware of the time, then stubbed out her smoke and sailed down the short corridor to the bathroom and her shower. "I also got that coleslaw and potato salad you love so much," she called back to him as she was closing the door, "and don't wait for your brother… believe it or not, he called and said he'd be a little late."

"Good," Kieran replied, snatching up the remote for the television and the video game controls. "I hope he never comes home."

"What's that?" His mother's muffled voice reached him through the door and over the running water.

"Nothing," Kieran assured her. "I said okay."

༄

It was after one o'clock in the morning when Kevin finally arrived home for his babysitting duties. He awoke Kieran as he stumbled down the hallway searching for his own bedroom, then retraced his steps back to his little brother's room and threw open the door. There was a pause as he hung silhouetted in the door frame, reeking of booze and an odd, chemical odor. Kieran tried to pretend he was still asleep by keeping his breathing steady; then Kevin switched the light on.

"Just wanted to make sure the boogeyman hadn't gotten you," he slurred, his long, dark hair framing a lean face that might someday be handsome. His heavy-lidded blue eyes slid over Kieran with amusement.

"There's no such thing," Kieran responded, the barbeque sauce now sour in his stomach.

"You better hope not, as much time as Mom leaves you alone."

"*You're* supposed to watch me," Kieran blazed in defense of their mother and much against his own best judgment.

"Is that right?" Kevin asked. "Wouldn't that be the job of your daddy?"

Kieran winced at the allusion to their separate fathers.

"At least I look in on you to make sure you're alive," Kevin added. "Who else would?"

This was a question that Kieran had no wish to dwell on and it hurt his pride that he was, in fact, very glad to see his brother. "Get out of my room, Kevin, I'm trying to sleep," was all he could think to say.

Kevin chuckled and said, "You're such a tool," then turned and began to close the door. Halfway out he stopped and asked, "Hey, what's for supper, little man?"

"Ribs," Kieran answered, turning his face to the wall. "They're in the fridge."

Kevin closed the door without turning off the light.

"Turn off the light," Kieran shouted.

"Switch is on the wall," his brother shouted back as he made his uncertain way to the kitchen.

☙

The following morning being a Monday, Kieran dressed himself in his usual jeans and T-shirt, ate a bowl of cereal glazed with sugar and drowned in milk, and left for school in plenty of time to allow for wandering. His mother, having arrived home just after six a.m., was sleeping the first of what she called her "shifts," having long ago discovered what most night workers learn—it is almost impossible to sleep through the daylight hours; no matter how dark the room, or silent the house—it's just unnatural to the human condition. Therefore, she would arise sometime in the early afternoon, putter about the house, then return to her bed once more as the day wore on. Kieran made his own way on such mornings.

As to Kevin, he remained behind the closed door of his bedroom, snoring, snorting, and occasionally shouting incoherently while in the grips of his alcohol and drug-induced unconsciousness. The hour of the day was of no matter to him and that it was a school day of even less import. Kieran knew that his brother would deal with the consequences of his actions in his typical laconic, amused fashion, because, he had, as he confided to Kieran, "an ace up his sleeve"—he did not *care* if he was thrown out of school. Surprisingly to Kieran, who never brought attention to himself and asked for nothing, the administration went out of their way to keep his brother in school, offering accommodations such as specialized schedules and classes that the average student could only dream of in stupefied envy.

Kieran made a point of kicking Kevin's door on the way out but was rewarded with only silence for his effort.

Kieran's ride to school would not normally have taken him through the woods, but this day he bumped along the narrow path, veined with exposed roots, until he popped out at his vantage point of the previous day and braked to a dusty halt. The two-story, yellow-and-green house appeared just as anonymous as its neighbors—only two of the cars from the previous day remained and all the blinds were drawn. There was nothing whatsoever to distinguish it from its bland, modern counterparts and Kieran felt a pang of disappointment.

Rolling down the slight incline and into the street, Kieran turned to pedal slowly past the front of the house. He had almost completed this pass when he glimpsed something in the shadows between the front door and the wall of the garage. Almost hidden amongst the fronds of a voluminous, green plant with long, slender leaves, pointed and sharp-edged, a carved figure peeked out at him. Even at a distance, Kieran's young eyes took in the unmistakable curves and voluptuous proportions of a tiny naked woman. He looked away and then back again in astonishment—did they have a naked dancing woman on their front porch? And did she have four arms?—his front tire scrubbed the curb and wobbled dangerously before he was able to regain control of his bike.

At the nearby bus stop, an overweight, pimply kid, two years his senior, laughed and shouted something obscene at him, but Kieran paid no mind so enthralled was he at his extraordinary discovery. Turning for another pass, he saw a slat in one of the blinds near the statue lift to reveal a triangle of darkness, then fall once more into place. Sensing a trap he reversed himself—further reconnaissance would have to wait; though he knew it could not wait long, for the desire to possess was hard upon him.

☙

Kieran's school day was interminable and his distraction so great that he was twice called to account for it. Worse still, his English teacher caught him in the midst of a feverish attempt to recreate with pencil and paper what he had only glimpsed that morning. Her sudden intake of breath at the generous proportions he had endowed his sketch with had been his only warning, and as this was a young teacher, whom he found especially attractive and nice, he was mortified. Though shocked at his depiction, she had nonetheless simply ripped the page from his notebook, wadded it up, and without word or comment consigned it to the trash basket. Even so, her gasp and his own blazing face told his classmates all they needed to know, and for the rest of the day he was treated to the nickname "Perv."

But, with the ringing of the final bell, all of these trials were forgotten and left behind, as he rocketed out of the schoolyard ahead of the rush. So great was his hurry that he stood on his pedals, pumping down the streets until he made the turn onto Palomino Drive, and even then he drove on, desire replacing reason and stealth with boldness and inspiration.

Riding at breakneck speed, Kieran aimed at the curb he had collided with earlier in the day. Then, at the last possible moment, jerked the bike into the air and leaped the barrier to resume his juggernaut across the soft green of the strangers' new lawn. The façade of the house remained unchanged, its windows still blinded to the outside world. The figurine that had danced in his mind all day hove into view as he turned to parallel the veranda, and her naked exuberance burned away his earlier imaginings. She was like nothing he had ever seen before.

She did, indeed, have four arms and was as black as the space between the stars of a winter's night. One of the arms wielded a scimitar, its blade curved and cruel as a shark's mouth, while another brandished a human head. The remaining arms appeared to have been captured in graceful motion in keeping with the thick, shapely leg raised in the act of a merry pirouette. Kieran applied the brakes just short of the porch and twisted the handlebars to execute a sudden, sliding stop, intending to launch himself onto the veranda and test the weight of the prize he must possess, and if it were possible, make away with it at that very moment. That was when his front tire flew off.

His collision with the soft, new fill of the lawn drove the wind from his lungs, but saved him from breaking any bones, and he rolled once before coming to a stop, splayed out on his back with his head at the feet of the sword-wielding goddess. From this vantage he could see that her enormous, blood-red tongue protruded at him in derision and that she sported a necklace of grinning skulls, whilst round her waist were strung a belt of human hands. Perhaps more ominously, she did not dance, but stood atop the body of a prostrate male. As his vision grew dark with the lack of oxygen, her form appeared to loom ever larger over him in triumph and he could see now that her allurements included a third eye on her forehead.

Suddenly, his lungs inflated, and his sight cleared like the passing of a squall line. He leapt to his feet, all action and resolve once more, clambering onto the porch to seize his prize. He did not recognize himself in this newfound boldness and hurried to complete his task before his current incarnation abandoned him.

Even as he took hold of the slick, cold stone of the statue, he could sense its solidity. Whatever it had been carved from was incredibly dense and heavy, and it only took one attempt at lifting it to convince him that he would require assistance for this task. The old woman appeared at his elbow as if for just that purpose.

How had he not seen her? The front door stood wide open; she had made no attempt at stealth. He stood slack-jawed in her presence, both due to her extraordinary appearance and the fact that he had never, in all his thieving, been caught in the act before now. He didn't know what to do. Would her sons rush out, seize him and call the police?

Shuffling toward Kieran, she raised her hands in what was now a familiar gesture, even as he began to back away towards the edge of the porch. She was once again garbed in vibrant colors, though this time of gold and green. Up close, Kieran could see that her arms, face, and exposed midriff were networked in wrinkles, her dark countenance sunken and dried-looking; any resemblance to the abundant and curvaceous statue long since sloughed off with great age. She continued to advance on Kieran, shaking her pressed hands as if in supplication and speaking all the while in her lilting birdsong language. Kieran stumbled backwards off the veranda and only just managed to keep his footing. He glanced at the open door. Stopping at the edge of the porch the old woman pointed to the statue of the goddess. "Kali," she whispered. "Kali."

Kieran looked to the statue as well. "Kali," he repeated.

The old woman smiled, revealing good and numerous teeth, then laughed. "Chop, chop," she said, "chop, chop."

☙

Kieran sat in the blue glow of the computer screen in the silent house reading the words he had conjured up from the ether, "Kali, the Dark Mother, is the fierce and fearful form of the mother goddess and is adorned with awesome symbols," it began. "She was born from the brow of the Goddess Durga during a great battle with evil forces and became so enraged that she began to kill not just the enemies of Durga, but all things. In order to stop her, Shiva threw himself under her feet. So shocked was she at this, that she stuck out her tongue in astonishment and ceased her homicidal rampage."

"Shiva," Kieran said, trying the word on for size. He made a note to look him up as well, then read the article through. It explained that Kali's black complexion symbolized her transcendental nature, whatever that meant, and her nudity showed that she was beyond false consciousness, while the garland of human heads stood for the letters in the Sanskrit alphabet and symbolized infinite knowledge; the severed hands liberation from karma, her sword the destroyer of the eight bonds that bind man, her three eyes, the past, present, and future—the sum total of which meant very little to Kieran other than to endow the object that he desired with yet greater power and allure. Hadn't his bike been knocked to pieces by merely approaching it?

Turning away from the screen, he looked across the dim, empty living room. From somewhere in the walls, a pipe knocked several times as the water within it cooled; then all went silent once more. His mother was still on night shift and he could count on Kevin to be either absent or disinterested in his whereabouts. Slipping on a black, vinyl jacket with a ripped seam at the cuff, he searched through Kevin's room until he located his brother's woolen navy watch cap and pulled it down to his eyebrows. Then he took several towels from the bathroom closet and went out to the aluminum shed in the backyard.

The shed leaned drunkenly against the chain link fencing and it took him several attempts to force the warped door and locate the beach wagon he had stolen the summer before from the Richardsons. Several minutes of frantic effort followed, as he struggled to free it from the towering accumulation of eclectic, rusting property he had appropriated over the past several years. When he was finished, he didn't bother to try to restore the items he had strewn onto the patchy lawn, but left them as they lay, exposed and now worthless.

He lined the bottom of the wagon with the towels and, as soon as he felt it was dark enough, began to tow it toward the street, passing his crippled bicycle as he did so. His "new" bike stood propped against the back wall of the house, out of sight of the neighbors. The chubby kid at the bus stop, who had laughed at his near mishap the day prior, was the unwitting donor. Kieran entered the woods before moonrise and made his certain way to Palomino Drive.

Though it was not yet ten o'clock, the neighborhood appeared empty and lifeless. The work-a-day world had locked itself in for the night and the street belonged to the stealthy and feral. Kieran crossed the silent street pulling his fat-wheeled wagon behind him. He did not hesitate or think any more on what he was doing, as it was only through calm focus and deliberate action that he achieved the cloak of invisibility he required. This was a skill he had taught himself long before, and it had been his mistake to have abandoned this the day before in his excitement—this was how he had been caught by the old woman. Pulling the wagon onto the lawn, he made for the darkened corner of the porch where Kali dwelt.

As he neared the alcove, the moon began to peek over the treetops and its first pale light glistened on the statue's black skin, revealing her raging, three-eyed face and sword-wielding upraised arm. Kieran paused, his concentration derailed by the vision, then brought his hands together in front of his face and bowed his head—he hoped that this might placate any resistance to her transference to his keeping. After several moments, he stepped up onto the porch, seized the statue and began to walk it, by ever so carefully rocking it on its base, to the edge of the porch. Other than his breathing, it was accomplished in remarkable silence. Leaving her at the edge he stepped down to the lawn and centered the wagon beneath her—this was the dicey part.

Taking hold of her two upraised arms, Kieran tipped her forward and let gravity do the rest. With an audible thump, she landed amongst the towels and the night was still. Yet all had not gone well. The tiny hand clasping the grisly head remained clutched within his own, even as the dispossessed glared at Kieran in frozen rage from the bottom of the wagon, the scimitar still within her possession and poised to strike. He shivered and stuck the broken hand into his jacket pocket. "Superglue," he whispered.

Even with this setback, no lights had come on within the house, and it only remained for him to make away with his prize. He began to tow the wagon to the street and the safety of the woods beyond and didn't see the boy waiting at the head of the path that was to be his escape route.

The punch to his chest knocked Kieran to the ground, and for the second time in as many days, he suffered the sensation of having the air driven from his lungs. The half-moon, which had now climbed well above the trees, threw his assailant's face into shadow as he leaned over his victim, yet Kieran recognized him—it was the boy from the bus stop.

"You little loser," he chortled. "Did you honestly think I wouldn't know it was you that stole my bike? Everybody in town knows you're the biggest thief there is. You must be retarded to think I wouldn't—you sure look it."

Kieran gasped a lungful of air at last.

"And sound it," the boy added. He reached down and placed all his weight on Kieran's narrow shoulders and breathed a stench of meat and gravy into his face. "Does your mom do retards, too? She does everybody else, my dad says."

Kieran struggled to rise, but it was useless. "Screw you, fatty," he hissed.

The fat boy sat on his victim, then punched Kieran in the right eye, just hard enough to cause sparks of pain to dance in his occluded vision. "You shut up. I'm gonna take this statue… thing," he waved his hand at the wagon, "and you're gonna bring my bike back first thing in the morning… get it? And it better be in one piece, moron. Do… you… understand… me? I sure hope so… for your sake." He stood up and took the handle of the wagon in his pudgy hand and began to saunter down the moonlit street with Kieran's prize in tow. "If my bike's okay, I might… just might, I said, give this statue of your mother back to you." He never bothered to look back.

Kieran hauled himself up from the dewy weeds and dirt, tears of shame, more than hurt, running over his sallow cheeks. "Chop, chop," he sobbed at his assailant's broad back, "chop, chop."

სა

The sirens wailing through the neighborhood woke Kieran even earlier than usual, and he hastened to the window—a dark, oily column of smoke rose in the near distance. It was not yet light outside, so he knew his mother wouldn't be home yet. In fact, it was probably she that had dispatched the police and fire departments to the scene, he thought with some pride, even as he probed the swollen, abraded flesh around his right eye.

He didn't dare take the bike and so had to run the three blocks to the scene of the fire. He arrived panting and out of breath, and felt his knees go wobbly and his vision swim as he recognized what was left of the fat boy's house.

Only the lower floor remained, its blue vinyl siding drooping like melted icing on a cake; the windows now gaping, scorched eyes sporting schizophrenic mascara. Charred and broken timbers commemorated the memory of the second floor bedrooms, while the odor of liquefied plastic almost masked the greasy, sweet tang of what could only be—must be—burned pork.

Kieran glanced about in near panic at all the neighbors that had gathered at the awful spectacle, sick with an unreasonable feeling of complicity, and fearful that others might sense it as well.

A fireman that Kieran thought his mother might have dated at some time spotted him and called out, "Get back from there, kid… don't make me tell you again!"

Kieran did as he was told and scurried off to the far end of the property line and nearer the separate garage. There, he came upon two young men in blue jumpsuits, almost hidden behind a screen of ambulances, struggling with someone, or something, on the ground and cursing between gasps of held breath. As Kieran shifted closer, without leaving the edged shadows of early morning, the scene revealed itself in unwelcome clarity—they were struggling to sheath the charred and contorted figures of what must once have been people into black, zippered bags. One of the corpses awaiting their ministrations was not much larger than Kieran and he felt the blood drain from his face and wondered if he were about to faint, then forced himself to look away. It was then he spotted his wagon next to the back door of the garage;, a tiny scimitar raised in triumph from its depths.

Without thinking, he walked directly to it, took it by the handle, turned, and began to haul it behind him down the street. In spite of his fears, no one took any notice of him, and he walked home without challenge.

"Where in the hell did you get that thing?" Kevin asked. "It's wicked!"

Kieran had been so engrossed in gluing on the broken hand that he had failed to hear his brother approach. He jumped to his feet, placing himself between the statue of Kali and Kevin, all his plans to keep her hidden amongst the clutter of their tottering, one-car garage dashed by his brother's unexpected appearance.

"She's mine!" was all he could think to say.

"Easy, my little psycho… who said any differently, huh?" Kevin advanced on Kieran's prize, unable to take his eyes from it. "Oh yeah, my man, you have scored big with this. She's Hindu, right? Goddess of something, right?"

Kieran held his ground, made uneasy by his brother's rapid-fire speech and questions. Usually, if he didn't know something, he would act as if it were unimportant or trivial; it was out of character for him to show such enthusiasm.

"Don't touch her," Kieran warned.

Kevin was standing over both boy and carving now, scrutinizing the amazing figure, his face a rapacious mask, his eyes all dark pupil. "What does somebody pay for something like this?" he asked aloud. "That's what I'd love to know. A few thousand wouldn't surprise me… maybe more."

Not once did he actually address his little brother. Kieran felt as if Kevin didn't see him at all, and he didn't like the odor that seemed to pulse from his brother's sweat-sheened skin. It reminded him of hospitals and industrial disinfectant. He took a step back and collided with the statue of Kali. Even as he spun about he could hear it totter on the loose wooden planks of the garage floor and only just caught it in time. The reattached appendage flew off with his clumsy embrace and skittered beneath a bench.

Turning, he shouted into his brother's face, "Get out of here, Kevin! And don't touch her, you stupid crankhead, she's mine."

Kevin took a surprised step back, his face pale and blank. "No one said different… I hear you. Whoa… what has gotten into you, little brother? You gone all schizoid, or something? Just came in to check on you—mom's a little worried, that's all… what with the black eye and all, and you being more of a psycho than usual, that kind of thing. I could give a rat's ass myself."

He took another step back and his face grew crafty and bold. "But if I did want… that," he pointed at the voluptuous warrior, "I'd take it… hear me?" He stuck his tongue out in imitation of the object of their dispute, then withdrew it again.

"No you won't," Kieran blazed back.

"You've got to sleep sometime," Kevin teased. "Not me, though. I can stay awake for *days*." The next step back took him out the door and Kieran was left with only the medical stench that trailed his brother like a following ghost.

For the next three nights, Kieran slept on a pallet in the garage at the foot of Kali.

༄

The morning of the third night, Kieran was greeted by his mother when he came into the kitchen from the garage. He knew right away that something was wrong; she stood between him and the cereal boxes in the cabinet, still in her house coat and smoking.

"I need to know what's going on," she began, "why you are sleeping in the garage, for God's sake, and where is your brother?"

Her words were rapid and urgent, and her anxiety frightened Kieran.

"It's stuffy in my room because that window still sticks…"

"Stop that," she demanded. "I don't have time to listen to that nonsense just now. Where is Kevin? Did you know he hasn't been here, or at school, in three days? When is the last time you saw your brother?"

Kieran was stunned into silence by his mother's vehemence, even as he struggled to understand the situation—Kevin was missing? Her fear entered him like the wet, charred smell that still hung over the neighborhood. Tears stood in his mother's eyes.

"I don't know…" Kieran began, fearing that somehow he might be held responsible, that somehow he might *be* responsible, though for what, he wasn't certain. "Three nights ago," he whispered. "I'm pretty sure."

"Three nights ago," his mother repeated in a near wail. "Oh God," she cried. "Then it's true, he *has* been gone that long! When the school called, I thought he had just been playing hooky; it never occurred to me that he wasn't coming home at night. I just thought I was missing him 'cause of the shift work.

"Why didn't you tell me, Kieran? And why are you sleeping in the garage? What's been happening around here… can you please tell me?"

Her pleas cracked that fragile thing that he carried about in his chest, and tears began to leak from his eyes. "I didn't notice he wasn't here," he confessed, feeling ashamed. "I'm sorry, Mom, I'm sorry. We had an argument and…" he trailed off, uncertain how to proceed without revealing his secrets.

"An argument about what?" she asked, sensing a clue, a thread that might lead her to her eldest son. "Tell me."

"Over something of mine," he hedged. "Something he wanted, but I said no, that's all. I don't think I should have to…"

Even as he spoke, he recalled his bike flying apart on his first attempt at possession of Kali, and the words of the old woman, followed by his pummeling at the hands of the fat boy on the night of the theft; the inferno that followed. He also remembered Kevin approaching his hard-won prize, greed and avarice etched into his features, and it was clear to him what must happen next.

His mother's words pierced his thoughts and he looked up to find her crying. "I want you to go out, right now, and talk to everybody you know and find out if they've seen Kevin. Are you listening, Kieran? I mean everybody."

"Yes ma'am… okay," he agreed, already turning for the door.

"I'm gonna get on the phone to the department," she continued, sniffling. "I know Kevin's been a handful and maybe some people think he's delinquent or something, but he's my boy and I'm gonna…"

"Wait," Kieran demanded, alarmed at the thought of the police entering into the matter. Once they arrived, his freedom of movement would be curtailed. "Just let me try and find out something," he pleaded. "Once the cops get involved no one will say anything."

His mother didn't answer, but studied him warily.

※

Now that his mind was made up, Kieran could not return the ominous, black carving fast enough, though he did exercise caution upon lowering her once more into the wagon. His repair of the broken hand was just visible, and it was his desire to return the Dark Mother without further damage.

Kieran didn't bother to wait until night, as he felt certain the old woman knew quite well who had stolen her property in any case. He paused only at the foot of her driveway in order to gather his courage for the last leg of his penitent journey. The house awaited him with the same blank countenance of his previous visits.

As he hauled the heavy wagon up the smooth drive, the front door opened and the old woman, dressed this day in scarlet, and accompanied by her eldest son in his grey suit, stepped out onto the porch. Kieran thought they appeared to be expecting him.

Swallowing the knot of fear that threatened to choke him, he completed the final few steps and brought the wagon to a halt at their feet, stopped, brought his hands together and bowed. They responded in kind. Then the old woman laughed with delight and pointed at the contents of the wagon, even as her son stepped down and lifted the statue of Kali from within, returning it to the spot from which Kieran had taken it. They appeared well pleased altogether.

Extracting several bills of large denomination from his wallet, the son offered them to Kieran, who stared in bafflement. He backed away, dragging his now-empty wagon with him. "Thank you," the man said in accented English. "Thank you very much."

"I just want my brother back," Kieran said, still backing away.

The man appeared puzzled, as if he were having trouble translating Kieran's words. "Your brother?" he repeated. "Yes, I hope so. Good luck with that, my young friend."

"We need him back," Kieran said once more, as the vultures across the street began to launch themselves into the air in their clumsy morning ritual, and the old woman placed flowers at the feet of Kali.

༼༽

When Kieran returned home, the police had already arrived—his mother had not been able to wait, Kevin was still missing, and there was no light he could shed on his brother's disappearance. His mother did not go in to work that day and allowed Kieran to remain at home as well. After the officers had departed, they spent the entire day together watching old movies on TV wrapped in a comforter on the couch. The phone never rang.

That evening Kieran heated up canned soup and prepared tuna fish sandwiches for their supper, but his mother barely tasted hers, and at some point he went to bed and must have fallen asleep. The sound of his doorknob rattling woke him and he sat up in bed, puzzled as to how he had gotten there, and switched on his bedside lamp.

Kevin, looking drawn, haggard, and years older than he should, peered at him through fingers raised to shield his tender eyes against the light. "Hey loser," he said, his voice sounding dry and unused, "why's mom asleep on the couch? I miss somethin' around here?"

Kieran vaulted out of his bed and threw his arms around his bewildered brother, causing him to stagger. "Kevin," he cried into the folds of his brother's jacket. "Kevin!"

Kevin pushed him away to arm's length, staring blearily at his younger sibling. "I must have," he rasped, "I must have missed something alright, for all… *this*," he grinned at Kieran, "hugging me and all."

"Where have you been? Mom's worried sick about you. Where have you been?"

"Been?" Kevin repeated, as if really trying to remember. "Out," he concluded.

"For three days?"

"Three days?" he repeated Kieran's words once more. "You sure it's been three days, Lil' Bro'?" He could see from Kieran's expression that he was. "Oh, huh. How 'bout that? Do you know I have no earthly idea?"

"I thought *she* had you," Kieran began to sob.

"*She*… who?" Kevin asked, puzzled and alarmed at his little brother's unusual display of emotion. But Kieran remained mute on the subject.

Kneeling down, Kevin took his hands. "No, K-man, there's no 'she'… not that I remember, anyway," he joshed. "But I'll tell you something, freaky boy, wherever I was, it wasn't good, that much I do know, and I'm not ever gonna go back there again. I mean that, little brother… I'm turned inside out."

"Me too," Kieran agreed, dragging a sleeve across his running nose.

From the darkness of the living room they could hear their mother stir and call out in rising tones, "Kev… is that you, Kevin?"

"Is she gonna rip me a new one?" Kevin asked with a lopsided grin.

"Oh yeah," Kieran assured him. "She loves you, Kevin… me too," he added.

"I know that," his brother replied; then turned to face their mother as she thundered down upon them, screaming his name.

Mariel
(2012)
Second Place EQMM Readers Award/Nominated for a Derringer Award

The neighbor watched Mariel approach through his partially shuttered blinds. She cruised down their quiet cul-de-sac on her purple bicycle, her large head with its jumble of tight curls swiveling from side to side. He thought she looked grotesque, a Shirley Temple on steroids. Ratcheting the bell affixed to her handlebars for no apparent reason, she stopped in front of his house, and he took a step back from the window.

His house was one of three that lay along the turnaround at the end of Crumpler Lane and normally she would simply complete her circumnavigation of the asphalted circle and return to her end of the street. This time, however, Mariel's piggish eyes swept across his lawn and continued to the space between his house and that of his neighbor's to the north, who despised the child as much as he did, if that was possible. A crease of concern appeared on his freckled forehead and he took a sip of his cooling coffee.

Suddenly she raked the lever of her bell back and forth several times, startling him, the nerve-wracking jangle sounding as if Mariel and her bike were in his living room. He felt something warm slide over his knuckles and drip onto his faux Persian carpet.

Hissing a curse about Mariel's parentage, he turned for the kitchen and a bottle of stain remover. "Hideous child," he murmured through clenched teeth. "Troglodyte!" What was she looking for? More than once he had chased her from his property after he had found her snooping around his sheds and peering in his windows. Though he had complained, her mother had proved useless in controlling the child. She was one of those "single moms" that seemed to dominate the family landscape of late and had made it clear that she thought he was overreacting.

He recalled with a flushing of his freshly razored cheeks, how she had appeared amused by the whole thing and inquired with an arched brow how long he had been divorced—as if the need for companionship might be the real motive behind his visit! He felt certain that on more than one encounter with the gargantuan and supremely disengaged mother, that he had smelled alcohol on her breath, cheap wine, if he had to hazard a guess.

But what now, he wondered? Usually, Mariel crept about in a surprisingly stealthy manner for such a large girl, but now she commanded the street like a general, silent but for the grating bell that even now rang out once more… but for what?

Forgetting the carpet cleaner, he set down his morning mug and glided stealthily back to his observation point at the window. He felt trapped, somehow, by this sly little giant so inappropriately named "Mariel." What had her mother been thinking, he asked himself with a shake of his graying head, to assign this clumsy-looking creature such a delicate, feminine name? When he peeked out again it was to find Mariel's bike lying discarded on his lawn, the girl nowhere to be seen. The crease between his eyes became a furrow and he rushed through his silent house to the kitchen windows.

Carefully parting a slat of his Venetian blinds, he looked on the path that led between his property and the next and on into the woods. A large head of curly hair was just disappearing down it and into the trees. A shudder ran through his body and beads of sweat formed above his upper lip like dew. *Damn the girl*, he thought, feeling somewhat nauseous as suspicion uncoiled itself within his now-queasy guts.

Unbidden, the image of the dog trotted into his mind, its hideous prize clasped between its slavering jaws. It had reeked of the rancid earth exposed by the recent torrential rains. He remembered with a shudder of distaste and a rising, renewable fury how it had danced back and forth across his sodden lawn, enjoying its game of "keep away." He remembered the shovel most of all, its heft and reach, the satisfaction of its use.

"That was her dog," he breathed into the silent, waiting room, then thought, *Of course it was… it* would *be*. His soft hands flexed as if gripping the shovel once more.

※

Standing over the shallow grave, Mariel contemplated the exposed paw. The limb showed cinnamon-colored fur with black, tigerish stripes that she recognized at once. She hadn't really cared for Ripper (a name he had been awarded as a puppy denoting his penchant for ripping any and everything he could seize between his formidable jaws), but he had been *her* dog.

As he had grown larger, his destructive capabilities, coupled with Mariel and her mother's complete disregard of attempting to instill anything resembling discipline, had resulted in a rather dangerous beast that had to be kept penned in the backyard at all times. Mariel had served largely as Ripper's jailer.

As she couldn't really share any affection with the dog, or he with her, they had gradually grown to regard one another with a resigned antipathy, if not outright hostility—after all, she was also the provider of his daily meals which she mostly remembered to deliver. It was also she that managed to locate him on those occasions when he found the gate to his pen unlatched (Mariel did this from time to time to see what might happen in the neighborhood as a result) and coaxed him into returning. This was the mission in which Mariel had been engaged this Saturday morning in early November. She saw now that she had been only partially successful, Ripper would not be returning to his pen.

Looking about for something to scrape the loose earth off her dog's remains, she pried a rotting piece of wood from a long-fallen pine tree and began to dig into the damp, sandy soil. Grunting and sweating with the effort, her Medusa-like curls bouncing on her large, round skull, Ripper was exposed within minutes. Whoever had buried him had not done a very good job of it and the slight stench of dead dog that had first led her to the secret grave rose like an accusing, invisible wraith. Mariel wrinkled her stubby nose.

Ignoring the dirt and damage being done to her purplish sweatshirt and pants, which matched her bicycle, she seized the dead creature by his hindquarters and dragged him free of the grave. Letting him drop onto the leaf litter of the forest floor with a sad thump she surveyed her once-fierce companion.

He looked as if the air had been let out of him—deflated. His great fangs were exposed in a permanent snarl or grimace, the teeth and eyes clotted with earth. Mariel pushed at his ribcage with a toe of her dirty sneaker as if this might goad him back into action, but nothing happened, he just lay there.

She thought his skull appeared changed and squatted next to him to make a closer examination. As she brought her large face closer, the rancid odor grew stronger yet, but Mariel was not squeamish and so continued her careful scrutiny. It *was* different, she decided. The concavity that naturally ran between Ripper's eyes to the crown of his skull was now more of a valley, or canyon. Mariel ran a finger along it and came away with a sticky black substance clinging to it. The stain smelled of death and iron.

Having completed her necropsy, Mariel stood once more and surveyed the surrounding woods. The trees had been largely stripped of their colorful foliage by the recent nor'easter, but her enemy was not to be seen. Though she did not mourn Ripper's untimely passing, she did resent the theft of her property and its misuse and concluded with a hot finality that someone owed her a dog.

She kicked Ripper's poor carcass as a final farewell then turned to leave and find a wheelbarrow in which to transport him home once more. She knew of several neighbors who possessed such a conveyance and almost none were locked away this time of year.

It was then that something within the dog's recent grave caught her attention—something that twinkled like a cat's eye in the slanted beams of daylight that filtered through the trees. Dropping to her knees, Mariel thrust her chubby hand into the fetid earth to retrieve whatever treasure lay within. When she withdrew it once more it was to find that she clasped a prize far greater than any she could ever have imagined—a gold necklace, it's flattened, supple links glistening like snakeskin and bearing a pendant that sparkled with a blue fire in the rays of the milky sun.

Mariel had no idea as to what, exactly, she had discovered, but her forager's instinct assured her that she clasped a prize worth having.

Without hesitation, she gave it a tug to free it from the grasp of Ripper's grave, but found that her efforts were resisted. She snatched at it once more, impatient to obtain her prize, and felt something beneath the dirt move and begin to give way. Encouraged at the results of this tug-o-war, she seized the links in both hands now and rocked back on her considerable haunches for additional leverage.

With the dry snap of a breaking branch, the necklace came free and Mariel found herself in full possession. The erupted earth, however, now revealed a yellowish set of teeth still lodged in the lower jawbone of their owner. Several of these teeth had been filled with silver and as Mariel had also been the recipient of such dental work, she understood that the remains were those of a human. A stack of vertebrae were visible jutting out from the dirt, evidence of the result of the uneven struggle, though the remainder of the skull still lay secure beneath the soil.

Mariel's grip on the pendant never wavered as she regarded the neck of the now-headless horror that had previously worn the coveted necklace. With only a slight "*Ewww*," of disgust, she rose in triumph to slip the prized chain over her own large head, admiring the lustrous sapphire that hung almost to her exposed navel while ignoring the slight tang of death that clung to it. She felt well-pleased with the day's outcome, Ripper's demise notwithstanding.

With her plans now altered by this surprising acquisition, Mariel dragged her dog's much abused corpus back to the grave, tipped him in, and began to cover Ripper and his companion once more. When she was done, she studied the results for several moments, then thought to drag a few fallen branches over her handiwork.

Satisfied with the results, she turned for home once more, pausing only long enough to slip the necklace beneath her stained sweatshirt. Mariel did not want to have to surrender her hard-won treasure to her mother, who would undoubtedly covet the prize and seize it for her own adornment. Besides, she had things she wanted to think about and did not want anyone to know of the necklace until the moment of her choosing, especially, the three men who occupied the homes on the cul-de-sac. It had not escaped Mariel's notice that only those three had easy access to the path that led into the woods and passed within yards of the secret grave.

☙

Watching her emerge from the trees and march past his house, the neighbor studied her closely but could read nothing from her closed expression. Other than her clothes being a little dirtier than when she went in, she appeared the same as always and he breathed a sigh of relief.

It was silly, he thought, as he saw her raise and mount her bike, how one unpleasant child could instill so much unease. It was because he was a sensitive man, he consoled himself—he had been a sensitive boy and with adulthood nothing had really changed. He had always resented the unfeeling bullies of the world, child or adult. Children like Mariel had terrified him when he had been a schoolboy and apparently nothing had changed in that respect either.

The sudden jangling of the bell caused him to gasp and his eyes returned to the robust figure of Mariel. Surveying the surrounding houses with her implacable gaze, Mariel studied each of the three on the cul-de-sac in turn, coming at last back to his own. He shrank from the window once more, his heart racing.

Then, with a thrust of a large thigh, her bike was set in motion and she pedaled from his sight with powerful strokes. "Damn her," he whispered as his earlier concerns returned with such force that his blood roared within his ears.

Finding an overstuffed chair to settle into, he peered around the plush, dim room with its collection of his own paintings on the wall, while around him songbirds began to chirp and sing from their cages as if to restore and calm him. He smiled weakly in gratitude at their effort even as Mariel's imperious face returned to his mind's eye with a terrible clarity. He closed his eyes against her, massaging his now-throbbing temples with his soft fingertips. If she had discovered anything in those woods, he asked himself, she would have come out screaming, wouldn't she? He lowered his head into his sweaty hands, while a blood-red image of Mariel shimmered on his inner eyelids… Wouldn't she?

☙

Mariel had no trouble engineering her encounter with Mister Salter. He worked on his lawn from early spring until the cold and snow of January drove him indoors. As long as there was any light she knew that her chances were good of finding him in his yard. So after she was delivered home by her school bus and enjoyed a snack of cream-filled cupcakes she pedaled her bike directly to the cul-de-sac and his property.

Salter watched her approach with a sour expression meant to ward her away. Not troubled by such subtleties, she came to a sudden halt in his driveway causing a scattering of carefully raked gravel. Salter's expression darken at this and he shut off the leaf blower he had been using, its piercing whine fading away. Man and girl observed each other from several yards apart as his corpulent Labrador waddled toward Mariel, thick tail wagging.

"Bruiser," Salter warned.

The dog ignored him and continued on to Mariel, pleased to be patted on his large head. Salter's complexion went darker yet.

"Can I do something for you?" he asked, his tone clearly inferring the opposite.

Mariel regarded him without answering, fingering the necklace she had retrieved from its hiding place before going out. Salter fidgeted beneath her round-eyed stare. "Be careful of the dog," he muttered, "he might bite."

As Mariel had recruited Salter's dog during her many secret forays, she knew this to be untrue. She often went into Salter's garage where he kept the dog food and fed the animal while he was away teaching shop at the high school. Bruiser was always pleased to see her as a result. As if to emphasize their relationship, the dog laid its great head on her thigh.

This was too much for Salter, who turned his wide back on her and went to pull at the cord that would start his treasured leaf-blower.

Mariel glanced at the well-worn path that led from Salter's backyard and into the woods. "I have this," she said, pulling the necklace from her shirt and allowing it to fall down over her plump stomach. The sapphire shone in the late day sun like a blue flame. Her eyes remained on Salter, even as her small mouth puckered into a smile of possessiveness.

Looking over his shoulder, Salter halted and turned back. "Where the devil did you get that?" he managed. He took a few steps closer as Mariel backed her bike away an equal distance. Bruiser's head slid off her thigh leaving a trail of saliva.

Seeing this, Salter stopped and studied Mariel's prize from where he stood. "Did your mother say you could wear that?" he asked.

As the girl did not reply, but only continued her unsettling scrutiny, he added, "Does she even know that you have it? For that matter, how the hell could your mom afford something like that… provided its real, of course?" Forgetting himself, he took another few steps, but Mariel was already turning her bike to coast down his driveway.

"I know you've been coming onto my property," he called to her as she picked up speed with each stroke of her powerful legs. "You'd better stop sneaking around here… it's called trespassing you know, I could call the cops." His voice grew louder as she added distance between them. "And maybe I will the next time," he offered.

"Did you steal that?" he called out meanly as she disappeared around the curve.

Mariel only looked back as she sped up the street and out of sight of the cul-de-sac. A small smile played on her puckered lips. She scratched Mr. Salter off her list of suspects.

༄

Mariel surprised Mister Forster in his own backyard, having glided silently across his still-green lawn. His back to her, Forster was busy feeding and talking to his flock of tiny bantam hens and didn't notice her arrival. The hens themselves pecked and grumbled within their pen, concerned only with their meal.

Several times in the past, Mariel had attempted to better make their acquaintance. On one such occasion, Forster had found Mariel within the pen itself attempting to catch one of his miniature chickens, feathers flying about in the air amid a cacophony of terrified squawking. He had been livid with rage at her incursion and had joined the ranks of other neighbors who had visited her home to complain to her mother. Mariel had learned to be more careful since that encounter and had not been caught since, but neither had she been successful.

"They're funny," she lisped.

Forster spun around scattering the remainder of the feed from the bowl he was using. "Oh," he cried, as the small, black fowl swarmed his shoes and cuffs for the errant seeds. "Oh," he repeated, then focused on his unexpected visitor. He brought a hand up to his heart and gasped, "You scared me half to death, Mariel. I didn't hear you come up and you nearly scared me half to…" he caught himself. "You usually ring that little bell of yours," he finished with a limp gesture at her bike.

Man and girl regarded one another across several yards of grassless, churned-up soil… evidence of poultry. A worn path into the woods separated them. Mr. Forster set the metal bowl down and opened the pen door to come out. Mariel responded by turning her bike in the direction from which she had come.

The older man appeared to note the child's wariness and slowed his steps, easing himself through the door and taking his time in closing and latching the wire-covered frame. When he turned once more to Mariel it was to find her holding out a large jewel pendant that hung about her neck from a gold-colored chain. She reminded him of the vampire-slayers in horror films attempting to paralyze and kill their undead foes with a crucifix.

"My goodness, Mariel that is some necklace you have there. It's lovely. You are a very lucky girl to have that."

Mariel continued to fix him with both her gaze and the pendant while her lips vanished into a grim, pensive line. Forster stared back. "Was there something that you wanted?" he thought to ask at last.

The sapphire wavered in her grip and she slipped it once more beneath her top. It appeared to have no power over this man either. As she puzzled over her lack of progress in her investigations thus far, Forster took two steps closer.

Only slightly taller than Mariel, he had no more than fifteen pounds over the ten-year-old, so she was not as intimidated as she might have been with other men in the neighborhood.

"It's the hens, isn't it?" he ventured. "You appreciate them like I do." He glanced back over his shoulder at the chicken coop. "I was probably a little hasty last time you were here," he continued. "I should have thought… but when I heard all that commotion and came out to find someone in the pen…. Well, I should have realized that you were just as fascinated by them as I am." He studied Mariel's broad, unintelligent face for several moments. "Would you like to hold one?"

Mariel's gaze flickered somewhat at this invitation. The thought of actually holding one of the softly feathered birds had become something of a Holy Grail for her and her breath caught at the idea.

Turning, Forster retraced his steps to the coop and within moments returned stroking a quietly clucking hen. Mariel smiled and reached out both arms for the coveted bird, but Forster stopped a few paces short of her. Still running his hand over the bantam's glossy feathers, he nodded at Mariel, and said, "Show me that necklace again, why don't you? I was too far away to be able to see it well. How about another look… I won't touch it, then I'll let you hold Becky." He smiled at Mariel and held the bird a few inches away from his chest to indicate his willingness.

Retrieving the necklace from within her shirt, Mariel held out the pendant for him to study, her small greedy eyes never leaving the near-dozing hen. Forster leaned forward onto the balls of his feet to study the stone for several moments. At last, he exhaled and murmured, "You should be very careful with that, Mariel. That's exactly the kind of thing that grown-ups will want to take from you." Leaning just a little closer, he asked, "Does your mother know you've got that?" And when she fidgeted and didn't answer right away, added, "I wouldn't tell her, if I were you… she'll want to wear it… and keep it… for sure. Any woman would."

Stuffing the necklace back down her shirt, Mariel thrust her arms out once more for the agreed-upon chicken. Forster carefully placed it within her thick arms and smiled as Mariel's normally glum face began to light up with the tactile pleasure of the silken bird. In her enthusiasm, she began to run her sticky hand down the hen's back with rapid movements, even as "Becky" began to squirm and protest volubly at the excessive downward pressure of her strokes. The contented clucking became the frenzied cackles of a terrified chicken in the clutch of a bear cub.

Seeing that Mariel's technique required more practice and refinement, Forster made to take the bird from the grinning schoolgirl, but she turned away with her prize as if she meant to keep Becky at all costs. With that movement, however, the hen was given just the opening she required to free her wings, flapping them frantically in her escalating desire for freedom.

Startled, Mariel released the bird, which in a whirlwind of beating wings and flying feathers covered the short distance to her coop in awkward bounds only somewhat resembling actual flight.

Mariel was left with nothing but a few of the errant feathers and her hot disappointment.

With a frown of both disapproval and resentment, she pushed off on her bike and made for Crumpler Lane. Behind her, Forster called out, "They just take a little getting used to, Mariel. Come back when you want, and I'll teach you how to handle them!"

After she had gone away, he turned to his precious coop to ensure that Becky was returned and properly locked in for the night. Then, with a sigh, went up the back steps and into his house, turning on the lights in room after room as darkness fell.

☙

Mister Wanderlei was next on Mariel's' list and she was not long in cornering him. She found him that very Saturday as he was painting the wooden railing of his front porch.

Stopping at his mailbox, she gave her bike bell several sharp rings to gain his attention. He glanced over his shoulder and smiled at her.

"Hello, Mariel," he called while lifting a paint brush in salute. "Another few weeks and it will be too cold to do this."

Mariel could think of nothing to reply and so rung her bell once more. Setting the brush on the lip of the can, Mister Wanderlei stood, wiping his hands on his old corduroy work pants. "Is that a new bike?" he asked.

Nodding her big head at this, Mariel thought to add, "My grandma bought it for me… I didn't steal it."

Wanderlei smiled and answered, "I never would have thought so." He ambled down the steps in her direction.

Fumbling with the necklace, Mariel only just managed to bring it out from beneath her top as he drew near. This caused

Wanderlei to halt for a moment as he took in Mariel's astounding adornment.

"Goodness," he breathed at last. "That's some necklace for a little girl. Where did you get that?" He ran a large knuckled hand across the top of his mostly hairless skull.

As she had done with Salter and Forster, Mariel realigned her bicycle for a quick escape should it prove advisable, one foot poised on a pedal. She remained silent.

Fishing a handkerchief from his pocket, Wanderlei set about wiping his face and near-naked pate. "Such things cause great temptation," he said at last. "Of course, I know that you're too young to understand what I mean exactly." He glanced up and down the street, then turned his gaze onto her once more.

"Where I work, there are men who have killed for such baubles." A slight frown crossed his face. "Do you know where I work, Mariel?"

In fact, Mariel did know, as one of her uncles had pointed him out to her during a visit between incarcerations. She nodded.

Wanderlei studied her face with interest, then said, "Well, then you know that I've spent my life amongst a lot of very bad people." His eyes had taken on a sparkle that was beginning to make Mariel uneasy. He took another step and she eased her rump upwards in preparation for escape.

"Are you Christian?" he asked in a gentle tone. "Does your mother ever take you to church?"

Mariel frowned, unable to follow Wanderlei's drift. Even so, she nodded out of nervousness.

"Is that right?" he smiled, showing no interest in her necklace. "Really, what church would that be?"

"We go sometimes," Mariel whispered, for some reason not wanting to lie outright to this man. "We're Cat'lics."

Wanderlei's expression became one of disappointment. "Oh, I see," he murmured. "That would explain the love of gold and baubles," he remarked, as if Mariel were no longer there.

Mariel rose up and pushed down on the waiting pedal, having learned what she needed to know.

Wanderlei looked up as she pulled away, his expression gone a little wistful now. "You and your mother are welcome to attend the services here at our house anytime you want," he called after her. "God accepts anyone that has an open heart. Do you have an open heart, Mariel?"

༄

That night, as Mariel lay awake in her bed, she contemplated her efforts to date at exposing Ripper's murderer and felt the keen bite of disappointment. Though blessed with flashes of innovative vigor, her intellectual resources had been taxed by the whole affair, and now she stared out of her curtainless window until her thoughts drifted away like tendrils of fog and she thought of nothing.

The backyard was bathed in the cold illumination of a full moon that created black and white etchings of once-familiar objects. Ripper's empty chain-link pen was captured near-center frame of her nocturnal reverie, its gate standing open, forever awaiting his impossible return. A spill of shadow ran like blood from the doghouse and onto the brilliant concrete pad it rested upon.

Mariel felt her eyelids grow heavy, while above her the ponderous footsteps of her mother measured the distance from her bathroom to her bed. This was followed by a groaning of bedsprings and a loud yawn, then silence descended over the household. Outside, something glided from out of a tree, only to vanish within the deeper shadows of the forest. Mariel's eyes began to close.

As she was drifting off, she saw something moving along the darkened tree line that formed the natural boundary of her yard. At first, as she was often a nocturnal traveler herself, this did not alarm her. She had spent many a night prowling Crumpler Lane and its environs. On more than one occasion she had allowed herself into the homes of their neighbors using keys that they had hidden beneath flowerpots and paving stones. In fact, her midnight forays and cool boldness had become something of a neighborhood legend.

This had been several years before however, after the loud divorce of her parents and the splitting of her family into a Mother-Daughter/Father-Sons arrangement. Mariel had thought that she would discover her brothers were sleeping over at some neighbors' house but never seemed able to catch them at it. When the state's child services were brought in, her mother took drastic action and placed a latch on her bedroom door.

Watching, trance-like, Mariel witnessed the figure detach itself from the shadows and emerge, glowing, into the moonlight. The man looked familiar, but the bright, ghostly light only served to erase his features. He glided across the littered lawn of her backyard in a direct line with her bedroom window and a small, shrill alarm began to sound in Mariel's head. She struggled to come fully awake and sit up.

The man disappeared from view as he reached the wall of her house and for the first time sound entered into the hushed scene. Mariel heard the scrape of something metal and remembered the rusty ladder that lay beneath her window. She hadn't needed that ladder since her mother ceased locking her in at night—whether from drunkenness or apathy, she didn't know or care—and it had lain, discarded and forgotten, in the rank grasses of her backyard. It was this sound that set her in motion.

Awake now, she slid from her bed and began stuffing her pillows beneath her blankets. Once done, she dropped to her hands and knees and began to crawl to the closed bedroom door.

Behind her a head rose within the frame of the window. Mariel froze as soon as she saw its elongated shadow begin to crawl up the opposite wall, even as she lowered herself into the welter of dirty clothes and discarded dolls and toys that formed the tangled landscape of her room. She sank from sight within the camouflage of her own environment.

Peering out from beneath a damp towel that she draped over her head, Mariel saw the silhouette swivel, then focus on the lumpy bed revealed in the moonlight. For several moments the scene remained frozen in this attitude. Then the window began to squeak like the tiniest of mice.

Mariel knew that she could call out to her mother and perhaps, if she had not had too much to drink, awaken her to the peril she faced. But this was not part of Mariel's rapidly forming plan.

Instead, she snaked an arm upwards for the doorknob. With any luck she could ease herself out into the hallway as the intruder made his way into her room, then… use the latch that she, herself, had been confined with so many times before. As for the window, she had simply to race around to the back of the house, tip the ladder over and he was caught like a rat! Then, and only then, she would yell bloody murder! Wouldn't everyone be surprised at what she had accomplished? Mariel began to grin beneath her covering.

She found the doorknob and began to turn it. From behind her came the hiss of clothing sliding over the windowsill followed by a soft thump. Things were happening a little faster than she had planned so she tried to hurry a bit more. She could hear her own breathing as she slithered into the opening she was making.

Then Sailor began to hiss and yowl, only just now deciding that this stranger in his room was not welcomed. Mariel looked back over her shoulder, she had completely forgotten Sailor.

The cat had been a gift to her mother from a former boyfriend who had worked on a clamming boat, hence the name, "Sailor." Naturally, he took up with the one member of the household that cared nothing for him—however, Mariel was not above putting him to good use.

Without a word, she sprang to her feet and snatched the fat orange cat from the nest he had created within her bed coverings. With a screech of protest he was suddenly airborne in the direction of Mariel's would-be assailant, his claws fully extended in a futile attempt at air-braking.

When the two met, it was the nocturnal visitor's turn to vocalize, as he screamed like a woman in labor, whether from pain or terror, Mariel could not know. From above there was a great concussion as her mother's considerable bulk was set in motion.

Mariel, consigning Sailor to whatever fate awaited him, flew for the door once more, slamming it behind her and latching it all in one movement. A tight smile appeared on her chubby face as she raced for the back door, even as her name was loudly heralded with her mother's rumbling approach.

Tripping over the uneven doorsill, she spilled into the silvered yard just in time to see the intruder fling himself from the ladder and begin his headlong flight. She had not been fast enough! Her disappointment rose like bile in her mouth. But even as her mother blocked the moon from view and began to scrabble at

Mariel with sweaty, fleshy hands, she noted with some vindication that her enemy had fled in the direction of the cul-de-sac.

☙

The Sheriff's K-9 unit tracked the burglar unerringly from Mariel's window to Mister Salter's backyard, the scent leading them right into Bruiser's territory. There, the sleepy, overfed dog, alarmed by the night's doings, and mysteriously free of confinement, managed to engage the interlopers in a snarling, slobbering, snapping exchange of canine unpleasantness. In the end, he was re-incarcerated, but not before spoiling the search. Mariel knew all of this from eavesdropping as the officers briefed her mother in the living room.

When the policemen asked Mariel if she had gotten a good look at the man that had made his way into her room, she studied the dirty knees of her pajamas for several moments, then mumbled, "I *think* it was Mister Salter." Though she had never *really* gotten a good look at her assailant, Salter appealed to both her logic and sense of justice based on both the dogs' tracking and the fact that she liked him the least of anyone in the neighborhood. The officers glanced at one another after her pronouncement, then departed to invite Mariel's neighbor to accompany them to the station for further questioning.

After they left, Mariel had a very difficult time falling to sleep—it had been an exciting evening. When, at last, she did drift off, it was with the pleasant sense of a job well done, mission accomplished.

☙

As the following day was Sunday and Mariel's night had been a long one, her mother allowed her to sleep in well past noon. When she did awake it was with a ravenous appetite and a fierce curiosity about the results of her efforts on the neighborhood-at-large. It seemed to her that an act of such magnitude would result in seismic changes on Crumpler Lane. So after two heaping bowls of frosted cereal and a glass of chocolate milk, she mounted up and set off to reconnoiter her domain.

The day was bright and fine, but as it was mid-autumn, the sun remained low in the sky and a distinct chill could be felt through her inadequate windbreaker. Racing down the lane, she swerved to drive through all leaf piles that awaited pick up, scattering the labor of her adult neighbors with her willful passage. When she arrived at the Salter household she did it twice, and then rolled to a halt one house away to watch for any outrage.

None was forthcoming. The house remained closed and silent. There were no cars in the driveway either, and Mariel imagined Mr. Salter's wife and teenage daughters down at the police station weeping and pleading for his freedom. She felt confident that the cops would pay them no heed and might even arrest them as well because they were related to him. She smiled at this thought, though she had hoped to be the unmoving object of their pleas herself.

Mariel heard a footfall behind her and, without sparing a look, began to pedal away.

"Mariel," A voice called to her softly… urgently.

After placing a safe distance betwixt herself and the voice, she spun around to see who had called out to her. It was Mr. Forster.

He stood by his mailbox, which was entwined in ivy. He smiled at her and said, "I was trying not to startle you… sorry."

Through the near-skeletal trees behind him the cold disk of the sun peeked through. Mariel waited.

He nodded his neat head at the Salter home. "What a ruckus last night, huh… police and everything… goodness, I didn't know what was going on around here."

Mariel watched his face and noticed that he had whiskers today.

"Scared the hens nearly to death, I can tell you that! They don't like a lot of commotion. Of course, I'm not telling *you* anything you don't already know." He glanced at the Salter residence, then asked, "What *did* happen last night? I figured if anyone knows what went on it would be you. You're our neighborhood policeman… er, woman, that is."

Mariel felt her chest expand with pride. "Come on," he waved her forward, "we can feed the hens while you tell me all about it."

Forster turned and began to walk back up his drive. Mariel followed. When they reached the backyard he took up a pan of feed and handed it to her and she began to scatter it for the hens. Within moments they were busy scratching away at the soil around her feet.

"So what *did* happen, Mariel?" Forster asked after a period of contented quiet.

Mariel felt herself beginning to smile and tried to suppress it. "Mister Salter came in my room," she managed by way of explanation, while gauging her chances of seizing one of the glossy black hens.

"He did?" Forster gasped. "Why on earth would he do that?"

Mariel's small lips twisted. "Don't know," she said at last.

"Hmmm," Forster hummed, then added, "maybe he was trying to steal something… what do you think?"

Mariel shrugged and said nothing. The pale sun, sinking ever lower, cast lengthening shadows across the wooded backyard.

Forster leaned toward Mariel and asked in a confidential tone, "You haven't told anybody about that necklace, have you?"

Mariel's small, pale eyes flashed up and back down again, then she shook her head causing her curls to bounce in agreement.

"Good," Forster assured her. "That's very good… not even your mom, though?"

Again she shook her head.

"How about some hot cocoa, what do you say? It's getting chilly out here and the hens will be alright for a while." Again he turned and walked away from Mariel without looking back. At the top of the steps he held the door open for her and patted her on the shoulder as she passed within. Mariel felt his fingers run over the necklace beneath her pullover as the slightest pressure—a fly walking across her neck.

He crossed to the stove where a kettle was already pumping steam into the fussy, over-heated room. "Lots of sugar?" he inquired.

Mariel nodded even as small beads of sweat formed along her hairline—the heat was a palpable force. There was also a peculiar, not altogether pleasant, smell in the house.

"Sit… sit," he waved at the round table that was placed within the arch of the bow window. Between the gingham curtains Mariel could see the backyard with its chicken coop and the darkening woods beyond. Ripper flashed through her memory and then was gone.

"It's for the birds," Forster called to her as he spooned cocoa mix into a mug and poured the hot water. "They can't take the cold, you know—the songbirds. Most of them are from South America." He swept an arm toward the ceiling of the room and

Mariel saw them for the first time: dozens of cages mounted at various levels within the kitchen and continuing on into the rest of the house. Whipping off the parka he had been wearing, Forster slung it onto a nearby chair. He wore a T-shirt beneath as mute testament to the hothouse atmosphere of his home.

"They're always quiet when a stranger comes in… but they come around when they get used to you."

As if on cue, first one, then another, began to sing and the house soon filled with their tropical chorus. Mariel thought she had never heard anything so beautiful and rose as if on strings. Gripping the cage nearest her, she peered in at the tiny, vibrant creature. The colors of its plumage, brilliant blues and reds, shimmered with the rise and fall of its delicate breast. Forster was still busy making the hot chocolate, taking far more time at it than her mother ever had, and Mariel lifted the little latch to its cage to reach in and…

"Don't!" Forster screamed, spilling some of the cocoa from the mug he had in his hand. "Don't touch them, Mariel!" The birds, all of them at once, went silent.

Starting, Mariel drew her hand back but not out. It was not her nature to surrender the initiative without good cause. The tiny bird regarded her sticky, chubby fingers without alarm.

"They're very delicate," he added, while looking for an uncluttered surface to set the mug down on, then added under his breath, "Not that you would know anything about that, you little *Neanderthal.*"

Mariel *didn't* know anything about that, nor did she know the meaning of the strange word he had used, but she did know when she was disapproved of, this was something of which she was keenly aware. But of far more importance, *she recognized Sailor's handiwork from the night before.*

Forster caught her gaze and looked down at the long, festering scratches that ran down his arms, then back up at Mariel. "I despise cats," he hissed very much like one. His pupils shrank to tiny dots as his neck tendons distended. "I just wanted the necklace, Mariel… that's all. I have my reasons, as I'm sure you know."

Mariel said nothing and the room filled with a thick, clotting silence.

Forster nodded, as his face rearranged itself into something less savage. "If you give it to me now, we can still be friends," he promised, "you can still have your cocoa. It's just that the necklace is important, it might be recognized if you wear it around. It's not really worth anything otherwise… it's cheap, paste jewelry… something a whore would wear—something a whore *did* wear." He set the mug down and took a sudden step across the slight distance that separated man and child.

"You killed Ripper," Mariel pronounced, seizing the songbird in her fist.

Forster froze in mid-step. "Don't," he gasped, even as he watched the bird's tiny, futile struggles within Mariel's pudgy grip. "Please… don't."

Mariel withdrew her fist with the bird firmly in her control. Backing up to the door, her sweaty free hand groped for the handle while Forster watched her every movement, his eyes sliding back and forth as the heat-swollen door resisted her efforts.

As she turned a little to gain more leverage, he eased a step closer, taking advantage of Mariel's distraction, his long fingers reaching out for her nest of curls.

Mariel's fist shot up, the tiny head of her captive swiveling this and way and that in its panic, its black, shiny eyes blinking and blinking.

"Okay," Forster halted once more, his hands coming up palms outward, "okay, please… please, don't hurt him, Mariel… please."

At last, she succeeded in throwing open the door, letting a cold wind rush through the stifling kitchen.

"Maybe," she answered, backing out onto the porch, her eyes never leaving his as she pulled the door closed behind her. The latch snapped into place like a hammer blow in the now-silent room. From the porch Forster heard a muffled giggle and the sound of clumsy footsteps.

He took a long step, then had to grasp the edge of the table to keep from falling, his legs grown too weak to support him. After several moments there came the ratcheting of a bike bell. "Oh God," he moaned, "Oh God, what am I going to do?"

Finally, as his breathing quieted, he looked up and around him as if just awakening. Lifting the mug he had prepared for Mariel, he drank its contents down in one scalding gulp, then walked from room to room turning on every light. All around him the air began to fill with the song of a new and sudden day.

Returning to the kitchen he sat at the cluttered table, and after a while, sagged forward, laying his head to rest on the placemat. As his eyelids began to flutter his breathing grew very rapid and he began to pant like a dog, perhaps like Mariel's dog, he thought. Then it slowed once more to become reedy and shallow. Trying to lift a hand to reach out for the empty bird cage, he smiled and muttered, "The speech of angels… the language of God."

From other rooms his choir sang on.

༄

Though Mariel had been successful in keeping the necklace a secret, the songbird proved another matter altogether. Between its near continuous song celebrating the unfettered freedom of Mariel's bedroom, and Sailor's constant yowling and scratching at her closed door, the secret was soon out. The following morning Mariel's mother discovered the colorful little creature flitting about Mariel's room, leaving its droppings wherever they happened to land. Neither she nor Sailor was amused.

Remaining mute in the face of interrogation served no purpose in the end, for her mother had heard from other mothers on the street about Mr. Forster's fussy relationship with birds. An unsettling suspicion began to dawn on her.

Snagging the contested bird within the worn fish net from an old forgotten aquarium, she confined it within a perforated bait can left behind by her ex and set off down the street. Mariel followed on her purple bike at a distance, silent, resentful, and a little fearful, but curious for all that.

When Forster failed to answer her repeated knocks, Mariel's mom marched her formidable bulk to the rear of the house where she found his hens scattered about the yard and far into the woods. Upon seeing her they stormed forth with hungry shrieks. Ignoring them she mounted the rear steps, grunting with each, to peer in through the glass of the back door. Forster sat slumped at his table and would not respond to her repeated poundings. An empty mug with a teddy bear painted on it rested next to an outstretched hand. As keen as her daughter, the long scratches that festooned his bare arms did not go unnoticed.

Turning with a gasp, she swept back down the steps, through the now-fleeing hens, and back up the street to her home, carrying Mariel in her wake by force of will and dire threats. The police responded within minutes of her call.

☙

Mister Salter was released from custody with a muted apology from the police, even as Forster was bundled away for autopsy. It appeared Mariel had misidentified her assailant in the darkness, a common enough mistake even for an adult. For his part, Salter threatened lawsuits all around.

As to Forster's motive for breaking into Mariel's bedroom, the general consensus was the obvious one. But as he was dead, the matter was laid to rest with his body.

Mariel, as a reward for her brave defense of herself, was allowed to keep the bird, and though it was not a dog, she was very satisfied with the exchange. As for the necklace, she continued to keep it a secret from her mother and wore it only when out of the house. Ripper, forgotten in all the excitement, remained in his shared and secret grave, an arrangement that also suited Mariel, as she had no wish for her possession of the necklace to be challenged in any way.

Reyna
(2019)

Reyna lay between the sheets of her small bed, the house around her quiet in the coolness of the dawn, her brothers and mother sleeping, her father not yet returned from his night shift at the gas station. Around her the room took form and color with the coming of the unseen sun, its distant radiance tinting the walls a rose-petal pink.

Glancing to her left the eleven-year-old saw her wheelchair awaiting her as it did every day. Beyond it stood a small table on which her parents had placed statues of Our Lady of Guadeloupe and Saint Padre Pio. A spray of flowers formed a backdrop to the little shrine. Reyna's mother often brought home flowers to place in a vase next to the Blessed Virgin, flowers that she had rescued from the homes of the wealthy people she cleaned for each day.

On the wall opposite, the faces of young pop stars alternately beamed or pouted down at her, faces that filled her heart with secret yearnings.

With a sigh, Reyna closed her eyes to them, took a deep breath, and focused her thoughts, tunneling deep within herself for that hidden resource, that spark that glowed there always, if not always brightly. It took all Reyna's concentration to find and grasp it, to gently coax it into an incandescence that would fill her inert body. After a few moments, she was looking down on herself. It always began this way.

Knowing that she didn't have much time, she paused only long enough for a glance, a reassurance that her body would be there to come back to. Once Mama woke Mateo and Gabriel, Reyna feared someone coming into the room and discovering the empty husk of her crippled body and mistaking it for coma . . . or worse yet . . . death. They had suffered so much already because of her accident.

Her first out-of-body experience had been a fumbling, and somewhat terrifying, tour of her small room. On her second attempt she had fared better, exiting her room and drifting through her family's tiny bungalow like her own ghost, eventually discovering Mateo's collection of dirty magazines.

Reyna had been shocked, though not surprised, as Mateo, being the eldest, was always precocious and full of mischief. Naturally, she revealed her findings to Mama later that morning— little Gabriel had to be protected from such influences, as he was the youngest and idolized his older brother.

It was only after her mother asked how she knew of the hidden magazines that it occurred to Reyna what she had done. She had the choice of telling the truth or lying. She lied, telling Mama that she had overheard Mateo discussing the nudies on the phone with a friend. She couldn't think how to explain the truth.

Later that morning she heard Papa confronting Mateo over the magazines. He was restricted to the house for seven days, except for scheduled school activities—he was on the football team at St. Charles Borromeo and had to make practices.

Not knowing how his parents had discovered his secret stash, he accused Gabriel and made him miserable the whole week Mateo was grounded. Reyna swore not to snoop after that.

She had been unable to resist, however, when her mother's wedding band went missing.

The simple gold ring never left her finger till she pinched her hand shifting furniture one day while working. Arriving home later that evening with a swelling hand, Reyna's mom complained that the ring was hurting her and used some liquid soap to get it off before the inflammation grew worse. Exhausted, and in some pain, she went to bed early. When she awoke in the morning, the swelling had subsided somewhat, and she thought of the ring. It could not be found.

Though Reyna's mom and her crew worked long hours cleaning and neatening other people's homes, her own was less tidy, and showed the results of two active boys and parents who worked long hours. Unable to recall exactly where she had taken the ring off, she spent a fruitless hour searching for it before having to leave for work again. Reyna's father did likewise, having come home to the crisis and been enlisted. After lifting and sifting through furniture, cushions, and strewn clothing, he, too, gave up, seeing Mateo and Gabriel off to school, then going to bed to catch a few hours' sleep. Reyna had heard everything through the open door of her tiny room.

With the house now silent, and her tutor not due for an hour, she closed her eyes, stilled her breathing, and tunneled inward searching for the ember. Finding it more easily each time, she seized it, blew it into life, and rose from her inert body like an exhalation. Moments later she drifted through the house, an invisible cobweb floating along the ceiling, her view of the cluttered floor below that of a hawk circling a lonely, distant field. Studying the mix of surfaces that presented themselves in search of a glint, a glimmer, of the lost gold ring, she discovered nothing. Willing herself to descend, she repeated the process, skimming along the carpeted and hardwood landscape of her home. When even the stained tiles, tub, and toilet of the bathroom revealed no evidence, she hurried to her parents' bedroom and slid beneath the door.

Ignoring her father's gentle snoring, she slipped beneath the bed and scrutinized the lightly furred surface of the hardwood floor. Within the dusty cumulus a golden arch shone in the dim light, and she glided over to it—her mother's wedding band lay trapped in a crevice between the wall and the floorboard's edge. Were she not above it she would never have seen it.

That afternoon, after both her physical therapist and her tutor left for the day and her papa came in to visit, she told him where to find the ring. There was nothing else she could do, as she lacked the power to move any object.

Upon hearing this, her father tilted his head to one side and asked, "How could you know that, Reyna?"

She shrugged in answer and he left the room. A few moments later he returned with the ring, the expression on his stubbled face a mix of joy, disbelief, and perhaps, Reyna thought, a touch of fear. "How?" he repeated. "Did one of the boys hide it as a joke and tell you?"

"No, Papa," she answered. "I just knew." Again, she couldn't think how to describe her newfound ability.

"Just like St. Anthony—the finder of lost things," he murmured, supplying his own answer. "God gives what's needed."

"Yes, Papa," she replied, smiling. "He does."

After that Reyna noticed that everyone treated her differently than before, even the boys, with a deference that she'd only seen when older relatives, or their priest, came to dinner. She wasn't sure she liked it.

It had been the story of Padre Pio that had begun it all. Shortly after the inexplicable accident that made her such a burden, Reyna's mother placed the little statue of the saint in her room. "He was a worker of many miracles, especially healings," Mama explained, setting the portly and bearded ceramic figure next to the one of the Blessed Virgin. "He was so holy," she continued, "that he had the stigmata at times—the wounds of the cross—just like Jesus! Can you imagine?"

Reyna found that she didn't want to; the thought of bleeding wounds both frightened and sickened her. Since the car had run her down, she had become very squeamish about such things. Seeing this on her face, her mama added, "Did you know that he could also be in two places at once?"

"I wish I could be," Reyna responded without hesitation. "If I could, then I would leave myself behind and go outside.… go wherever I wanted to."

"Well, I don't know about that, but I do know that we can pray for his intercession and healing… and that is what we'll do."

"Yes, Mama," Reyna answered, and she did, but it was the thought, the idea, of bi-location that fascinated her.

It was during one of those prayerful meditations that she found she had been granted the same ability as the miraculous monk—she left her body and was free.

And today she was determined to venture outside the house.

Feeling much as she imagined a balloon might, Reyna bobbed along the ceiling, struggling to master her ethereal self and control her movements. Taking a last look at the pale girl with her long dark braids and thickly lashed eyes closed in apparent slumber, she crossed the room to the window, paused for courage, then passed through it and into the wakening world.

Preening himself on a glistening holly tree, a cardinal caught her attention, and she entered his tiny, fragile body as quickly as a thought, something she had not intended to do, nor even knew she could accomplish.

As if startled, or struck by a stone, he threw wide his brilliant wings, and before Reyna knew what was happening, took flight, and she with him.

Darting from tree to shrub, shrub to bush they dashed along, Reyna as startled as he now, even as she was exhilarated by the bird's speed and aerial dexterity. Feeling breathless, though she knew it was only a feeling, she focused herself and found her proud host calming, as well. Lighting on a branch, his head turned this way and that, as if searching for Reyna, his tiny heart beating hard. Reyna soothed him with thoughts like soft strokes, her will subsuming his instincts, and soon he began to sing—he was hers.

But what to do? Reyna feared just going along for a ride, uncertain where they might end up. She wasn't sure she could find her way back.

Then it occurred to her—her school. She had not been back since the accident on her way home. She missed her teachers and friends, missed playing with others.

She knew how to get *there* and back. She was sure of it.

The bright-red bird launched itself, abandoning its usual pattern of short, cautious flights and winging straight and level across the shingled roofs of Reyna's neighborhood, following the streets that she knew well from having walked to school and back so often with her brothers.

It had been that one rare day she walked home alone that everything had come unraveled. Mateo had stayed on at school for football, or maybe it was soccer, Gabriel was at home with a bad cold. That was the day she could neither remember with clarity, nor explain—why *had* she turned back after safely crossing the street and run into the path of an oncoming car? The driver couldn't avoid her, according to his testimony. The only witness, a large, long-haired man in coveralls whom the driver had caught a glimpse of, was never located. Her life, and those of her family members, was forever changed in that moment.

To care for Reyna, her father had to work night shifts while her mother worked days. In this manner one was always available (even if sleeping). Reyna's sense of guilt for these hardships was profound.

Passing over the very spot where her family's troubles had begun, she looked down on the suburban intersection, which appeared no different from so many others—two-lane blacktop framed by cracked sidewalks and shaded by trees whose leaves were tinged with the yellow and russet of coming autumn.

She and her cardinal alighted on one of these. Reyna saw no evidence of what had happened to her at this very spot almost a year ago—no scattered books, no blood—all trace of the accident gone. *Why did I turn back?* she asked herself for the thousandth time.

With that thought, she felt herself leaving her little host and saw him flit quickly away through the canopy of branches. This time, however, she felt herself not rising, but sinking, dropping through wavering layers of shadow and light, like a diver descending to the bottom of the sea.

Before she had a chance to become frightened, she stopped and found herself exactly where she had been before the sensation overcame her—looking down on the fateful intersection.

Fewer cars were parked along the streets now, and the sun was much higher in the sky than it had been moments ago. A group of children were crossing the street, the boys laughing and shoving one another, the girls ignoring them, speaking with their heads close together. All of them wore backpacks or carried books and wore the uniforms of St. Charles Borromeo. Reyna could see from the direction they walked that school had just let out. But how could that be? It wasn't time yet.

As the children reached the other side of the street a battered white panel van pulled up to the curb nearby, its engine coughing into silence. A large, heavy man sat behind the wheel, his big arm resting on the open windowsill, a cigarette clasped between his thick fingers. Beneath a great tangle of shoulder-length bushy hair he peered across the street and down the sidewalk.

Reyna looked in the same direction as the man... and saw with a start her own self approaching... alone. It was *the* day... the moment drawing near.

The man flicked the cigarette away and opened the driver's door, stepping out. She could see now that he wore coveralls stained with dark splotches, like a car mechanic. Taking a few ponderous steps, he arrived at the van's side door and slid it open. Leaning in, he appeared to busy himself with something inside. A faint mewling came from a cardboard box he was reaching into.

Reyna looked back to her former self in her school uniform of plaid skirt, white blouse, and knee socks, scanning for traffic before crossing the shadowed street. Satisfied, she stepped out. The big man turned, smiling, his grizzled jowls quivering.

"Hey there! Wanna see some newborn puppies?" he called to her from the opposite curb.

Reyna saw herself hesitate in the street, still several yards from the van and its open door. As if on cue, the pups began to sing and whine.

"Take a look," he offered. "You can have one, if you like."

She saw herself smile just a little as he held up one of the squirming, fluffy creatures for her inspection, its eyes barely open, its belly soft and pink.

Don't, she ordered her former self, beginning, at last, to remember. *Keep going.... Run home!*

But it was no good. These things had already happened; Reyna of the year before would make the same choice as before—the puppies were adorable, irresistible.

Her smile wide now, her former self hurried toward them, closing the distance.

The big man's arm shot out like a piston, seizing her in a terrible grip, and hauling her toward the waiting van.

With a small cry of terror, Reyna watched as she tried to pull in the opposite direction but was dragged forward. She saw now the interior of the van and a second larger wooden box behind the cardboard one containing the puppies. It had a lid like a coffin and an open padlock dangling from a clasp mounted on its side. She understood in that frantic glance that she mustn't allow herself to be placed in that box; if that happened she would never see Mama and Papa or her brothers again.

In desperation she bit the man's grubby hand, her small, sharp teeth sinking deeply into the thick flesh. His blood tasted of salt and iron.

With a high-pitched squeal he snatched his hand away, releasing her. Reyna turned and ran as hard as she could in the opposite direction, aware only of an impending roar and a rushing shadow before everything went black and red.

Responding to a call that his wife had gone into labor, the driver was hurrying to the hospital a half mile away. Reyna knew her former self would not recall any of this.

Unable to watch the bloody carnage done to her by the vehicle, she hastened to reverse the process that had brought her back to this day, ascending like a scream through the filmy elements of time and catching up to the present.

Moments later, she opened her eyes in her small sad bed, her wheelchair standing guard nearby.

Beyond her door she heard Mama in the kitchen and smelled the aroma of the dark, thick coffee she and Papa liked. Across the hall she heard Mateo and Gabriel arguing. Soon, Papa would come home, tired and bleary-eyed from his night shift. He and Mama would kiss as they always did, and she would hurry off to work herself. Reyna would lie in her bed and wait for her tutor, wait for her physical therapist, wait for her visiting nurse, wait for her life to someday resume…

"No!" Reyna cried to the pop singers on her wall, the statuary on her table. "Saint Padre Pio, I don't want to wait any longer! What can I do?"

As if in answer, there was a pecking at the window. Looking over she saw the cardinal peering in at her.

An idea began to form in her mind.

If having inhabited this beautiful tiny creature had created a bond between them, then how much more of a connection might be formed with her earlier self? If she could not will the earlier Reyna to avoid the trap laid for her, could she not reunite her present and former selves to do so? Armed with foreknowledge of their fate, Reyna could simply take another route home, avoiding the terrible intersection and its rapacious troll altogether.

But having conceived the possibility, Reyna understood that it wasn't enough to avoid her fate at the hands of the monster. There must be justice, as well—for her year of pain and suffering, for the hardships imposed on her parents, for the innocent driver, and perhaps for the other little girls who would not, or did not, escape. There must be a reckoning, and it must be now... and she thought she knew a way.

Heedless of her family finding her vacant body, Reyna once more closed her eyes and sought out the transforming energy within her broken frame. Within moments, it seemed, she was hurtling back to the moment, the place.

She met herself traipsing down the buckled sidewalk and entered her younger self. The merging of her past and present selves only resulted in a tremor within her brain, a small pebble disturbing a placid pond.

How wonderful to feel her legs once more, to be walking beneath the autumn elms, smelling the aroma of burning leaves, catching glimpses of a faint blue sky between the branches overhead. It was exhilarating to be whole and free once more... and she intended to stay that way.

Nearing the intersection, she saw the big man sitting in his rusty van, smoking. He was looking in her direction. She could not yet make out his expression. She freed one arm from her knapsack and let the bag dangle from the opposite shoulder. Without breaking stride, she unzipped it.

Looking back up, she saw that the ogre had tossed his cigarette onto the street and was exiting the cab of his vehicle. He turned away from her to slide open the van's side door, leaning in to stir the pups. A faint whimpering and yipping reached her ears, and terror pierced her like a sickness.

Forcing herself forward, Reyna entered the intersection and walked toward the other side.

Turning around, the monster held a squirming puppy in one giant hand, the hand she had bitten, and this reminded her that she had tasted his blood—he was human. Her resolve swelled once more.

With a hitch of her narrow shoulder she allowed her schoolbooks to fall out onto the street from the open bag.

Squatting to gather them up, Reyna called out to him, her teeth near chattering, "Hey mister, would you help me?" Somehow, she smiled.

He looked confused at this unexpected development. She had not even allowed him to make his pitch about the dogs. Reyna noted him taking a quick look around before answering, "Sure... I'll help you. Then you can come look at my puppies. You'll love them."

She kept smiling at him across the twenty feet that separated them. "Okay!" she answered.

He turned to place the puppy back with its siblings. Reyna teased some papers out from between the pages of a book while he was distracted.

Smiling also, the big man lumbered toward her, his bloody eyes gleaming and eager. Reyna allowed the breeze to send the papers fluttering along the asphalt. As he knelt, she sprang up to chase them.

Thwarted, he called after her, "I'll pick these up and you—"

But he never got to finish. With a roar of acceleration, the car raced into the intersection just as Reyna knew it would, the young father-to-be distracted and on the way to the hospital. The man in the coveralls was kneeling, turning just in time to see the grill of the car before it smashed into him, sending him and Reyna's books flying. She screamed and turned away. A pedestrian coming upon the scene pulled out his cell phone, shouting to the stunned motorist, "I'll call nine-one-one!"

When all was silent once more, she turned back. Scrambling from his vehicle, the driver rushed toward the coverall man, who lay on his back. Splashed with crimson, his large frame appeared crushed and deflated, his eyes wide as if studying the scudding white clouds above.

"Oh my God!" the young man cried. "I've killed him!"

In the distance a siren began to scream.

Only just beginning to understand the magnitude of what she'd done, Reyna went to him and placed a hand on his shoulder as he knelt over the big man. Startled, he looked up into her face, tears streaming down his own.

"He was trying to get me into his van," she told him in a clear, steady voice, and pointed at the waiting, open door of the battered vehicle.

"What?" he asked, unable to focus on her words.

The siren drew closer.

"He wanted to put me in a box," she explained.

The young man turned and looked to where she was pointing.

"A box?" he repeated, still not understanding.

A police car pulled up to the scene, its siren fading as the officer exited and hurried toward them.

"You'll see," she promised. "It wasn't your fault."

And with those words, Reyna focused herself on the task of returning, separating her selves once again so that she could go back. She had to go back and see.

When her eyes opened again in the early-morning gray of her room, the aroma of the coffee was still fresh, her brothers' argument ongoing. It was when she heard her papa laughing at something her mother said that she dared to hope.

Turning her head a little to the left, she looked for her sentinel through slatted eyes—the wheelchair was no longer standing guard; her little statue of Saint Padre Pio was missing, as well.

"Reyna!" her mama called down the hallway. "We're waiting breakfast for you! Wake up, you sleepyhead!"

Throwing back her covers, Reyna leapt to her feet, and with a cry of joy rushed to join her family.

The Hangman
(2016)

As I was packing up the house today, emptying shelves and drawers into cardboard boxes, I came across a book that I hadn't read since I was a child. It was one of those adventure tales full of pseudo-science and improbable derring-do, with a marvelously illustrated jacket showing the young hero, Tom Swift, employing his latest world-beating invention. Once upon a time, I had relied heavily upon the boy genius for companionship.

I flipped open its cover for a glimpse into my youth and a newspaper clipping fluttered out like a dusty autumn leaf. I retrieved it from the floor with a grunt and unfolded it with as much care as I could, the brittle edges flaking at my touch.

Within its folds lay a photo perched atop a news column, a mugshot provided by the police according to its caption. The grainy black and white picture showed a young man in his early twenties with an over-bite and narrow, slitted eyes, his gaze off to the left of the lens and downcast.

The article, dated April 1978, gave his name as Tommy Locke, age twenty-four, a known narcotics user, and a suspect in a recent drug store burglary; a fugitive. I knew Tommy, of course, which is why I had saved the story.

It seems appropriate that I should chance upon this picture of Tommy, dead now for nearly forty years, as my wife of almost that long recently, in her only moment of cruelty, predeceased me. I had not seen it coming, was not prepared, and don't know that I can ever recover. Our home is now haunted, so infused with her essence that it is killing me to remain here. So, I'm closing it up to take an apartment nearer our children. This is my last day—a day for the dead, it seems.

Finding a chair unoccupied by packing material, I lower myself into it and gaze into the face of Tommy Locke, a childhood friend. What happened between us when we were kids changed so much for me… yet, in the end, so little for him. The newspaper item was proof of that.

For some there is no justice… only suffering.

༄

As children we are often confronted with mysteries, though seldom of the Hardy Boys variety. The actions of our playmates can be puzzling, even disturbing, but in the self-absorbed way of children we let those behaviors pass unchallenged… unless they impinge on our own pursuits, of course. At least this was so when I was a child in the fifties and early sixties, a time when children seemed to be everywhere, like some cloning experiment gone terribly awry.

In those crowded days it was difficult to walk a block and not attract bored and curious fellow travelers, usually barefoot boys in jeans and dirty T-shirts, who would pepper one with such intellectual challenges as, "What'cha doin'?" "Where ya goin'?" and "Wanna play?"

My typical response being something along the lines of, "Nothin'," "Nowhere," and "I guess so."

These early attempts at meaningful conversation were carried out in Columbus, Georgia, where, for at least half the year, we excelled at sweating. Air conditioning was only a rumor in Lester's Meadows—nine square blocks of two- and three-bedroom houses with but a single bathroom and crammed with bunk beds—a neighborhood where we kids stood around streaming salty water like young seals.

Yet, despite the heat, we did sometimes move about, and on occasion even vigorously. But when we did it was either to chase someone down, escape being caught, or to defend ourselves with whatever martial talents we possessed.

For variety, we played war.

War, as played by us boys, and sometimes Bonnie Shaver (whom we were afraid to make go away), was mostly fun. Sometimes it wasn't, due to some knucklehead refusing to be dead when you had clearly, and indisputably, shot him.

The other big challenge was with which army you served. Not everyone could be in the U.S. Army. Sorry, but that's the way it was. If they were (as was evident even to us kids raised during these dark times), who would be the enemy? You gotta have someone to fight… and beat. There weren't a lot of volunteers. You can see our problem. No pay, no benefits, and you get killed at the end.

But we did have the Lockes.

Maybe most neighborhoods have a family like the Lockes, though I hope not for the sake of that family. Like many in our neighborhood, theirs was a large brood—five or six kids. No one was ever sure. Several other families were in the same situation. Head counts kept changing. With so many of us running around adults grew confused or just pretended we weren't there. We showed up for supper anyway.

In a neighborhood where everyone was sweaty and had fathers who worked in sheet metal shops, textile mills, bottling plants, or, in the case of the more educated, were appliance repairmen, culture consisted largely of TV programs and comic books. No one had much time for, or interest in, being sensitive. What went on in our various households was understood by us kids to be "normal." We were all normal, maybe some less than others—which brings me back to the Lockes.

They had it hard even by our standards. Their father was a drunk and a bully (mostly of his kids; his wife too when he was feeling ambitious). We had lots of drunks in the neighborhood, but Mr. Locke was low and mean as well. Even the other drunks despised him. Our insanely alcoholic neighbor across the street knocked some of his teeth out one glorious afternoon.

Mr. Locke hated me, and I despised him right back. He believed I was teaching his boys treason… and he was right. His boys were beaten down, fearful, and nervous—I counseled disobedience, evasion, and escape, and often led by example. They rarely followed me far before turning back.

His girls… well, I'm not sure… but something. At eleven, girls were pretty much invisible to me, except for the aforementioned Bonnie Shaver whom I feared, and the chocolate-eyed and honey-skinned Vanessa Cordelle, who made me feel light-headed and hollow-gutted whenever I stood near her.

But kids are ruthless, we all know that, and the kids of Lester's Meadows were no exception. Remember our dilemma with fielding an opponent? The Locke Boys made great Nazis, superb Russians, and passable North Koreans. They didn't like it, but it seemed they lacked the will to resist. It was probably just easier, and certainly far better than being left in the dugout.

This arrangement mostly worked… until the day it didn't.

It was late spring in 1964 and we were playing cowboys and outlaws. I guess we were looking for a change of pace. I'm sure you can guess who drew the short straws.

The only problem with the Locke boys playing the bad guys was that they lacked both energy and malice. My memory of the brothers was that they could rarely attain actual running speed; it was more of a lurching movement akin to those nightmares where you can't pick your feet up even though there's something really, really horrible bearing down on you. Nor would they put up much of a fight.

The Locke brothers had only one defensive move in their repertoire, and it went like this: The one being pursued would run away (sort of) and when I closed the distance in order to tackle and capture him alive (if possible), he would suddenly drop to the ground like a fifty pound sack of flour, causing me to trip over him and go sprawling into the dirt. I'm ashamed to admit how many times I fell for this… literally. In my defense, I wasn't alone. By God, it was maddening, though! Perhaps there was something in the waters of Lester's Meadows. I sure hope so. It would explain a lot.

In spite of such challenges, and after a pitched gun battle, the younger of the two, Tommy, was apprehended and brought to justice. He suggested that we hang him.

No, I'm not making that up. It was his suggestion. That much was never contested.

We thought this a capital idea.

As is the way of boys, a rope was secured and a tree selected. Oddly, or perhaps not, all of this was taking place in the front yard of a family that had no boys—the home of the soft and golden Vanessa Cordelle. I leave it to you to conjecture our collective male motive for being there.

Her father wasn't home or he would have chased us away. He didn't much care for other human beings and this was well known. The mom was an Italian war bride, spoke little English, and was rarely seen at any time. God knows what she must have thought of the sweaty mob of boys who had commandeered her property. Perhaps, having lived in war-torn Europe, she thought it was normal.

Tommy tied the rope around his own neck and climbed up to sit in the crotch of the tree. Kevin Bradley, a wiry kid with glasses and a crewcut, climbed the springy mimosa after him and secured the other end to a higher branch. Then, having pronounced him guilty as sin, we all stood around for a few awkward moments as the realization slowly dawned on us that we couldn't *actually* hang Tommy. With a collective shrug we began drifting away to continue the game—after all, there was another Locke still at large.

As we were leaving, Kevin offered to untie Tommy so that he could climb down, but Tommy just shook his round, close-cropped little head and stared off into the distance as if disappointed with our lack of follow through. So we left him there as we swept 'round to the backyard to renew our pursuit of frontier justice.

Sometime later, don't ask me why, I decided to check on Tommy and see if he was ready to come down from the tree yet. It was starting to seem a little stupid even to me. Rounding the corner of the house, I found his situation unchanged—Tommy just sitting in the cradle of branches staring out at nothing, the rope still circling his neck. The whole picture began to make me nervous.

Calling out to him, I asked, "Tommy, you wanna come down?"

Turning his head, he stared in my direction as if he couldn't yet see me.

I came a little closer. "You wanna get down now, Tommy?"

His face puckered a little, like someone waking up cranky.

When I reached the base of the tree, his bare, dirty feet were level with my face. His toenails looked like he chewed them. "Tommy, why don't I untie you so you can get down from there?"

Why he hadn't untied himself had yet to occur to me.

He blinked.

"Leave me alone," he murmured, as if he was speaking to a ghost.

"I'm gonna go get your brother," I said. "You should get down."

"Leave me alone!" he repeated with more force than I had ever heard from one of the Lockes.

His eyes were a shimmering blue, like a pool empty of swimmers.

He began climbing out on a limb. And right then, I knew exactly what he was going to do.

"I'm just gonna untie you, Tommy," I said, and hiked myself up into the spot that he had vacated.

"Don't get near me!" he commanded, his voice rising.

I angled upwards toward the branch where the other end of the rope was tied.

"Get away from me!" he screamed, like I was crowding him. I was further away than I had been and getting higher. The fragile tree trembled with our movements.

Shouting could be heard from the back of the property—the eternal dispute over who was dead and who wasn't.

"I'll jump!" Tommy shrieked.

My fingers tugged at the stubborn knot.

"I will… I will!"

Suddenly the fronds of the mimosa thrashed into life, the entire tree dipping then rising. Fragile blossoms, like tufts of pink cotton candy, rained down.

Losing my purchase, I scrabbled for a branch to keep from plummeting to the earth. The rope next to my face had gone taut as a dowel rod, tremors coursing through it like electricity. Looking down, I could see the top of Tommy's head as he spun at the end of the rope, tiny scars visible through his short hair, like pale worms beneath the flesh.

Leaping like a monkey, I started down. Tommy's fingers were clawing at the rope around his neck. I could see now that the tips of his toes were just touching the grass beneath him like a dancer *en pointe*. This had probably saved him from breaking his neck. Meanwhile his face was turning the color of an eggplant, his body spinning slowly around as he strangled. I could hear him gasping for breath.

All I could think to do was to seize his legs and lift him to relieve the pressure on his windpipe. Then I began yelling bloody murder!

There must have been a lull in the backyard debate because the thundering herd rounded the corner of the house and sped toward us. Kevin hurtled up the tree as if it was horizontal and a few seconds later his end of the rope fell to the earth. Tommy flopped over onto me carrying us both down.

Someone managed to loosen the noose and pull it over his head. A raw, bloody ring was burned into his neck, but he was still breathing. When he opened his eyes they were starred with ruptured blood vessels. After a long moment they sought my own… and held.

I couldn't fathom what was coming.

"He pushed me," Tommy croaked, tears running down his dirty cheeks, his bloody gaze sliding away from my own with the damning words.

Silence descended, the accusation burrowing into a dozen ears. Everyone was looking at me.

"That's a lie!" I gasped. "He's lying!" I couldn't believe what I was hearing. "I saved him!"

Not only was I unjustly accused, but I had been robbed of being a hero by the very person whom I had rescued! Looking to those around me for support, I was met with silence and stares; my face flamed. Even then I could see how it might look to the others. "It's just not true!" I managed, stopping as tears threatened to add to my humiliation.

"He did so…" Tommy insisted, his ragged, injured voice carrying the weight of moral authority.

The other boys drew back from me, uncertain now, the slight shuffling of their feet creating a gulf between us, Tommy's words making me a stranger.

At some point adults arrived on the scene and Tommy was hustled away, the rest of us sent home to our parents.

Stumbling into my own house, I found mom on the phone. As I shut the door, she turned toward me, her face white with shock, the phone receiver still to her ear. Her expression was like the last candle in the church guttering out. I lay face down on the couch and cried until I had no more tears.

☙

Tommy was fine in the end, his neck healing, his voice returning to normal. A few days later, despite my repeated protests of innocence, Mom dragged me down to the Locke household to apologize.

My old man seemed to have had his doubts about Tommy's story, but held his peace, and in the end I had to spit the words out. It was my story against the victim's and what kid, after all, would hang himself? The play-acting had just gotten a little out of hand. It was an accident, that's all I had to say—all that anybody wanted to hear from me. We were all normal... yes?

Tommy's dad smirked as I choked out the words, his piggish eyes watering with satisfaction. When I had finished, he said, "You stay away from my kids. I don't trust you... never did... and now... nobody else does neither." He was fighting back a smile.

Mom hustled me away from there without looking back. I think even then she sensed she had made a big mistake. She didn't tell Dad what Mr. Locke had said; she knew it would cause a fight. I wanted to tell him myself but was too humiliated to speak. In time it seemed pointless to say anything.

That summer the other kids gave me a wide berth, their parents uneasy with my presence. You can guess my new nickname. I took to reading and spent a lot of time in my room, or stretched out with a book in a wheelbarrow in the backyard. That was when I tried to read the entire "Tom Swift—Boy Scientist" series, of which there were a thousand, I think.

Once we were all back at Rosemont Elementary things began to return to normal, and as time went by, and nothing else happened, other kids began to show up at my house again. Not many… but a few—oddballs and outcasts—kids like me—kids I had hardly been aware of before the hanging.

As the months went by and the days greyed and shortened, even the Locke brothers joined in again, though only in other kids' yards, or on the street—neutral ground. After all, what choice did they have? They were still Lockes.

Tommy kept his distance, seldom meeting my gaze, but not for the reason our friends thought. Only he and I knew why.

A few weeks after my forced apology, I had managed to waylay Tommy as he was cutting through a patch of woods. It was a popular shortcut on the way home from school. He was not surprised. It was the way of things then.

After a brief scuffle, he admitted that he had lied and swore that he was sorry, though he offered no explanation as to why. But even as I sat atop him amidst his scattered schoolbooks, both of us panting like dogs and my fist hovering over his face, I already knew the answer.

In that moment when our eyes had met as he sat in that mimosa, I had seen everything—the sadness… the fear… the desperation. He had been looking for a way out of it all. And when I had thwarted that, he'd had to have a scapegoat—me—the hangman. How could he have faced his old man otherwise? How could he have explained it to him?

Though I had gotten my apology that day, there was no one else to hear it, and I would never be looked at in the same way again, never be allowed to return to my former self.

But I knew the truth, and I knew his dad, and for Tommy's sake, it had to be enough.

It wasn't, of course. Not for Tommy— the newspaper article from '78 went on to say that the police had discovered their suspect hanging by his neck in an abandoned garage on lower

Broad Street. There was a small photograph of this sad, leaning structure mid column. According to the reporter, lodgers at a neighboring boarding house had complained of an odor.

Tommy's second hanging was only the inevitable ending of the first.

As we had both learned that hot afternoon at the foot of the mimosa tree—for some there is no justice… only suffering.

Neighbor
(2014)

Evan saw him first but didn't say anything to the others. He didn't want any trouble with the new neighbor, especially since they were all playing hooky from school. But Frankie noticed him anyway.

"What's *he* lookin' at?" he growled to the others.

Evan and Kit-Kat turned their heads in the direction Frankie was looking.

"I think he's just readin' or somethin'," Evan offered. A magazine, or catalog, rested on the man-next-door's lap as he sat in a lawn chair on his patio. It lay open, but it did not appear as if he were reading. He was staring in their direction. His dark-framed glasses obscured his eyes behind their thick lenses.

"Dude… he's starin' right at us," Frankie insisted.

Kit-Kat, so called because of his predilection for the chocolate wafer bar of that name, took a bite of the same and said, "Man, he is one weird-lookin' dude."

"Dudes," Evan pleaded, "stop starin' at him… he's not starin' at us; it just looks that way." If the neighbor came over to complain to his mom when she got home from work, she would know that he had skipped school again.

"How can you tell?" Kit-Kat inquired. "You can't even see his eyes, man."

It was true. The light reflecting off his large glasses rendered them opaque.

"He's prob'ly wondering why we're not at school," Evan offered.

"What business is it of his?" Frankie challenged. "It's *none* of his freakin' business," he answered his own question. "Screw him!" He said this last looking straight back at the neighbor, who was separated from them by a sagging chain link fence, and about thirty yards of distance. "Turn the music up!" he commanded.

Kit-Kat complied automatically, his round placid face expressionless, even as Evan protested, "Dudes, he's gonna call the cops about the noise!"

The bass thump of the hip-hop beat they had been listening to swelled in volume, the voice of the singer emphatic and threatening. The neighbor continued to stare at them, his expression unreadable—a balding man in his mid-fifties, pale and slug-like in his cheap lounger.

After several more minutes of this the neighbor set his magazine down onto the concrete of the patio, rose, and went into his house. A page of the abandoned reading material lifted and fluttered with the slight breeze, then lay down once more.

"Hah," Frankie crowed, "what a puss!"

"You better hope he's not callin' five-o," Evan said, turning down the radio even as he spoke.

"Speakin' of pusses," Kit-Kat replied with a glance at Evan's hand on the volume knob. Evan refrained from turning it off altogether.

Minutes went by, and when the neighbor did not return, and no police showed up, the three friends resumed their slothful postures in the wobbly aluminum chairs they occupied: legs thrust out, arms dangling, occasionally bringing a cigarette to their slack mouths. A cool breeze started up and Evan shivered once, convulsively, like a dreaming dog. He wished he could put a jacket on over his black T-shirt, but Frankie and Kit-Kat disdained such accommodations to the weather, so he refrained.

"Somebody walked on your grave," Kit-Kat remarked. "That's what my great-auntie says when you do that."

"Your great-auntie is full of it," Frankie said. "If you've got a grave, then you're in it, jerk-off, and Evan's sitting right there. That's the stupidest saying I ever heard."

A lawn mower coughed into life and began to roar and pop. All three boys turned their attention next door again as the neighbor rounded the corner from his garage pushing the machine. He began to mow his back lawn… very slowly.

Evan thought the mower sounded unnaturally loud, as if something were wrong with the muffler. He had seen his new neighbor mow his lush yet meticulous lawn several times before and never noticed it being so loud. The pudgy man reached the far end of his yard and turned around to do another swath. He took tiny mincing steps as if his feet hurt. The boys' music was drowned out by the racket, but the man showed no signs of personal discomfort. A weak beam of sunlight revealed a flaky, raw-looking scalp.

"You've got to be kiddin' me!" Frankie shouted. He cranked up the volume once more, but it was useless against the neighbor's lawn mower. "Are you kiddin' me?" he now asked the world at large.

Eyeing the neighbor, Kit-Kat stripped the wrapper from another treat and began to munch. His pebbly complexion took on a reddish hue. "He's dickin' with us," he murmured between bites.

"You guys hungry?" Evan shouted over the roar. "Ma bought some cold cuts yesterday! They're in the house," he added.

Turning as one, his friends shrugged and slouched after him.

☙

The bologna was really for Evan's and his little brother Eric's school lunches, but Evan was not going to sweat the small stuff now. He lathered some mayonnaise onto slices of white bread and stacked them with the cold, greasy-tasting meat. Pouring sodas all around, he sat and began to eat with his friends.

After several minutes of this, Kit-Kat remarked around a mouthful of gooey bread and meat, "Hey, Numbnuts finished with his lawn." They could hear the raucous thump and boom of their music once more. It sounded lonely out on the patio.

Shoving his chair back across the sticky linoleum flooring, Frankie rose and went to the kitchen window, sandwich still in hand. After studying the scene for a bit, he observed, "Naw, he still has some mowin' left to do—looks like he had to go out; his car's gone." Turning back to Evan, he asked, "Don't you have any mustard in this house, dude?"

Fishing out a crusty-looking jar from the back of the fridge, Evan turned around to find Kit-Kat missing. "Where'd Kit-Kat go?" he asked, handing the jar to Frankie. Then he heard the mower start up again.

"No… he's not…" Before Evan could finish, the engine coughed into silence once more and he heard the rattle of the fence being vaulted. Kit-Kat rushed back into the room from outside, his face red with suppressed laughter.

"Dudes…" he exploded, pointing at the kitchen window, "…dudes!"

Evan rushed to the window and looked—the mower appeared to be exactly where the neighbor had stopped it, but the bed of daffodils that bordered the house were sheared and scattered across the lawn like dabs of butter. "You…" Evan began over the gales of laughter behind him. "… you mowed his flowers, dude."

The neighbor's car eased back into his driveway. Carrying a red plastic bottle of machine oil, the shapeless little man made his way to the backyard. He stopped over the mower. He appeared to be studying the tracks it had made in the grass. Evan saw his face rising to follow them to his flowerbed and the carnage that waited there. "Dudes…" Evan breathed. They crowded to the window beside him.

The neighbor turned his face in their direction as they all three ducked back from the window. Standing motionless, he appeared to be looking right through the walls at them, and even Kit-Kat and Frankie went silent. Peeking from behind the curtains, Evan saw no change in the man's bland expression, the eyes still opalescent behind their lenses.

Returning to the mower, he uncapped the oil and added some, then some more. When he started it again it smoked like a diesel train, the exhaust as loud as before. Evan noticed the slight breeze that had chilled him earlier drifted the smoke over the sparse grass of his own yard. Within minutes the boys retreated, coughing, into the living room.

"Dude," Frankie observed hoarsely, "he added *way* too much oil to that bitch!"

☙

That Saturday the boys hit the dirt trails that were woven through the woods behind Evan's house. Coursing along miles of rutted paths, their dirt bikes whined like giant wasps, the sound rising and falling with the sudden twists and turns of their progress.

The woods were littered with rusty barrels they had dragged in to mark turning points. Other debris lay along their path as well—the accumulated detritus of countless teens nourishing themselves on candy bars, sodas, and the occasional prized beer can.

Evan saw Kit-Kat throwing up dirt some twenty yards ahead of him, struggling to bull his way through a mud hole. Frankie was lost to sight, having disappeared around a bend in the trail ahead, blue smoke marking his passage.

Wobbling deeper into the churned-up black goo, Kit-Kat thrust a booted foot out to steady himself, found no support and began to topple over. "Shit!" he cried out.

Evan saw his chance and gunned his Yamaha onto the sliver of solid earth that formed the rim of the mud trap. As he passed, Kit-Kat collapsed onto his right side in the mud, his bike lurching a few feet beyond, spewing mud over him as it did so.

"Haw!" Evan called out, streaking past his downed buddy. His helmet skewed a little with his movement, and he had to take a hand from the handlebars to twist it back around so that it wouldn't obstruct his vision. He gave this a fleeting thought, as he had adjusted the strap just before they set out.

Rounding the same curve that Frankie had gained moments before, he opened up his throttle as he settled into the straightaway that led to the next obstacle—a large mound of dirt that provided a near vertical climb, followed by a heart-lurching descent. He felt a slight tremor run through his front tire and forks. Glancing down and back, he could see nothing he might have run over to cause it. He turned back to the upcoming hill, lowering his center of gravity on the motorcycle, and focusing on the summit through the dirt-spattered screen of his helmet visor.

Frankie was just cresting it, his bike lifting into the air at the crown and then nosing over and disappearing with its descent. Evan felt the vibration again like a small electric jolt through his fingers and elbows. There was no time to reconsider it. He gunned the bike into its climb up the slope.

Pushing skyward, he could sense that his tires had found Frankie's tracks and were having an easier ascent as a result of it. The summit approached with dizzying speed and then he was airborne. Feeling his stomach fall away beneath him, he struggled to ignore the sensation and focus on maintaining the bike's posture—it was essential to nailing a good landing and continuing his run. Like Frankie before him, he nosed it over and held his breath.

As the blue horizon of the sky fell away to ragged treetops, followed by the churned, ruined earth of their racecourse, Evan's front wheel touched the sloping path milliseconds ahead of the rear tire. "Nailed it!" he thought, even as that same tire came free of the front forks, launching him over the handlebars and into the path of his now-tumbling motorcycle. His helmet flew from his head with a snap that stung his throat.

Somersaulting onto the hillside, his back slammed into the earth even as his downward movement continued, his motorcycle appearing over him now, upside-down and tumbling. "It's gonna get me," he thought, but lacked the air in his lungs to scream.

The crippled motorcycle, with its engine, transmission, and gear-laden rear wheel, smacked the soil next to his now-bare head, and then leapt up once more, carrying on beyond him, its greater weight giving it momentum. Evan slid along in its path, dazed and grateful.

Reaching the bottom in a slurry of stones and loosened earth, he came to rest next to his wrecked bike. Finally able to draw air into his lungs once more, he gazed up into the blue above him, his left wrist screaming, his right cheek deeply scratched and embedded with bloody pebbles and dirt.

Frankie's face, framed in his helmet visor, suddenly blocked out the sky. "Dude!" he said, his voice muffled by his head gear, "Dude!"

*

On the ride home, tuning out his mom's diatribe on how dangerous off-road biking was, how lucky he had been, and how he would never ride again so long as she took a breath, Evan tried to think about what went wrong. He and his dad, on one of his increasingly rare weekend visits, had gone over Evan's bike with a fine-tooth comb, changing the oil, checking the tire pressures, and testing the torque on the various nuts and bolts that held it together. Everything had been perfect. It was a second-hand motorcycle, and his dad, a car mechanic at a local dealership, had been adamant about maintenance. The helmet, resting on the floorboard between his feet, had been new.

"No way this happened," Evan thought as the world ripped by the car window. His cast-encased wrist and bandaged cheek throbbed even though he was groggy with painkiller.

"You're so lucky that you're a rightie and it only broke that one little bone… that… that… *scrap-oid*," his mother's voice pierced the fog. "If it had broke your arm you'd be in a real mess, wouldn't ya?"

"*Scaphoid…*" he heard himself correcting her. A colorful diagram of human wrist bones lay in his lap—a gift from the emergency room.

"Oh… sorry, Doc," Ma fired back, "I'm still working on my medical degree, and we ain't got to wrist bones yet—I should smack you." She whipped the car into the oil-stained driveway and braked. "Listen you—you take yourself inside and lay down—you got pretty beat up today."

She ran a rough hand along his narrow face, being careful of his bandaged cheek. "I'm so glad you're okay, sweetie. When I think what might have…" Evan was embarrassed to see tears in his mother's eyes and looked away.

She gave him a little slap on his good cheek to get his attention. "I've got to get back to work—we can't afford me to miss any time." She had lost her last job due to a drinking binge when she fell off the wagon. "Now get on in the house—your little brother's probably worried sick about you. I'll come straight home," she promised as Evan slid out of the car. She blew him a kiss and backed out into the street.

Standing in the drive, the helmet dangling from his good hand by its broken strap, he saw his neighbor standing in his driveway, as well. He had rolled a gleaming metal tool cabinet out of his open garage and appeared to be cleaning a set of wrenches with a rag and gas. Holding a silver socket wrench up that winked and glittered in the pale sunlight, he brought his opaque gaze around to meet Evan's… and held it. After a long moment, a tiny smile played across his plummy lips.

With a gasp of belated understanding, Evan stumbled for the front door. Falling through and slamming it behind him, he leaned against it breathing hard. He could feel his heart thumping in his narrow chest. With his good hand he flicked the door lock.

"Holy shit," his little brother gasped from his reclining position on the couch. "Ma was right—you are *messed up*! Does it hurt?" The television screamed with laughter. Sliding the bowl of cheese puffs off his chest and onto the cluttered coffee table, Eric sat up, his eyes on Evan's face. "Ev… you okay?"

Evan studied the strap of his helmet more closely than he had done before—the nylon had given way where it attached to the inside of the helmet. As he scrutinized it through his dilated eyes he could see that the tear was almost clean, not ragged. It had separated in a straight line, with only one side appearing to be a bit torn, and only at the very edge. It had been cut almost through with a very sharp blade, something like a box-cutter, he thought.

He could picture the neighbor making himself at home in their unlocked garage while he and Eric were at school and Ma was at work, loosening the bolts then turning his attention to the helmet, almost slicing through the strap at a seam well hidden within the headgear.

"Sonofabitch," Evan thought, "they were just *flowers*!"

He shuddered and pushed off from the door. Crossing to the couch, he dropped the helmet onto the floor and collapsed next to his brother.

"Ev, you gonna be sick or somethin'?" Eric slid a few extra inches toward the far end of the sofa, while securing the cheese puffs.

"Shut up," Evan told him. "Just shut up."

He tried to think what to do.

As soon as he finished telling Frankie and Kit-Kat of his suspicions, Evan knew he had made a mistake. They all three stood staring at the empty spot along the garage wall where Evan's Yamaha used to lean.

Frankie stubbed out a cigarette beneath his scuffed combat boot, the laces dangling like tentacles. "He must really think he's some kind of badass," he murmured.

"Looks like a queer uncle to me," Kit-Kat remarked between drags on his smoke.

"Well," Evan persisted, "whadda ya think? Should I tell the cops?"

"Oh yeah," Frankie answered. "I can really see them gettin' behind you on this."

Kit-Kat snorted.

"You really think they're gonna take your word over Numbnuts next-door there?"

"What about the bolts?" Evan returned. "What about that strap?" He gave the helmet a kick for good measure, while cradling his cast in his right hand. The scarred headgear spun like a top across the cluttered concrete floor.

"Dude," Kit-Kat interrupted, "they're just loosened bolts; it's just a frayed strap. It'll be your word against the slug's next door. Who you think they'll believe?"

Frankie had wandered over to the side window that looked out on the neighbor's property. After a period of silent contemplation, he remarked, "He loves that lawn of his—it's beautiful. I love it too."

Kit-Kat snorted again.

Evan dreamed of hornets that night. Ma had gone out on a date with a guy she met at work, and Eric had fallen asleep in front of the television. His hand still throbbing in spite of the extra painkiller he had taken, Evan had lain down on top of his unmade bed and fallen instantly to sleep.

His dream-self stood beneath a papery gray ball that hung suspended beneath the eaves of his home. From within it there issued a faint angry buzz. Picking up a branch that lay at his feet, he poked the nest with the tip. It rocked a little, and he noted that he had punctured the hive with a small hole. He could feel his palms sweating and his mouth growing dry and cottony, and wondered why he was being so foolish. But he couldn't stop—it was a dream.

He poked it again… a little harder this time.

Now the whine within grew more strident, and a few of its occupants crawled out to investigate, studying him with their hard multi-faceted eyes. Their wings flexed slowly up and down over their glistening bodies.

Breathing harder, Evan willed himself to wake up. His eyelids fluttered and his lips tried to form words.

Instead of waking, he gave the menacing paper ball a good whack with the stick.

The sleeping Evan moaned in fear.

The whine became a furious and concentrated buzz—the sound of a table saw. Erupting now with tiny black and yellow bodies, the hive crawled with wasps, their thoraxes pulsing with anger, their stingers barbed and dripping.

"Ma…" he heard himself say aloud into the cluttered room. "Ma…?"

"No," Eric said, shaking him by the shoulders, "it's me! Evan, wake up! There's something going on next door!"

"Help me!" Evan cried, coming bolt upright, as the buzz of the hornets reached a terrifying crescendo, stinging and swarming over his face.

"Evan!"

His eyes, at last, flew open. The whine was all around him.

"What?" he cried over his pounding heart and the terrific noise.

"Next door, at that weird guy's house—come look!"

Stumbling after his brother, Evan peered out the kitchen window into the darkness. The rise and fall of angry insects filled the air, even as beams of light cut back and forth across their neighbor's front lawn.

"What the…?" Evan breathed, even as he saw lights coming on in the house next door, and the dirt bikes, both singly, and in twos, turning their headlamps toward the wood line and disappearing down the dark trails within. "No… oh, no—they didn't!"

As quickly as they had come, they were gone, the angry sound of their passage fading into the night.

The neighbor's front porch light came on.

Diving toward the light switch on the wall, Evan doused the overhead.

"Ev…" Eric asked, a tremor in his squeaky voice, "… what's goin' on, man?"

"Be quiet!" Evan commanded, creeping back to the window.

The neighbor stood on his front stoop beneath the porch light, his tiny pink feet peeking out from beneath the cuffs of pale green pajamas. Motionless, he surveyed the carnage that had been done to his lawn from behind his ever-present glasses. Evan could see that his friends had ground and cut the velvety turf to pieces. Broken sprinkler heads spouted water, adding to the soggy, churned-up annihilation.

Turning his eyes back to the neighbor, he found the little man gazing back at him. Though he knew the man could not possibly see him in the dark, he took another step back, pulling Eric with him.

"What's wrong with you?" Eric demanded.

As he watched, the neighbor turned and went back into his house, shutting the door behind him. Next moment, the porch light went out.

No sirens followed, no cops were summoned.

After that, sleep eluded Evan. He couldn't get the neighbor's bland featureless face out of his mind, the blank smeared glasses seeking him out through the darkness. The silence that followed the departure of Evan's misguided friends was like a held breath.

☙

Flayed and torn, the neighbor's lawn lay like an open festering sore in the neighborhood. Each time Evan passed it he felt his neck bending, his face growing warm, as if he were, indeed, responsible for the past few weeks' events.

"What's wrong with that man?" his mom asked Evan one morning as she poured milk into his brimming cereal bowl. He still wore the cast, but with his good hand he was scooping cereal into his mouth. "I thought he was so particular about his yard—now look at it! That looks bad even for around here." Then she added with feeling, "Where's the pride?"

"Maybe he don't have the money to get it fixed," Evan offered around a mouthful of crunchy goodness.

"Sweetheart, he's got homeowner's insurance, I'm sure. And the damage those kids did to his property *had* to exceed his deductible!"

Evan wasn't sure what a deductible was but got the point—their neighbor wasn't repairing his property because he didn't want to. And this made him worry even more, though he couldn't say why.

"You didn't see any of the boys that did it?" Ma asked for the umpteenth time.

"I *already* told ya—*no*! It was dark; I didn't see *anything*… or *anyone*! You don't even know it *was* boys… it coulda been girls."

Ma gave him a look, "Yeah… *right*."

"For Christ's sake, Ma," Evan cried, standing up from his chair and stalking away from his unfinished breakfast.

Before he could get out the door she called after him, "Them boys are gonna get ya in a lot of trouble one of these days, Ev!"

He was already in a lot of trouble, he thought—his neighbor wanted to kill him.

Slamming the door behind him, Evan hurried past the neighbor's house, resisting the urge to look over at it. Without Ma to give him a ride, he would have to hurry if he didn't want to be late for school.

A damp wind was rising, and Evan looked up to see a bank of low, dark clouds gliding across the sky. Shaking his long bangs from his eyes, he lengthened his stride as the first heavy drops began to fall.

☙

By the time Evan got home from school, the rain had blown up into the season's first nor'easter. As he heated up some chicken fingers in the microwave for his and Eric's supper, the rain rattled the window, while the wind rushed around the house like a phantom train. When there was a lull in the volume of the television program, they could hear other things, as well: the creaking and groaning of the house as the gusts teased and pulled at it and, sometimes, what sounded like someone running across the roof from one side to the next. Each time, the boys would glance at one another, then look quickly away again.

Squirting some more ketchup onto his chicken, Eric complained, "I wish Ma would get home."

"Eleven o'clock," Evan replied, "that's when she finishes the late shift." He wished she were home too. The storm and its noises made him edgy and nervous.

Taking his plate back to the kitchen, he set it in the sink with half a dozen other crusty dishes. He should probably rinse them off and put them in the dishwasher, he thought. Then, remembering the cast on his hand, and that he had not emptied the dishwasher after its last use, decided that Eric should do it instead.

Glancing up from the sink, he noticed the neighbor's house was dark but for the back porch light. That was odd, he thought, to leave a back porch light on when he was gone. It should have been the front porch light.

Looking toward the front of the strange man's property, Evan caught the glint of light on wet metal. His car was still in the drive.

Suddenly he heard the front door slam open and his heart leapt into his throat.

"Ma," Eric called out from the living room, "you're home!"

Evan heard his mother struggle to close the door to the wind, "Yeah, they let us go early cause of the storm—they're worried about power outages. Turn that damn television down, Eric. Are ya deaf?"

Evan let out a sigh of relief. He was glad to hear her loud, hoarse voice.

He also heard a mechanical rattle and whine from somewhere out in the storm and darkness—faint, but as furious as the hornets in his earlier nightmare. The sound faded as he went to the front of the house.

"Hi Ma," he called out, even as he became aware that something was happening—something bad. It was almost as if the pressure in the room was suddenly increasing.

Swelling in volume, the groan of a dying giant filled the air, accompanied by the thrashing of a thousand wings. They all stood frozen, looking at one another. Then the giant struck the roof of their little rancher a mighty and thunderous blow, causing white dust to descend upon them in a choking fog. From Ma's room came the crash of breaking glass and falling debris. The entire house shook to its foundations.

Then the lights went out and they all began to scream and cough.

☙

By the light of a clearing dawn, Evan gazed trance-like at the huge ragged spur that pierced his mother's bed. The jagged branch had punched through both mattress and box springs. The rotten pine it was attached to could be seen through the hole in the roof it had made, its scaly length extending across the tiny backyard to the wood line where its broken stump still stood.

After a frantic call to their dad, who had come out in the storm with a couple of his buddies to rig a tarp over the hole, they had all slept in the boys' room. But with their nerves thrumming from the night's events they had gotten little sleep.

"My god," Ma whispered. "If I hadn't worked the night shift I might have been…" She didn't finish the thought, as there was no need to.

Eric clasped his mom around her waist.

Evan looked out to the black stump squatting at the edge of their lawn. He heard Eric mumble, "I love you, Ma." His mother answered, "You, too, Pumpkin."

Starting for the back door, Evan said over his shoulder, "I'm just gonna see if there are any other trees about to go."

"Always the optimist," his Ma called after him; then, "Be careful, you!"

The lawn was a green and yellow sponge, soft and squishy beneath his sneakers. Bark lay scattered across the yard as if the pine had exploded. Thinking of the rattle of the rain against the kitchen window, Evan wondered why the tree hadn't fallen in the direction the wind had been blowing.

Another sound teased the edges of his memory but eluded him.

Arriving at the stump, he halted, feeling his soles sinking into the soggy carpet of pine needles and mulch. He could see at a glance that the tree had been rotten throughout. It had been inevitable that it should fall. The edge closest to the house appeared smooth, almost even. Kneeling, he ran his good hand over the surface. It was *very* smooth.

As he rose, he caught sight of a small patch of mud, clear of debris. It contained a fresh shoe print. The heel impression actually contained a small amount of rainwater from the night before. If it had been there before last night, Evan realized, it would most certainly have been washed away by the torrential rainfall. The memory of the strange sound returned to him, and he knelt once more at the base of the stump. There were unmistakable teeth marks on the side of the trunk facing the house—chainsaw teeth.

Rising, Evan's thin legs went wobbly and his vision blurry. Steadying himself against the stump, he ran his right hand over his eyes, turning to look back toward the neighbor's house. As his vision cleared, he saw that it looked dead—no pale face peered out from its windows.

It wasn't possible… was it? Evan asked himself. Nobody *really* tries to kill someone over some stupid flower bed… do they?

The image of the man's blank passionless expression, his merciless insect-like stare, returned to Evan with force, and the dizziness swept through him once more. He tried to kill me, Evan thought with despair, remembering his shattered dirt bike. And now he almost killed Ma.

Stumbling toward his crushed home, he tried to think what to do. There had to be some way to make him stop. He would confess—tell Ma everything that had happened. She would go to the police, and they would believe *her*. She was an adult—they spoke the same language.

As he entered the kitchen he halted long enough to down several painkillers—more for courage than for his throbbing wrist. Washing them down with a glass of tap water, he heard voices in the living room. One of them was a man's voice—*Dad's back*! Evan thought. *Just wait till I tell him everything that loser tried to do. He'll probably go next door and tune that creep up—that'd be even better than having him arrested.*

Skidding into the living room, Evan was brought up short, his words still in his throat. The neighbor stood framed in the doorway. In his hand was a chainsaw.

Evan was certain he must still be asleep—this was all just a prolonged nightmare— this *had* to be the part where he would wake up! Swimming within the huge lenses of his glasses, the neighbor's small pupils fixed on him, mantis-like, over his mother's shoulder. He was close enough that Evan could see the flakes of eczema tiling his raw-looking face and scalp.

Turning to him, Evan heard his mother say from very far away, "I'm glad you're back, sweetie…. Mister Brimson here, has offered to saw the tree up for us… isn't that nice?"

Speechless, Evan continued to stare, while the little man's murky gaze never wavered from his face.

"Evan? Are you alright, honey? You didn't take too many of those painkillers, did ya? I told ya to be careful of that. I know you got a bad paw, sweetie, but Mister Brimson thinks you can help him out by pulling branches away after he's cut 'em loose. You feel up to that? Eric's not big enough."

The smeared lenses remained fixed… patient… waiting. So many things could go wrong—chainsaws were dangerous things.

Evan fled through the back door on the leaden legs of nightmare—he had not known what a coward he was until that moment.

☙

Evan spent the morning sitting atop the hill that had nearly killed him a few weeks before. Smoking cigarette after cigarette from his crushed packet of Kools, he listened to the sporadic whine of the chain saw in the distance. It set his teeth on edge, and he seethed with anger and humiliation. In a single bold strike, the repulsive little man had chased him from his own home and was now removing all evidence of his murderous nature.

After a few hours, the sound stopped and did not resume. Evan stubbed out the last of his smokes in the damp earth and rose to make his way home through the dripping woods.

The tree lay in evenly cut sections across the backyard, like a giant child's Lincoln Logs set. The neighbor had done a professional job of work. The tarp Evan's dad had rigged up had been rearranged to properly cover the hole in the roof now that the great branch had been carved up and removed. The neighbor was thorough… meticulous.

Slinking in through the back door, Evan was relieved to find his mom alone in the kitchen. Apparently the mantis-eyed man had gone home. Ma sat with her back to Evan, and as he came up beside her she started and glared up at him. The bourbon bottle on the table in front of her was a third empty. An empty glass stood next to it.

"Well… there you are!" she greeted him with an ugly smile. "Now that the work is done, the big man returns!"

Ma's flannel shirt and jeans were damp, the knees of her pants muddy. The shirt was sticky-looking with sap, and pine needles were caught in her tousled, dark hair.

"It's that *dick* next door…" Evan began, "… I think he might have notched that pine so it would…"

"Getting to be more like you dad, evr'y day…" she cut him off, "… so hep'ful… so goddamn dependable!" She struggled to her feet and stood glowering at him with bulging, bloodshot eyes. "I'm goin' out," she announced. "I haven't been out in ages, and I need to get out of this stinkin' hellhole."

"Ma," Evan protested, "you can't drive like this—you've been drinkin'!"

"No shit, Sherlock… what was yer first clue?" She brushed past him. "I'm gonna have a shower and a nap, then Caitlin's comin' by to pick me up—we're goin' out for a while."

Evan hadn't seen Ma touch the bottle for months and guilt swept over him like a black tide. "Where'd ya get the bottle?" he demanded.

Turning unsteadily, Ma regarded him for several long moments. "That little man you've got yer panties in a wad about… well, he ain't s'bad. When he saw how upset I was, he brung me a bottle over—*after* he finished doin' all the work around here, I might add—sayin' I deserved to relax a little." She turned back toward the bathroom. "And he got *that* right, by God!"

As the bathroom door slammed, Evan noticed Eric watching from the living room couch. His eyes were swollen and red; streaks of moisture ran down his plump cheeks. Now that Ma had picked up the bottle again, they both knew what to expect.

☙

On the third day of Ma's absence, after Evan explained to her boss once again about how she was too sick with flu to come to the phone—about how they were considering putting her in the hospital, it was that bad—Eric came home late from school.

Irritated, Evan noticed the mud he tracked into the house. "Hey, loser, you wanna try wipin' your feet… huh?"

Eric backtracked to the door mat.

As Evan pulled the fish sticks out of the oven and slammed the metal tray onto the greasy range top, he shouted, "Where you been, anyway? You shoulda been home an hour ago."

"Oh," Eric began sheepishly, as he shuffled back to the kitchen doorway, "Mister Brimson gave me a ride home from school. We stopped off for some tacos. I guess I'm not that hungry now."

"Whadda ya mean… he gave you a ride home…?" Evan felt his vision growing dark, his scalp prickling. "Don't be getting' in the car with that weirdo, dumbass!"

"He don't seem all that bad, Ev. He was just passing by as I was walkin' home and offered me a lift. He said he was starvin' and did I mind if he stopped off for some tacos. Then he bought some for me too, 'cause he said he didn't want to eat in front of me. I don't know, Ev, he don't say too much, but… he seems like a pretty nice guy."

Evan was regretting not having put Ma and Eric in the picture now, hating the feeling of outraged betrayal that was welling up in him at Eric's words. "You don't understand…" he began, but Eric cut him off.

"Oh, he did say as to how I might could help him plant some flowers in his backyard, if I wanted to… that he would pay me 'cause he needed help with it." Eric's eyes gleamed at the idea of pocket cash—spending money was in short supply in their household, and if Ma didn't get back to work soon, would be for a long time to come.

"No!" Evan shouted, burning his good hand on the baking pan at the same moment. "You are not to go over there—d'ya hear me, Eric? I will beat yer little ass, if ya do!"

Tears started in Eric's eyes, and he shouted back, "He said you might be this way, Ev… that you might not like me getting' the job over you! He said to tell ya, if ya did, 'Then why don't you give 'im a hand with it yourself!'"

Slamming the pan down, Evan stalked out of the kitchen and across the driveway to his neighbor's lawn. It still looked as if moles the size of small dogs had burrowed through it, and the recent rains had turned the exposed soil black. Puddles lay here and there, the entire expanse appearing to have suffered an extremely localized earthquake.

Attempting to stay out of the worst of the mire, Evan navigated in little hops and long steps to Brimson's front porch. Pressing the doorbell, he felt his legs shaking within his jeans.

Nothing happened, and he glanced around the devastation, his nose wrinkling in disgust as an odor of sewerage wafted its way to him from nearby. Near a sprinkler control valve recessed into the lawn but exposed by a broken cover, lay the cast iron lid to his neighbor's septic tank. It had been shifted several inches by his friends' dirt bike rodeo.

Evan turned to find the little man staring out at him from the shadows of his foyer.

Startled, he blurted, "I'm… I've… I… owe you an apology, Mr. Brimson. Well… kind of, you know. I'm sorry 'bout what happened with your flowers and all… and then…" he waved his cast at the lawn. "Well… all this, too, I guess."

The neighbor continued to watch through his thick lenses, the tiny pupils shifting smoothly from right to left with Evan's movements.

"It's just that… I… well… I didn't actually *do* those things, you know… that was something some friends of mine did. I guess they thought they were doing something good for me… I don't know… I'm just sayin' that… that… I guess I'm sorry that they did what they did and I didn't come to you about it." He sputtered to a halt. "I just wanna make things right now… okay?" Sweat was running down his armpits.

"Friends?" the little man asked in a smooth, low voice—the sound of air rising out of a hole in the dark earth. "Is that what you're worried about—friends?"

Evan shook his head, even as he studied his torn, dirty, sneakers. "No…" he found himself almost whispering. "Not so much them…"

"Who then," he persisted, "your mom… your brother?"

Now Evan felt his shaggy head going up and down in agreement, humiliating tears beginning to leak from his eyes.

Brimson took a small sudden breath, as if shocked at the depth of Evan's feelings. "It hurts to care about someone," he said in a casual tone, as if they were old friends, comfortable with one another. "That's why I don't… ever." After several moments, he added, "You'll get over it, I suspect," then closed the door as quietly as he had opened it.

That night, Evan lay in his bed in the silent house, the neighbor's words running through his head like a chant—"You'll get over it… you'll get over it."

Snoring softly, his little brother lay in the bed across from his own. He couldn't always be with him, he thought… it was impossible, and any day now Ma would wash back up as she always did, wrung out and vulnerable.

He couldn't go to Dad, though he wanted to so much—Pop had thrown in with his new family, having grown tired of all the turmoil in his old one, and Evan saw less and less of him each month.

The sunburst clock on the kitchen wall tick-tocked in the darkness of the house.

He dreamt again of the hornets, thousands of them. Looking down at his feet, he saw the crushed remnants of the gray hive, his stick, broken with the effort, lying beside it. The air vibrated with the sound of their furious wings, but they were nowhere to be seen. And he was so very hot.

Thrashing and grunting, Evan kicked at his blankets, attempting to free himself from their suffocating embrace. He just couldn't seem to get away from them.

Opening his eyes, it became obvious why—the glistening black and yellow bodies clustered over every inch of him, only his eyes had been left unobstructed, and even as he watched, the angry insects began to march across his eyeballs like a closing curtain.

Evan started screaming as they poured into his open mouth, stinging, biting, and choking him, transforming his body into the very hive he had destroyed.

∽

The neighbor woke to the sound of a lawn sprinkler spurting in uneven bursts from the front yard. Being a light sleeper he knew they couldn't have been on for more than a few minutes. His glasses were already on his face, even as his small feet slid into his bedroom slippers.

Suspecting an already damaged fitting had given way, he glided toward the front door, picking up a flashlight from an end table on the way. It would only require that he turn off the water at the main sprinkler control valve. He switched on the porch light. Peeking out a small window inset into the door, he reassured himself that no one was outside, then threw open the door.

The ravaged yard, the small segment he could see in the yellow light, lay as he had chosen to leave it these past several weeks. His rage, ever present and easily stoked, was only evidenced in the slight pinking of his soft cheeks, his wispy scalp.

Framed in the doorway, his breathing was rapid and shallow—he felt alive each time he thought of the flowers, each time he looked out over his raped and plundered property. His own children had been as stupid and callous as these, he thought to himself… their drunken mother just as worthless.

Switching on the flashlight, he stepped out onto the porch and played its beam across the muddy field. Within seconds he located the problem: It was the main control valve. He was not surprised, as he had noted on the night of the destruction the kids had broken the cover over it. The fitting had probably been damaged at that time, and now, had at last given way. Dirty-looking water gurgled up from it in a sad fountain.

Stepping gingerly through the sodden mess of his former lawn, he tried to avoid contaminating his slippers. Within just a few steps, however, they were clotted with mud. He refrained from cursing; cursing was a sign of low breeding. So he said, "Fudge," in a vehement whisper.

Kneeling down and holding the beam of the light over it, he reached into the cold water with his free hand, searching for the valve handle. A stench of human waste wafted over him, and he choked and sputtered. It was horribly strong.

He swept the light across the small patch of ruined grass that separated him from the septic tank. It revealed a perfectly round hole in the ground a few feet away—the cover from the septic tank had been removed. The heavy, cast-iron, lid lay inches away from the opening.

The pilot light of his indignation ignited a white-hot rage, though the flashlight in his hand remained steady, his fury a cold that burned.

Coming to his feet, he began to swing the cone of light along the edges of the yard, following the splayed shoeprints that led from the septic tank toward his house. Yet even as the peril of his situation dawned on Brimson, Evan was already stepping out from the shrubbery behind him, the same crowbar with which he had dragged the heavy lid off already whistling toward his neighbor's bare head. Evan gave him no time to react, as his plan depended upon striking right at this spot.

The thud of the metal bar connecting with the base of the man's skull launched an electric shock up Evan's good arm, even as it sent Brimson stumbling to his knees. Kneeling now before the open tank, he swayed to and fro like a drunken penitent, blood running down the back of his pajama shirt. "Oh God…" he moaned, "… oh God." There seemed to be no urgency in his plea, just a deeply felt horror.

Evan hesitated, even as his victim appeared to be gathering himself to try and rise once more. Then he thought of his sabotaged motorcycle hurtling toward him as he lay helpless on the hillside, his mother's room with the great, jagged branch thrust through her bed, his brother's cozy lunch with this sinister little man.

The next blow landed across Brimson's shoulders, hurtling him over the edge and into the putrid mess of his own waste. A loud splash from the pit was followed by a gust of air so foul that Evan began to retch, dropping the crowbar.

From within came the sound of sodden splashing followed by the weak cry, "Don't leave me… don't leave me in here!"

Picking up the neighbor's fallen flashlight with his good hand, Evan focused it on the scene within—the man who had terrified him was struggling to keep his head above the black sludgy filth of his own making. He was several feet shy of being able to reach the rim of the entrance.

"You shouldn't have said what you did," Evan said to the streaked face, the now-naked, blinking, mole-like eyes. The obscuring glasses had been lost in the muck. "I told ya I was sorry about everything… I meant it. But you shouldn't have said I'd get over caring about Ma and Eric… that couldn't ever happen… you wouldn't know that, maybe. But I couldn't ever let anything happen to them."

Setting the flashlight down and plunging Brimson into pitchy darkness, Evan picked up the crowbar once more. Hooking the iron lid with it, he reversed his actions of earlier that evening, dragging it to the edge of the tank, and then several inches over it. It was hard work with one arm and he heard his own breath rattling with tension and fatigue.

The splashing below grew less frantic, and Evan set the crowbar down once more to retrieve the flashlight. When he shone it down the hole the neighbor stared back up at him, his fleshy face pursed with disdain, his tiny eyes ablaze with hatred, even as he was losing the battle to stay afloat.

"No," Evan resumed, "I don't think you'd ever understand, Mr. Brimson… I'm not sure you even can… but *you're* the one that's gonna have to get over it, and this is the only way you ever will."

And with that, he tossed the flashlight into the stinking hole with its captive and pulled the lid the rest of the way across, dropping it into its circular framework with a satisfying clang of metal.

That night, the hornets returned, chasing Evan across a featureless gray landscape, stinging and stinging—even his screams could not make them stop.

☙

Opening the door, Evan found a police badge being waved at him. The policeman, a tall, heavy man with a flat-top and eyes as shiny as marbles, asked a question which Evan couldn't hear over the roaring within his head. In a single instant, a black bile of guilt rose in his throat, pushing the cleansing words of confession ahead of it. He felt his legs going weak and wobbly.

Ma was shouting something behind him as she walked into the living room from the kitchen. She stopped short when she saw the detective's badge. "What's this?" she challenged, still drying her hands on a faded, threadbare dishcloth. She shouldered up next to Evan, displacing him.

"Your neighbor," the officer repeated, tilting his head in the direction of Brimson's house, "when's the last time you seen him?"

"That guy next door?" Ma asked, while giving the policeman a quick once-over. "No idea." She brushed a little of her springy hair out of her eyes. "It's been a while, though… a few weeks, anyway. I figured he was on vacation, or somethin'."

"That long," the officer mused. "Hmmm…" He made a notation in a small writing pad he had exchanged for the badge and ID. "What happened to his lawn?"

Ma's eyes cut to Evan then back to the officer before he looked up from his writing. "I think he was digging up his sprinklers," she answered, "some kind of problem there."

"Must'a been a bad leak," the detective murmured.

Ma nudged Evan with a sharp elbow, startling him back into life. "What about you, honey? When's the last time you saw your favorite neighbor?" She turned a big smile on the cop, adding, "He don't like Mr. Brimson too much. I don't know why—seems like a pretty nice fella, if you ask me. Helped us out during that last big storm," she explained.

The officer looked up, meeting her eyes. "S'at right—that last storm? Have you seen him since?"

Ma shook her head in what she hoped was a coquettish manner.

"How about you, son, was that the last time you saw him, too?"

Evan stared back at the cop, whose pen hovered over the pad. "Yes," he managed after what seemed an eternity. His lips were so dry that he actually felt them pulling apart when he finally got the word out. "I… think so."

The cop kept staring at him, as if he were waiting for more. "You didn't much like him, huh?"

"I… no… I… not much…" Evan felt he might black out.

Turning to Ma, the big man said, "Kids sometimes have an instinct about these things."

"What things?" Ma asked, intrigued now.

"If he's who we think he is, he's not a nice guy."

Ma slid closer to the cop. "Whadda ya mean?"

He glanced at Evan, but as Ma didn't seem to object to his being present, he explained, "We think he's that guy from upstate that killed his family a few years ago. Remember that? Went from room to room killing them all in their beds—a wife, two sons, and a daughter—the youngest, the girl, was only eleven. Can you imagine that?"

Ma shook her head, not that she hadn't been tempted herself from time to time. "So you think it might be *him*, then?" She nodded toward the neighbor's house.

"Yeah, probably—we're lifting some prints from inside, and taking some DNA samples from combs, used drinking glasses, et cetera… but yeah, we think it's him."

Ma seized Evan's elbow and yanked him closer. "Oh my God, I let him in the house!"

Shaking his big head, the cop said, "I wouldn't worry too much about him from this point, Mrs.…?"

"I'm not a missus, anymore, officer…" Ma turned on the wattage again, "… I'm just plain ol' Lari… short for Laura… Laura Wallace."

"Anyway…" he resumed with a smile of his own, "… it looks like he got wind of us comin', got out of bed, called a cab for the train station, or airport, maybe, and got out of town—he didn't take nothin' but the clothes on his back. I don't think he'll come back here."

Looking relieved, Ma pulled Evan even closer, punching him on a stringy bicep. "I guess you were right, Ev… he *was* a bad man, just like you said—you got an instinct." Turning to the officer, she made the smile vanish and asked, "Will you be keepin' an eye on us in case he *does* return? We don't have a man in this house."

Looking thoughtful, the detective answered, "Yeah… sure, I'll… we'll… keep an eye on you… *all*… just to make sure you stay safe."

Smiling big now, Ma said, "Great… that'd be just great."

For the first time in weeks, Evan slept through the night.

Ibrahim's Eyes
(2007)
Winner of Ellery Queen Readers Award

Sean Lafferty slouched behind the counter of the Quik and EZ Mart and watched his reflection stare back at him from the plate glass doors that fronted the small store. If he stepped away from the counter his phantom self would vanish from the glass, sucked into oblivion by the remaining illumination. Sometimes, he would shift to one side or the other and his ghost would mimic him, wavering, or disappearing altogether as a pair of headlights swept across the store from a car entering the parking lot. When the headlamps were switched off, his pale doppelganger, drained of blood by the softly buzzing fluorescents, would reappear to resume its study of its earthly counterpart. This could go on for long periods of time, and often would but for the interruption of customers, yet the sign, the thought, the emotion that Sean kept looking for remained locked behind his own alien visage.

He knew that seen from outside, he would appear to be waiting for the Q&E's nocturnal patrons—nervous teenagers in need of condoms,; even more nervous young mothers who had miscalculated the diaper count and were now forced out into the midnight world, or perhaps a sudden brash invasion of young men intent on menace and calculating the odds of taking the store's earnings by force, or just sheer intimidation. The graveyard shift was a perilous, haphazard world and Sean's apparent alertness was not altogether a front. Once another human being appeared from the darkness beyond his image, Sean's attention was refocused, and he bid farewell to his mute self.

The customer that stepped onto the lighted stage beneath the working outside lights raised a hand in salute, and Sean did the same. Moments later he emerged from the pool of darkness that shrouded the double doors into the store.

"Those lights, Sean," the police sergeant pointed over his shoulder, "they been that way for months. Not smart."

"No sir," Sean agreed. "I keep tellin' Mr. Corrado about 'em." Sean was older than the officer by at least seven or eight years, but he could not refrain from calling him "sir"—it was the three stripes on his sleeve. A long time before, Sean had been a Marine, and it was the only time in his life that remained vivid in his mind. His present was hazy and insubstantial, and he just a ghost that haunted it. "He's busy opening that new store on the other side of town," he added by way of explanation. A long cardboard box of the tubes lay untouched in the storeroom, and whenever the manager thought to ask about them, Sean would lie and say that he had forgot to install them. This explanation would suffice as the harried Mr. Corrado scurried from crises to crises in stores that lay scattered across the city.

The policeman, a portly, but light-footed man, diverged from his course toward Sean, gliding over to the coffee stand. Sean watched as the sergeant chose a flavored coffee from the row of stagnant pots and proceeded to add a flavored creamer and two packages of sugar substitute to his choice. After stirring all these ingredients to his satisfaction, he waltzed over to the counter and plopped the concoction down in front of Sean, his breathing slightly labored.

"No charge," Sean assured him as the officer dug into his wallet.

This was a ritual the two men went through on a regular basis.

"You sure?" Sergeant Fullerton asked, fulfilling his half of the litany.

Sean nodded and the policeman raised his paper cup in a toast and then brought it to his lips. As usual, Sean noticed, he had filled it too full. With a gasp, the sergeant snatched the brimming container away from his lips with a muttered exclamation, "Damn… that's too hot!" Several spoonfuls of the steaming liquid sloshed over with his sudden movement and the policeman danced deftly away, avoiding getting any on his snug uniform. The stain the coffee made on the dirty linoleum was only noticeable for its gleaming liquidity.

"Don't worry about it," Sean murmured from his seat.

"No, hell, hand me some paper towels," Sergeant Fullerton demanded. "It's my fault… I'll clean it up."

Sean did as he was bid and reached under the counter where a roll was kept for just such situations. Tearing off several, he handed them across the counter to the sergeant who bent grunting to his task. Sean studied the bald spot that was developing at the crown of the officer's skull. His own hair had remained full and thick through the years and only recently had streaks of gray begun to show themselves. People usually thought he was younger than he was.

Sergeant Fullerton's voice came up to him a little strangled, "How come you're always on midnight shift? Ain't you got some seniority, or something? Been 'round here forever!" This last he said as he straightened up, his features flushed and congested looking.

Sean caught a glimpse of his own face across the room, his head a pale balloon floating over the policeman's shoulder. "Doesn't bother me," he said.

"I can't wait to get off night shifts," the sergeant complained. "Damn things'll kill ya!"

"It's quiet," Sean offered.

"Yeah, it's quiet," the policeman repeated as he surveyed the shabby, empty store. "Quiet until someone comes charging in here to rob you, and maybe kill your ass in the bargain. Couldn't pay me to sit here like a fish in a bowl, waitin' for some mangy cat to take notice!"

Sean's gaze drifted downward and he whispered, "No, sir."

The sergeant's voice softened, "Hell, you don't have to 'sir' me, Sean. How old are you, anyway?"

"Forty," Sean answered, looking back at Sergeant Fullerton now.

"Forty," the officer repeated. "You're kiddin' me, right? You don't look no forty. Hell, I'm younger'n you! What's your secret?"

Sean thought for a second, and then smiled. "I keep out of the sun."

Sergeant Fullerton stared for a moment, then guffawed, "By God, you do that!" He chuckled a few moments more, then grew serious. "Listen, Sean, you been watchin' the news?"

Sean shook his head. He rarely watched the news programs.

"How 'bout the papers? You been readin' what's goin' on in this area?"

Again Sean shook his head.

The sergeant studied him in puzzlement. "You ain't just stayin' out of the sun, you're stayin' out of life altogether. Maybe that's the real secret." It was the officer's turn to shake his large round head. "Anyway," he resumed. "There's a gang of some kind been workin' our end of the state pretty serious. They like stores just like this one—open all night, lone operator in the wee hours, deal largely in cash. Get me? It's not a snatch and run outfit, Sean. They mean business and they're not leavin' witnesses. They've killed three, so far… and they take the security tapes, the whole damn cassette recorder, if they have to."

Outside the store, a car cruised through the small, littered parking lot. As the headlights swept across the patrol car outside, they appeared to hesitate, then resumed the arc that meant they had continued on to the exit. A fissure of white gleamed through a broken taillight lens. Sergeant Fullerton, his back to the lot, did not notice, and Sean gave no indication of what he had witnessed. During the course of a shift, perhaps half a dozen cars would perform the same maneuver.

"So we don't have a clue as to what they look like," Sergeant Fullerton went on. "No vehicle description. Nothin'. But they do shoot. The state police have recovered three bullets from the skulls of three night clerks… all small caliber. A ladies' gun, a .25, I believe, and they use it up close and personal, execution style with a mean twist." He placed an extended forefinger against the soft flesh that sagged beneath his jaws. "Straight up to the brain pan. The last thing those poor bastards got to see was their killer's grinning face.

"I'm not tryin' to scare you, Sean, but I can't help but worry with you sittin' on the edge of town out here."

Sean was touched by the officer's concern. They really hardly knew one another. "Well," Sean ventured over a rising feeling of excitement. "It wouldn't do to have Mrs. Fisher or little Megan in here for me."

"No, I didn't mean that," Sergeant Fullerton continued. "Talk to Mr. Corrado about closing down early for a few weeks, until we catch these thugs. How much money can he make between midnight and eight that would make it worth it?"

Sean appeared to think this over as Sergeant Fullerton studied his face, noticing for the first time the vertical creases that ran from cheekbone to chin amidst the salt and pepper whiskers of the night clerk's five o'clock shadow. It occurred to the sergeant that, but for Sean's vague, wistful gaze, a certain hardness might lie at the core of the man.

"I'll mention it," Sean lied. "But we make a lot of money up to about two a.m."

"Not enough," the policeman assured Sean as he wedged a travel cap onto the cup of coffee and turned for the exit. "I'll try to get cars out here as often as I can," he promised over his shoulder.

"Thanks," Sean said to his own image as the glass door swung closed behind the sergeant.

☙

Sean slept poorly that day. After the policeman's visit, a growing sense of alertness, a tingling nervous energy began to course through his veins. He felt like a person who had just awakened to a cry from another room, startled and uncertain as to its meaning. He was not afraid as a result of the officer's warning, but excited as he had been as a child watching a summer storm rolling across the landscape, its belly dark and full of lightning, the hot, humid air charged with menace and hidden meaning. So he was not surprised when he dreamt of Beirut.

The chaotic, crashing images of his dream would not have been recognizable as a geographic locale to anyone else, as they held significance only for the dreamer, but to Sean the very smell and taste of "The Root," as he and his fellow Marines had dubbed it, flooded his senses.

He stood on a third-floor balcony of the Battalion Landing Team's Command Post looking back over his shoulder. Somewhere to the front of the building he had heard the revving of an engine, and in the predawn quiet it seemed very loud. He was glancing back to see if the noise had disturbed any of his fellow marines in the room behind him, where most of his squad lay cocooned in their sleeping bags, but besides the usual grunts, snores, and farts of slumbering young men, they appeared unperturbed. Amused, Sean smiled and turned away. The dreaming Sean smiled also.

As his dream self watched the coming Sunday dawn tint the Lebanese sky with blood, a crash came to his ears, and a splintering of wood. The truck, or whatever it was, sounded much closer. Leaning over the wall of the balcony in an attempt to see what was going on, Sean was rewarded with nothing but the sight of a few heads popping out from the bunkers and makeshift shelters that dotted the edges of the airport tarmac. From somewhere below him there was the crashing of glass, and he counted two rifle shots. A moment later, a sergeant he thought he recognized charged out of the building's lobby and into his field of vision. Sean thought he had never seen someone run so fast before, or perhaps it was just an effect of the acute angle from which he watched. A husky voice from behind him called out, "Dude, what the f—k is goin'—" The sleeping Sean sucked in his breath. This is when it happened.

Suddenly he was flying, or more accurately hurtling through the air, over the very heads that he had just been smiling down on. Though he was enveloped by clouds that billowed grey and soft, he felt no sense of peace, as his breath had been sucked from his lungs and he was choking and on fire; an angel cast down from heaven. Other objects whistled by him in this celestial pollution—body parts and glass;, concrete and steel reinforcing rods,, boots and vehicle parts—all seeking new converts to their miraculous liberation. The maelstrom around Sean shrieked with the flight of unseen banshees.

Then, with an unceremonious thump, he was thrown to the earth like litter from a speeding car and left to stare upwards at a heaven obscured by tons of Ferro-concrete dust, while all around him objects, some horribly recognizable and others mercifully indescribable, fell from the sky like a hellish plague. He was alive.

This is where Sean would awake, just as he had awakened in the makeshift Battalion Aid Station a day later, bewildered at the sudden shift in reality, but largely unhurt. He would not believe the corpsmen that had insisted the entire Battalion Command Post was no more and grew combative when they had told him that two hundred and forty-one of his fellow Marines had died in the carnage of a truck bombing. He had known that this could not be true, as he was still living—could not be true. He could not have survived such a catastrophe.

A lieutenant with an engineering degree had tried to explain it to him, saying that it was likely the very explosion that had doomed so many within the building had lofted him along on a cushion of hot gases, setting him down with surprising gentleness as those same gases dissipated into the unconfined atmosphere. "A miracle nonetheless," the well-meaning officer had assured him. "Bullshit, sir," Sean had replied.

The following day he had been released for duty. Still angry over the inexplicable pessimism of his normally gung-ho fellow marines, he had strode directly to the site of the command post. It wasn't there.

Staring in incomprehension, he turned this way and that in an attempt to get his bearings. Somehow he had become disoriented and arrived at the wrong location. Its concussion, he had assured himself. That was the only possible explanation for his sudden loss of direction within the limited confines of his unit's area of operations. Had he not spent the last five months of his life dodging Shiite sniper bullets, Druze artillery rounds, and the occasional Syrian-made rocket right here in the Corps' stinking little piece of Beirut?

A corporal had walked towards him dragging a poncho liner full of something and dropped it heavily at his feet. "Pull your head out of your butt, Marine, and get this over to the morgue." Sean had stared back at the NCO blankly. "And when you're done, double-time back here… there's still a lot to clean up." He had hooked a thumb over his shoulder at the tons of rubble behind him. Only then did Sean allow himself to see and recognize.

The administration building that the Beirut Airport had given over to the Marines for their command post lay in the grave that the basement had provided, floor upon floor having collapsed in on itself after the Iranian Revolutionary Guardsman had driven his twelve thousand pounds of explosives into the lobby and detonated them. Sean had seen then… and believed. Then the poncho liner had fallen open.

☙

Climbing out of bed, Sean felt sore and tired, as if he had re-lived the experience his dream commemorated. Even so, the excitement the police sergeant's warning had engendered remained, and he felt unaccustomedly cheerful and optimistic. The possibility of a threat to his life had somehow reconnected him to the living world, awakened him as if from a deep, deep slumber. Pouring milk over his cereal, he gazed out his kitchen window at some children returning home from school. They were chattering like jays and darting about, the energy of youth rendering them unable to walk the sad straight line of adults, and for the first time in many, many years, he thought of Ibrahim.

In the days following the bombing, Sean had found himself more and more often manning Combat Post 69. This was due to the loss of personnel, and had the bombing not happened, he would have complained at such long pulls of hazardous duty. CP 69 was not sentry duty. CP 69 was where you provided target practice for the Shiite militia in "Hooterville," a slum otherwise known to its inhabitants as Hay-Es-Salaam. It was rumored that in the early days of the Marines' peacekeeping mission, when all had been well betwixt the peacekeepers and the Muslims, two lovely Lebanese girls made a habit of undressing in front of their window which faced the Americans' outpost. Hence, the name Hooterville. Sean suspected this had been wishful thinking on the part of some lonely marines, as the Muslim girls were known to be extremely, and disappointingly, strait-laced. Nonetheless, the name stuck.

But in the months of August and September, relations between the marines and all the factions involved in the Lebanese Civil War deteriorated, and CP 69 had become a very hot spot. They were shot at and rocketed from every quarter. Infuriatingly, the 'Rules of Engagement' laid down from on high made it almost impossible for the beleaguered troops to defend themselves. After the bombing, the marines, and Sean, found ways.

    One of the rules that Sean and the other surviving members of his company soon dispensed with was the prohibition on returning fire at a combatant that could not be clearly seen firing on them. As the enemy usually chose to shoot from the upper windows of the bombed-out buildings that overlooked CP 69, and then ducked back inside, this had always been impractical. Now, they always "saw" the militiaman, and after chasing him away from the window with a hail of bullets would follow up with a few well-placed grenades. This had the effect of silencing that particular room, and the marines could rest assured that at least one, if not more, militiamen would fail to answer roll call the following morning.

    After several days of this, there was a dramatic lessening of incoming fire. From several thousand rounds of small arms fire a day, and hundreds of rocket-propelled grenades and frequent mortar barrages, they were faced with what, as seen in comparison, was a desultory few hundred rounds and only the occasional grenade. The Shiite militiamen seemed to be thinking things over.

    It was during this lull that Sean and his newly-constituted squad discovered Ibrahim. Sean first saw him at the Lebanese Army checkpoint located across the street from CP 69. He appeared to be entertaining the soldiers with some kind of story that involved episodes of break dancing, and the government troops were enjoying the show. These soldiers were ostensibly the American's allies in their failing mission to keep the peace between all the warring factions in their country. However, experience had taught the marines that their commitment to that mission varied and appeared to be based on the quality of the opposition they faced. When they fought, they fought ferociously, but often they would stay their hand for reasons known only to them, much to the marines' consternation.

To Sean's eyes, the boy appeared to be about nine years old, small and spindly, with the large dark eyes and jet-black hair characteristic of so many Lebanese. He was assured, however, by a new member of his squad (a quick, nervous private first class from Indiana named Randy Colquitt), that Ibrahim was at least fourteen years of age. Randy had been transferred from his company to make up the losses Sean's had suffered in the bombing. It seemed the Corp was robbing Peter to pay Paul, as the unit that was supposed to relieve the marines in Beirut, had been diverted to a spot of trouble in someplace called Grenada.

"How d'ya know that?" Sean had inquired, while scanning the seemingly empty buildings in Hooterville. He had noticed several women cross an alleyway and enter one of them a few minutes before. They had all been draped in the traditional Muslim clothing. Sean thought they walked funny.

"Used to hang out in our AO. They say his parents were killed by the PLA… or the Shiites, or somebody."

Sean threw a look his way, then returned to scanning the blown-out windows across from their sandbagged position. "That right?" he asked. "Why's that?"

Colquitt turned away and slid down into their hole with his back against the wall. In the midst of firing up a cigarette, he answered, "Christians, I guess. That's what they say," he continued, blowing out a lungful of smoke. "I don't know."

Sean glanced once more at the Lebanese Army position. The kid had finished his dance and was looking in the marines' direction. He caught Sean looking at him. "Marines kick ass!" he shouted in passable English and waved.

Without thinking, Sean waved back. The kid started their way. "Damn," Sean muttered. "that little bastard's comin' over here."

Rising up from his crouch to wave him off, he caught a movement in the corner of his eye, then ducked so fast that he crashed into Colquitt and toppled him over onto his side. "What the—" the PFC spluttered.

Several shots rang out in rapid succession and Sean could hear them pinging off the street and the ricochets whining wildly away. The "women" had walked funny for a reason. He dared a peek over the side of their emplacement, and his mouth fell open.

The boy was doing his break dancing routine in the middle of the street. It was generally agreed that the Shiites were terrible marksmen, but Sean knew from experience that what they lacked in accuracy they made up for in volume. Every second the kid delayed brought him closer to that lucky bullet.

"Lay down some fire on that position," Sean demanded. Colquitt obeyed and began taking shots at the window. The fighters, who had doffed their previous attire, ducked away from the opening. One appeared to be clutching his throat.

"Good one," Sean said. "Keep it up!" He risked standing to a crouch and saw that the boy was now on his back spinning like a top, with his legs raised up in the air. "Get your ass in here, kid!" he shouted. The Lebanese soldiers had disappeared.

The boy leapt to his feet, even as he spun, and landed facing the militiamen's position, one arm raised in the air. From his small fist popped a middle finger. "You suck!" he assured the fighters, and then with a grin at Sean, began a mad dash for the marines' bunker.

"Sonofabitch," Sean muttered. Then they opened up.

Sean had never seen so many flashes from so many windows in all his time in "The Root." The sheer volume was deafening, and the whining of passing rounds was like being in a jar of wasps. The only problem was that they were all aimed at him as he stood slack-jawed watching the kid's race for safety. Snagging him by the belt, Colquitt yanked him down into the hole. The firing ceased at once, and moments later the kid vaulted the sandbags and landed, laughing and panting, amongst them.

"I do not believe you!" Sean gasped. "Kid, you've got some big ones."

"I guess," Colquitt agreed.

"What's your name?" he asked the youngster as he tossed him his canteen.

"Ibrahim," the boy informed him, his black eyes sparking with excitement.

༄

That evening when Sean arrived at work, Mr. Corrado was there going over register tapes. As he would often appear at unexpected times, Sean thought little of it. Nodding to Sean as he hung up his jacket in the storeroom, he returned to poring over the tapes through the thick, dirty lenses of his glasses. Sean shoved the gym bag he had brought with him beneath a work counter with his foot.

"How's it goin'?" Sean asked, as he extracted his time card from the holder on the wall.

"Good, Sean, good," Mr. Corrado mumbled.

Sean slid his card into the time clock, then returned it to the holder. "That's good," he said as he headed for the front of the store to relieve Megan.

"Oh, Sean," Corrado stopped him. "Just a minute… before you go out front."

Sean turned to his employer, curious. It was unlike him to engage in any but the most rudimentary conversations. He was not known for his "people skills."

"Listen Sean, I'm sure you're aware that there's been a series of hold-ups in the area," he ventured.

Sean nodded. "Heard somethin', yeah."

"Well," Corrado glanced towards the front counter and Megan. "I'm a little concerned, you see."

Sean felt his face growing hard. "Yeah," he offered.

Corrado ran a hand over the slick strands that failed to cover his gleaming pate, and Sean wondered, not for the first time, if there was some link between responsibility and baldness. It was something he had avoided since leaving the Corps twenty years before. "It seems they hit stores like ours," the nervous manager continued. "After midnight… your shift, that is." He glanced up at Sean as if for encouragement.

"And…?"

"The thing is," Corrado returned his gaze to the register tapes, "I'm thinking it might be wise to close at midnight… for a while… till they're caught."

"Closing *all* the stores then?"

Corrado glanced back up, a stricken look on his face. "This one's a little different, Sean… you're so far out here, on the edge of town. It's exactly the kind of place they seem to hit. The others are closer in… a little less vulnerable," he added.

"And I'm gonna pay the rent, how?"

Corrado began to gather the tapes, as if to leave, but found that Sean was standing over him. "Sean, this would be for your own safety. Did you know a clerk at the Putnam chain was murdered just last night? That's less than five miles from here." He had never seen Sean like this.

Sean took a step back, sensing he was going too far. "Mr. Corrado, I cannot afford not to work, that's one thing. The other thing is that I don't like gettin' chased off my hill by a pack of maybes… maybe they'll hit us, maybe they won't. I stand to lose wages, and you stand to lose a lot of money in the bargain. If I'm willin' to take the chance, you ought'a be, too." He took a breath and glanced out toward the front counter where Megan was staring at him and tapping her watch. "Mr. Corrado, you may not know this, but I was a Marine once. I know how to take care of myself."

Corrado had not known that and studied Sean for a moment before dropping his eyes. "I see," he said, rising. "If that's how you feel, then. You make a good point."

Sean could see the relief flooding the other man's face. The responsibility was no longer his. "Thanks," Sean said, turning to take over for his co-worker.

"But those lights out front, Sean," Corrado spoke with authority. "You've got to take care of those. Understood?"

"Understood," Sean agreed with a smile, and snapped a smart salute.

Corrado flinched, then hurried from the store as the witching hour struck.

༄

From midnight until two a.m. customers came in the usual spates of hurried, exhausted-looking individuals in need of last-minute cigarettes, milk, coffee, chips, and beer. When, at last, Sean judged that he would have the store to himself, probably until the six a.m. coffee rush began, he hauled out the ladder from the storeroom and set to work on the lights. Maneuvering it from one narrow aisle to the next, he loosened one fluorescent tube in each fixture, until the store was powered down to a drowsy twilight. After replacing the lights outside above the entry, he went out into the parking lot to judge the effect from the street and was satisfied with the results. The store still gave the impression that it was open for business, but had acquired a tired, careless appearance. Just as importantly, it would not be as easy for a passerby, or the police, to see what was going on within—certain to be attractive to anyone who might be casing the place, he thought.

After loosening all the light tubes in the fixture above the service counter and plunging his work area into a gloomy murk, he returned the ladder to the storeroom, only to reappear with a work lamp that he clamped onto a smokeless tobacco display next to the register. He now had only to reach out and switch off the lamp to return his work area to near darkness. Without rising from his stool, he bent beneath the counter and retrieved the gym bag that he had brought out from the back room after Megan and Mr. Corrado's departure.

There were two items within, the first being a large and powerful hand-held spotlight of the type used by emergency personnel. He placed this, with a thump, upon the countertop and off to the side of his workspace, but pointed directly at the entrance to the store. With a quick glance to ensure no customers were in the lot outside, he switched it on. The brilliant flash that reflected off the glass doors made him turn away with a curse, and he switched it off again. Anyone standing in front of him, he thought, would be blinded.

The second item he removed from the bag he placed on the shelf beneath the countertop, its cropped, double barrels pointing forward. The stock of the gun had been cut down as well, and the pistol-like grip that remained was within easy reach of his hand.

The customer was just entering the store as Sean's eyes came up to the level of the countertop. He was a tall, emaciated-looking man in his middle thirties, Sean guessed, with a dirty baseball cap pulled low over his long, greasy locks. Wearing a drooping mustache and several days' growth of beard, he started when Sean popped up from behind the counter. "Wasn't sure anyone was home," he stuttered, before changing direction and heading into the aisles. Sean noted that he kept one hand in the pocket of his frayed, oversized jacket.

"Nope, we're here," Sean replied. "That is, I'm here."

The man peered over a display stand of factory produced pastries as if to verify this information. Sean's hand rested on the gun beneath the counter.

The customer returned to his study of packaged cakes and donuts.

"Need help with somethin'?" Sean offered, while scanning the parking lot for the man's car. He spotted it just at the edge of the lot, almost out of sight of the store's windows. The lights were off, but Sean thought he could make out two heads within, silhouetted by a distant streetlamp. Was one of the occupants jumping up and down in his seat?

The man began to move, and Sean's attention shifted away from the car and back to him. He had made a selection and was carrying the box in both hands. Sean relaxed somewhat and brought both his hands to the counter in order to scan the tasty sponge cakes packed with a creamy artificial filler. The man seemed unable to look at Sean, his prominent Adam's-apple bobbing. He reeked of body odor, tobacco smoke, and a strange chemical-like smell.

"That it?" Sean asked as the fellow dug through his wallet.

"Yep," he answered, glancing back toward the door. "Open all night?"

"Sure are. Just me."

"Uh huh…" The customer turned to leave and had taken a few steps before remembering his purchase. "Damn," he said under his breath, snatching the box from the counter, and hurrying out into the parking lot.

Sean watched the man lope into the darkness, and his hand returned once more to the gun. After a few moments, there was the faint sound of a car starting and Sean saw headlights blaze into life. The driver took the farther exit, so Sean was unable to see the other occupants of the car, but he did see the telltale white gleam of the broken tail lens.

꽁

Though the company commander had put the word out that fraternization with unvetted civilians was prohibited, this was a rule observed in the breach as it applied to Ibrahim. The boy had long been a mascot at the fringes of the Marines' sprawling encampment within the airport, and as word spread of his display of bravura at CP 69, demand was high amongst the lower ranks for his company.

Demonstrating an appreciation of military politics far beyond his years, Ibrahim avoided the battalion and company command posts and officers in general, sticking to areas mostly populated by the enlisted men. He could be counted upon to show up wherever the "grunts" were breaking open their "Meals Ready to Eat," or MREs as they were commonly called, to make a repast of the marines' donations. His high spirits, reputation for fearlessness, and vehement hatred of the shared enemy made him a welcome guest wherever he went.

Sean tried to discourage the boy from joining the marines at their combat posts, but he would have none of it. It seemed his bloodlust was the equal, or greater than, that of the Americans. When Sean asked him about this, he replied, "Pigs," and pointed over the berm into Hooterville.

Colquitt chimed in with his own observation, "Bet you'd like to have one of these, wouldn't ya?" He shook his M-16 at the boy, and Ibrahim made a lunge for it. Colquitt snatched it out of his grasp. "I guess," he observed.

"You're Christian?" Sean asked the disappointed kid.

Ibrahim turned a hot gaze on the marine, then dug into his pocket. He thrust his fist out to Sean, then opened it to reveal an ornate silver cross on a chain cradled in his soiled palm.

"That's somethin'," Sean remarked. "How come you don't wear it?"

Ibrahim drew a forefinger across his throat and grimaced in answer.

"I guess," Colquitt said again, casting a glance into Hooterville.

Sean, for the first time, thought of the boy making his way home to the Christian Sector each night. "Big ones," he muttered.

That night, it was Colquitt's turn.

༒

The evening had begun with the usual desultory bursts of fire from the 'ville. It appeared that the Marines' determined response over the past few weeks had taken their toll on the militiamen, and for some time now, they appeared content to simply harass the Americans. Having just zeroed in on a fighter who kept returning to the same window, an accurate burst of automatic fire from the street level tumbled Colquitt down into the hole. Just like that, he was dead.

If Sean had been numb, almost comatose, over the great slaughter that had befallen his fellow marines and spared him at the battalion command post, he was no longer. He did not weep for Colquitt, though the pain and grief he felt for the young man, whom he had known only a few short weeks, was a more piercing hurt than anything he had ever felt. In the loss of Colquitt he at last experienced the anguish of all that had gone before—the great hole in the earth that had swallowed the young men he had sweated with, cursed at, trained with, fought with, complained about, shared both boredom and terror, now lay in his heart. The Corp did not have enough bullets for all he hoped to do.

The following night Sean returned to CP 69 with a powerful searchlight that he had stolen from one of the airport's warehouses. Friends in the motor pool had helped him rig it to a jeep battery that they had donated in support of his scheme, with the promise of more, as needed.

With some reluctance, his squad sergeant gave him the go-ahead, but promised to shut down this new enterprise the minute it went wrong. Sean assured him it would not.

Ibrahim was fascinated with the whole idea and could not stay away from the contraption, so Sean put him to work. "It's like this—" he explained to the excited youngster. "I'm gonna place the searchlight on top of the berm. You stay down in the hole with the battery. When I give you the word, you take this," and here he held up a cable with an alligator clamp on the end—"and attach it to this," and pointed to the positive terminal on the battery. "Got it?"

Ibrahim shook his head and grinned. "Got it," he promised.

Sean waited until it was completely dark, and the flashes of the AK-47 muzzles could be clearly seen, before he put things into action. Selecting a persistent nest of snipers, he swiveled the light until he felt he had a pretty good line on the shooters, then called down to Ibrahim, "Do it!"

The brilliance of the beam threw the entire side of the building it was aimed at into relief, each brick suddenly separate from the others in detail. The shooters were caught like moths pinned to velvet, their hands flying up to their eyes with a cry, their weapons clattering to the rubble-strewn floor of their position. Sean, situated well away from the light, wasted no time, but took both out with a controlled burst of fire, and then launched a grenade from his M-203 that finished whoever remained hidden within the room. "Kill the light," he called out to Ibrahim. The building returned to darkness as the members of Sean's squad scuttled up to slap him on the back and offer their heartfelt congratulations. Sean ruffled Ibrahim's tousled hair. "We got some," he said to the boy.

"Get some more," Ibrahim responded, his white teeth visible even in the gloom of the bunker, though it did not look like a smile.

The rest of the night was more of the same, and Sean's body count was becoming the stuff of Marine legend. It seemed to Sean that the militiamen were slow learners.

The next evening proved otherwise.

Sean and his section had no sooner relieved the combat post when they came under intense and accurate fire. It seemed that as soon as they shifted from one fighting position and began to return fire, they would be driven to another. Neither camouflage nor darkness proved a deterrent, and Sean was unable to place his search lamp on the berm for fear of the enemy's newfound marksmanship. He wondered if the Syrian Army had directly entered the fray at last. They lost one killed and two wounded.

At dawn, after the Shiite fighters had melted away and Sean's unit was being relieved in its place, Ibrahim bid his farewells and glided away to wherever it was that he called home. Sean glared at the destroyed buildings that grinned back like a mouthful of broken teeth and cursed. Something had changed, just when things were going his way, and he couldn't understand why. He shouldered his weapon and turned to leave, then noticed something about twenty yards out.

Cans. Ordinarily, he would have paid no mind to any of the debris and garbage that lay strewn betwixt CP 69 and Hooterville, but one can in particular had caught his attention. It appeared to be a gallon paint container that lay empty on its side, an errant bullet having punched through it and rolled it over. One side was coated with a greenish fluorescent paint. The paint reminded Sean of the kind the Americans used to dot tent pegs and other small, necessary objects so they could find them in the dark. He began walking towards it into no-man's land. Several voices were raised in alarm at his back and he called out over his shoulder, "Cover me." Even the bad guys had to sleep, Sean thought, though he really didn't care.

Looking down at the battered can, he was sure it was the same kind of paint they kept stored within the Marine compound. He lifted his gaze to CP 69. From the can to the spot he had placed the searchlight the previous night was a straight line. He looked from right to left. A series of cans, of all sizes, and roughly aligned, stretched away in both directions, and seen from this side, each painted a fluorescent green. Sean strode to each can, turned, and looked back at the marines' bunker complex. Each marked a prepared fighting position that could be targeted with the use of these glow-in-the-dark aiming stakes. Sean heard his sergeant bellowing for him to get back behind the line.

Turning his back to Hooterville, he selected a smallish can that had contained soup in gentler times and tipped it over. Being careful to keep his actions from being seen by interested eyes in the 'ville, he slipped a hand grenade from his vest, pulled the pin while keeping pressure on the spoon, and slid it into the empty can. It was a good fit. He left that can on its side and walked away, kicking over a few others at random before returning to his unit. Sean was satisfied that whoever had set them up would want to repair his handiwork.

ஒ

Sean briefed his squad on his discovery, and when they returned that night they were in a high state of excitement. They quickly settled in to await the unfolding of events.

Less than an hour into their vigil, the word came down the line that someone was moving out front and to the right of their position. Every head swiveled in that direction, straining their eyes and ears. Sean thought he heard the scrape of metal against a rough surface but could see nothing. Based on this, he calculated that their visitor was roughly two overturned cans away from his surprise. A few moments passed in deathly silence. It seemed the marines were holding their breath as one. Then, another faint scrape of metal. Silence returned and held this time even longer than the last.

"Sonofabitch," Sean said under his breath. "Get on with it!"

At last, Sean was rewarded with a repetition of the previous sound. It seemed their visitor was checking each of his ad hoc aiming stakes with great caution and due diligence. He was one cool customer, Sean thought.

Then nothing. Minutes of nothing. Sean began to become alarmed that somehow his invisible antagonist had gotten wise to the boobytrap that lay next in line. Sweat was running now beneath the collar of his flak jacket. Still there was nothing. No sound, no scrape of metal followed by an explosion. Nothing.

He looked around for Ibrahim but couldn't locate him in the trenches. Instead, he grabbed one of his fellow squad members and told him to stand by on the battery. Sean hoisted the searchlight up on top of the sandbags. "We can't wait," Sean whispered to the squad. "When I hit the light, fire 'im up!"

Sean brought his own rifle up to his shoulder, then called softly to the man on the battery, "On three. One, two…" He adjusted his aim to where he remembered the rigged can to be. "Three!"

Ibrahim was revealed as a chalky statue, frozen in the act of betrayal. Even as his arm flew up to shield his eyes, the can he was holding dumped its deadly contents onto the earth at his feet, the spoon flying away and setting in motion the three seconds remaining that he had to live. In those moments, an eternity to Sean, the little militiaman had just time to recognize his peril before looking straight into the faces of the marines. In the unforgiving illumination his eyes were as black as obsidian and glittering with defiant malice. He thrust his thin arm into the air, but did not have time to complete his signature salute.

☙

When the tall man in the baseball cap re-entered the store, Sean's head snapped up from his chest, and he realized that he had been caught napping. His head felt swollen with the wooly, disparate images; his limbs heavy and spellbound. There were three of them now standing together at the doorway looking at him. They could have been posing for a family photograph, Sean mused, even as he fumbled for the stock of the gun and switched off the lamp that shone down on him. They were not what he had expected.

He reached for the switch on the spotlight, then hesitated. The man and his bedraggled mate appeared to be urging the boy to approach Sean, whispering in his ear and shoving him forward. Sean was reminded of himself at that age, reluctant, yet eager, his parents coaxing him to sit on the mall Santa's lap.

The boy began his hesitant approach, his eyes on his dirty, scuffed sneakers. His parents, if that's what they were, drifted into the aisles on either side, peering over the display cases as they pretended to be shopping. Mesmerized, Sean watched as the child shuffled closer. Was he being sent to beg, he wondered? His finger rested on the double trigger.

At last, the boy reached the counter, the top of his shaggy head on a level with it. Sean glanced at the man and woman, who continued to play their bizarre and obvious game of peek-a-boo. The boy remained immobile, looking down at his shoes, even as he tugged at something in the pocket of his shabby hooded pullover.

Even as he felt the unreality of his situation, Sean determined that he must speak, say something to break the spell. "Mister," he croaked, his throat choked with sleep, "is there somethin' your boy…"

The gun the boy brought forth from his parka was a .25 caliber, just as Sergeant Fullerton had said, a ladies' gun that fit just as well in the hand of a child. As the boy's arm extended to its full length, Sean understood that the bullet that would issue from it would duplicate the trajectory the good sergeant had so graphically demonstrated the night before.

Knowing he could unleash a hail of buckshot that would pierce the thin partition that separated the child from this world and the next, Sean hesitated long enough to look into the boy's eyes, eyes that danced and sparked with a triumphant, inexplicable hatred—Ibrahim's eyes. Then, with a tired sigh, relaxed his grip on the triggers.

In a Dark Manner
(2013)

Father Gregory watched the woman from the shadowed recesses of the confessional. The last penitent, an ancient distracted by impending mortality, had stumbled out leaving the door ajar. That had been ten minutes before and no others had come forward. The half hour allotted for this sacrament had expired, but the little priest remained at his post, fascinated by the struggle he was witnessing, and hoping for a resolution that would culminate in the unburdening of a soul. Outside the church deep rumblings made the floor tremble while the stained-glass windows glowed and faded with racing clouds. *Vigil Mass will be lightly attended*, he thought.

He had noticed the woman earlier, as the comings and goings of penitents had afforded him glimpses of her from time to time. She was in her mid to late fifties and a tall woman, and he did not recognize her as a member of St. Brendan's parish. He found her to be slender, if large-boned, giving the impression of a former athleticism perhaps. Her graying hair, still showing streaks of straw-blonde, was straight and badly cut, as if she had wielded the scissors herself. She glanced sharply in his direction and he drew back into the shadows like a hermit crab.

After a moment scanning the near-empty interior of the small church, she appeared to make up her mind at last, and made straight for him with long strides, her peasant-style dress swaying as her sandals slapped the tiled floor. The plump Indian shrank back even further, awed by the approach of the giantess (he never ceased to marvel at the size of Americans). She filled the doorway, stopped, and peered in at him with narrowed eyes. Even in the comforting semi-darkness he could see that they were the color of cornflowers long faded by the sun.

"Ah… good afternoon," he offered, "Please do come in."

The woman eased the door shut behind her but continued to stand, glancing around the confines of the tiny room. He was reminded of a nervous mare in a narrow stall.

"I thought you'd be hidden behind a screen," she said.

Her voice was gravel and sand.

"Ha, yes," the priest answered, "those days are long since passed in most parishes… Vatican Two, you know."

Glancing down at the kneeler positioned to the right of the little curate's chair, she pointed at it. "There?"

Father Gregory looked at the kneeler as well, then back at the perplexing woman. "Yes, yes," he answered and waggled a long dark finger at the suspect piece of furniture.

Hiking up her long skirts, she allowed her knitted handbag to slide off her arm and onto the floor. By stages she folded her lanky frame downwards until her knees were properly positioned on the cushion of the kneeler and her sharp elbows rested on the padded crosspiece provided for that purpose.

"Like this?" she asked, folding her workman's hands into a prayer-like attitude.

"Yes," Father Gregory answered, growing more puzzled by the minute. "That will be satisfactory, dear woman, if it is comfortable enough for you."

She appeared to consider this question for several moments before answering, "Yeah, it's okay, I guess." She closed her eyes.

"Very well then, let us begin…. In the name of the Father, the Son, and the Holy Spirit." He sketched the Sign of the Cross in the air between them, then halted in confusion as she failed to mimic him in this.

In the silence that followed, she opened her eyes once more. "Do I start now?" she asked flatly.

"Well," Father Gregory ventured, uncertain himself now, "it's customary to begin with telling me when you last confessed your sins."

"Oh," she answered, "Okay… well, this is my first time then. Is that alright?"

Ordinarily, the priest avoided eye contact with the penitent so that they were not made uncomfortable by direct scrutiny, but in this case, he was unable to do anything but stare.

"How…" he began, then trailed off in confusion.

"I'm not Catholic," she offered, "Do you have to be?"

"It would be useful," he answered after a long moment, then added, "I must say, I have been a priest for many, many years but this is a first for me, dear lady, I hardly know what to say."

"Can you do anything for me?" she persisted.

"Do… well, let me think. What is it that you wish exactly?"

"Forgiveness," she snapped. "Isn't that what you do?"

Father Gregory studied the woman's seamed, yellowish face before answering. "Yes, of course, this is true. But in order for one's sins to be forgiven there must be a good and true confession, which requires a belief in the very Sacrament you are asking to receive and in the God Who grants it. Do you understand?"

"Is that a no?"

He shook his head. "Perhaps I should begin with a simple question—though you are not Catholic, have you been baptized? This would be helpful to know, at least."

"My folks were Methodists," she answered. "I was baptized when I was a girl, but that was a long time ago." A wistful smile played across her chapped lips and, for the briefest of moments, Father Gregory glimpsed an unexpected charm in the large, coarse woman. It vanished along with the smile. "I *fear* God, if that helps" she added, looking into his eyes. "I fear *Him*."

"That is a beginning," the priest agreed, "but more is needed."

She slumped forward onto the crosspiece as if she might lay her head upon it and rest. The air in the small room felt warm and cottony with the moisture of the coming storm.

Father Gregory risked placing a hand on her shoulder but felt her flinch with the contact and withdrew it.

"Perhaps it is enough for now," he said. "I will take you at your word and act in good faith in this matter, as it appears that you are in great need… desperate need. May I rely on the same from you… that you will act in good faith?"

She nodded.

"Good," he whispered, then added, "I will keep your confession confidential, of course, and will pray for your forgiveness, but I will not be able to grant the Sacrament of Reconciliation until you have taken instruction in the Faith and been confirmed into the Church. The Catholic Church," he added for clarity.

She raised her eyes to his once more, the moment of weakness banished as if it had never existed. "Meaning?"

"That while I am free to pray for you, I am unable…" he searched his English vocabulary for the correct word, "… unable to 'loose' you from your sins until you have professed your faith."

She appeared to think this over before answering, "That makes sense," she agreed, then added, "If you can make a bargain with the devil you shouldn't expect anything less of God, I guess. I'll do it then."

Father Gregory was made speechless once more. Running a hand over his sparse white hair he felt the damp of perspiration along his receding hairline.

When he had recovered himself, he said, "It might serve us both if you could explain the urgency of your need. Could you tell me that?" Even kneeling she was face to face with him in his chair.

"My granddaughter has a tumor," she said, her voice soft now. "It's the size of a golf ball in her head… and growing. The doctors aren't very hopeful. I haven't told my daughter their prognosis, but they expect me to. And I will… eventually, but only if I have to. She's all my daughter has… and they are all I have."

Tears brimmed over the woman's reddish lower lids. "It can't be this way," she went on. "I will atone… I will make it right no matter what it takes."

"I am so very sorry at this news," Father Gregory said after a few moments. "There is nothing more painful than this." He stood to his full five-foot-four height and took the grieving woman by her elbow, raising her up. He indicated a straight-back chair with a burgundy cushion. She sat down, and he resumed his own seat. They now sat side by side in the cramped quarters like fellow travelers on a journey. A low rumble rolled through the church like a passing train adding to the effect.

The priest folded his hands onto his belly and asked, "What is it that you wish to atone for… and why?"

"For a terrible sin, Father… a crime… a crime that I've gotten away with for decades… until now."

Father Gregory turned his face to her to find her staring down at her folded hands. "What sin is this?" he persisted, "And what do you mean… until now? Speak plainly… the time for dissembling is past."

"I killed someone. It was a long time ago and I was a girl at the time, but it wasn't an accident… nothing like it." The woman's face was set as stone. "I don't deserve to be forgiven, but my granddaughter doesn't deserve to die. I'll do anything to save her… I never meant for anyone else to be hurt!"

They sat in silence for several minutes before Father Gregory reached above his head and unlatched a small stain-glassed window, opening it like a door. "Do you mind?" he inquired. A stream of cool sodden air flowed into the room, while in the near distance, lightning glowed and vanished behind a grey tumble of approaching clouds.

At length he said, "Tell me."

☙

"She was beautiful and that was the beginning of why it all happened. There was little else that I could find wrong with her… and maybe that was part of the reason as well. When I think of her now… when I allow myself to remember, she was always smiling, and so tiny and graceful… not like me."

Father Gregory glanced at the woman as if she had somehow perceived his earlier thoughts, but she still stared into her folded, reddened hands.

"She was nothing like me," she continued, "and maybe that was part of it too. She was nothing like any of us."

"Us?" the priest inquired.

"We called ourselves the 'Witches'… the 'Witches of Camelot Beach'… you know, like the characters in *Macbeth*."

"William Shakespeare," Father Gregory murmured, nodding his head.

"It was Lizzie's idea—she read a lot… too much, maybe. There were just the three of us to begin with, and for many years. We all grew up together on the island here. Cindy Heenan's family went to this church as a matter of fact. Lizzie Ledbetter and I both went to the Methodist one. Anyway, we all went to school together at Camelot Beach Elementary and later on to Wessex High School on the mainland."

The woman paused for a long time, as if giving these memories careful thought. "My name is Helen Lucas," she confided at last, then looked over to her confessor and added, "That's my real name, not my husband's. He's dead now and, in any case, I dropped it long ago, after he left me and Linda for some young thing that I never even knew existed—until she stole my husband, of course." A bitter smile played across her face.

"Go on," Father Gregory urged. "Tell me about the killing… this is why you have come here."

Helen nodded, took a deep breath, and resumed. "Her parents had moved to Camelot Beach from somewhere in Pennsylvania. They seemed to have a lot of money. Her dad was a doctor over at Wessex Memorial Hospital while her mom stayed at home. She was Romanian, I think, very pretty, and always wore these gauzy flamboyant fabrics—we used to call her Madame Butterfly. That's what she reminded us of… a big, colorful butterfly. They seemed like a happy family. Sasha was their only child.

"Sasha," the priest repeated in a whisper. The girl's name floated there, filling the small space between them.

"Yes… it's pretty isn't it? It suited her. She was just like her mom, really, very beautiful, but in a quiet way. She didn't go in for brilliant colors or gaudy make-up. No, she was more like those wistful, lovely girls that you see in Renaissance paintings—the same small, oval face, pale as paper, but with beautiful splashes of color on her cheeks and hair so black that it shimmered blue in certain lights. She was… entrancing, really, that's the only word that fits."

Helen glanced at Father Gregory. "I'm sorry," she said. "I know this must sound silly to you, but it was very important to us at the time. We were all just impressionable girls. I was thirteen when she first arrived in one of my classes."

The priest waved her on. "Not silly at all," he corrected her. "Please continue."

"We were just developing, if you know what I mean, and for me it was a nightmare. I suddenly went from being just your average girl to this towering, gawky creature. I scared the boys to death, of course.

"As for Cindy and Lizzie, they had it just as bad in their own ways: Cindy blew up like a balloon—she had never met a candy she didn't like, but with adolescence she paid a terrible price—you can imagine the jokes she endured. Kids are brutal at that age.

"Lizzie was probably the luckiest in that she didn't become fat or too tall, but what had been cute as a little girl somehow didn't translate well into young womanhood. We had called her 'Pixie' growing up because of her turned-up nose and pointed chin. In high school the boys called her 'Witch.'"

"Hence, 'The Witches of Camelot Beach,'" the priest murmured.

Helen regarded him with new interest. "Exactly," she agreed. "We took the name as a show of solidarity; after all, we didn't have anyone else… until Sasha. Her coming changed everything.

"That year she arrived sometime after Christmas. We couldn't take our eyes off her: firstly because she was so lovely, but also because, in those days, we islanders didn't see a lot of strangers during the off season. She was exquisite and we all envied her immediately.

"Even in the beginning there was that undercurrent… subtle, barely noticeable, like a rip tide that you don't know you're in until you find yourself in cold, dark water a hundred yards from shore.

"I'll never forget one spring day that we were all out in the schoolyard playing a silly softball game when Sasha finally managed to hit the ball. I was playing first base and could've easily tagged her out, but none of the boys seemed in any hurry to retrieve the ball and throw it to me. She was safe by a mile and the guys on her team applauded and whooped it up like she had really done something spectacular. I couldn't understand it.

"Charlie Dunstan was acting as first base coach and I was thrilled—I had a crush on him that had lasted since fifth grade. He was one of those cool, dark types that girls find so irresistible. When the next hitter, a boy who was perhaps the only one as tall as me in the whole school, homered, Sasha was given the go-ahead by Charlie to run in. As she skipped away, happy and excited, Charlie said to me out of the corner of his mouth, 'She has the most beautiful lips, doesn't she?'

"Can you imagine, a thirteen-year-old boy making such a statement… and to me? He was so taken by her that he forgot I was even a girl."

Father Gregory felt her pain as keenly as she, for it was no different in faraway India for a plump, shy boy whose most attractive attribute had been a gentle, inquisitive nature.

"What then?" he urged.

"Well, one day, before school let out for the summer, we, the other witches and me, were sitting together at our lunch table when she walked over with her tray and said, 'Do you mind if I join you?'

"You could have heard a pin drop... we didn't know what to say so we just nodded. She slid in next to Cindy and smiled at me across the table. Just like that... she became one of us.

"None of us witches ever understood why she chose to join us, as she could have been accepted anywhere, but we weren't asking questions either. Without even knowing what she had done, she transformed us into something other than what we had been.

"That summer we did everything together, which is to say, for girls like us, we spent a lot of time lolling about our bedrooms together leafing through teen magazines and talking in whispers and giggles about boys—even Sasha. She could have had her pick, but she just wasn't interested in them, really.

"As we got to know her better we soon realized that she was younger than us somehow... less mature. Of course, I'm using the term in a *very* relative sense. She was just such an innocent. It wasn't that she didn't like boys, it was just that she found them *foreign*, I think. She had no idea of her effect on them.

"You'd think we'd have spent our summer on the beach since we lived right there, but we were terrified of going down there in our bathing suits. We instinctively understood that we'd be ignored at best, and openly ridiculed at worst. So we just kind of hid out... and Sasha seemed happy to be included. *She* could have gone down to the water; even at thirteen she was developing, and of course, since it was her, it was in the *right* way—even as petite as she was, her body was already filling out in all the proper places. The rest of us remained lumpy or fatty and the only thing we developed was bad complexions.

"That fall we started our first year at the high school. It was a nightmare. Firstly, the Witches were broken up. We shared some classes, but not many, and had to settle for quick whisperings in the crowded hallways between periods. We were freshmen and, as if that weren't bad enough, we were growing less attractive each month.

"If eighth grade had been painful, high school was an exercise in prolonged torture. Boys would whinny and stamp their feet when I went by. Poor Cindy would wait until the very last minute to rush to her next class just to avoid the remarks about her weight. I can't tell you how many times she swept by me in the hallway, tears streaming down her red, bumpy face. Sometimes she didn't even look up to see me.

"As for Lizzie, maybe it was worse for her. She grew dark. All the fun seemed to go out of her. From being a girl who had been our playful pixie she became quiet and angry. I noticed scratch marks and cuts appearing on her arms and legs. She would never say how they happened. She also started wearing make-up… lots of mascara and eyeliner.

"Sasha and I shared both homeroom and a lunch period. The only thing *she* had to fear was what the other witches could only dream about—boys. They couldn't take their eyes off her wherever she went, and that was helpful at lunch—when she sat with me I became invisible. It was a relief, really, even though I resented it, too.

"I'm not being completely fair; Sasha didn't get away scot-free either. The older girls in the school hated her, of course. They were jealous of the attention she was getting—even senior boys were asking her out, but she wasn't having any of it. Instead of this making the other girls happy, they just started saying she was stuck-up and a snob. Sasha was very confused and hurt by it all. She could never understand why everyone couldn't just be kind to one another."

Helen paused and Father Gregory risked a glance—the woman's expression was the slack face of the sleepwalker. Then she whispered, "When someone so beautiful is in pain, it's almost pleasurable to watch—secretly, I was glad that she suffered, too."

Father Gregory shifted in his chair as the room grew dark with the coming storm, the thick air trembling with the pressure of it.

"Continue," he said.

"My phys ed teacher convinced me to try out for the basketball team, because of my height, of course, and I got on. In fact," Helen smiled, "I got pretty darn good at it."

"Ah," Father Gregory observed, happy for some good news at last, "a place of acceptance… this must have been a blessing for you."

Helen chuckled, one dry stone tumbling across another. "Oh yeah, it was a real blessing. Now everybody assumed I was a lesbian. That was much better."

The priest felt his face grow warm. "I am very foolish," he offered. "Please do go on."

"We got through that year somehow and regrouped on the island that summer. We were like survivors from a shipwreck finding one another. Everyday felt like a reprieve—a miracle. We couldn't be together enough. The upcoming school year, the end of summer, was a storm still far out to sea… unknowable… terrifying.

"We mostly hung out at Sasha's. She had the biggest house and her own bathroom and television. Her room opened out onto a small deck where you could see the ocean two blocks away.

"That summer started off well enough for all of us: Cindy actually started to shed a few pounds now that she was out from under all that pressure, and Lizzie had begun seeing a therapist. Her parents had made her go and, at first, she had resented it terribly, but after just a few weeks she seemed to be happier, lighter… more like her old self. Nothing changed for me, but then, I don't think I expected anything to—I had resigned myself to what I was… to what I had become.

"The only problem was privacy. Sasha's mom, Mrs. Chessman, didn't work and would often come barging in with sandwiches or sodas, without knocking. Of course, it was her home and she was just being nice. Even so, we all resented it, except for Sasha. She didn't seem to mind in the least.

"Looking back at it now, I think Mrs. Chessman—she wanted us to call her Oksana—was happy that Sasha had made some friends. I also think she was a little surprised at her choices, and a little worried. She didn't know what to make of us.

"The other problem with Sasha's room was her dolls. It was a large airy space, but every conceivable surface was covered with dolls of every description: There were French dolls, German dolls, Dutch dolls with little wooden shoes, Barbie dolls, rag dolls, and even dolls the size of small children. The end tables, lamps, desk, bed, and chairs all wore pink skirts trimmed with white lace. It was like walking into a seven-year-old's room. Sasha was very happy there and never noticed the looks between Cindy and me; Lizzie's eye-rolling. We had to get out of there after a while.

"It was Lizzie who found our secret place… it would be her.

"We were all lounging about in Sasha's room one morning in early July when Lizzie showed up late, her expression smug, taunting. She looked at us all in that sly way she had and said,

'Come on… let's go. I want to show you something.' We all stood as if commanded and followed her out to our bicycles.

"Lizzie led us over to First Avenue and then south. It was a beautiful day; I remember the sky was so blue, a blue the color of…" Helen searched for the word, "the color of her cloak there." She nodded at the small statue of the Holy Mother that watched over them from an alcove. "And clouds like storybook sheep gliding across the sun, causing the street to go from light to shadow, shadow to light. We all felt like we were embarking on something exciting and important.

"Lizzie turned right at Thirty-fifth street and took us over to Dune Drive, then we headed south again. She was racing, her bottom rarely touching the seat. Every now and then, she would glance back to see if we were following, and grin. Then, without any warning, she turned left onto a driveway that led up into the high dunes. She only slowed because of the steepness of the drive. Cindy had fallen behind, her face gone as red as a beet, and Sasha was not far ahead of her. I was right on Lizzie's tail.

"The drive forked halfway up the steep incline and Lizzie swung to the left and around a curve. For a second she was lost from sight, hidden by the low, sweeping branches of white cedar and beach plum bushes that reached out into the driveway.

"When I rounded the curve, I had to stand on my pedals and skid the bike to a halt. She was stopped at a wooden bridge that crossed a narrow gully. A rusty chain was strung across it. 'We'll walk from here,' she announced as she hid her bike beneath the undergrowth. We all followed suit.

"Sasha asked between gulps of air, 'What is this place?' She looked uncertain, frightened.

"'Walk along the edges,' Lizzie directed us and started across. Cindy was puffing so hard that I stayed behind to help her—she wasn't the most graceful girl. Crossing the bridge, I saw why Lizzie had told us to stay to the edges: The cross-planks were rotted through in spots and the whole thing creaked and groaned.

"On the other side we continued to climb up the cracked, stained concrete of the drive. The sky could only be glimpsed between the laced branches of huge bayberry bushes and wind-twisted cypress. After another twenty yards we stepped out onto a large paved turnaround that lay at the base of a two-story house. Its shingles had gone grey with weather and age and it was clear at a glance that no one lived there anymore. The house seemed to breathe darkness.

"Lizzie was very pleased with herself. She pointed toward the back and announced, 'There's a pool and I've cleaned and filled it.'

"We all just looked at her.

"'I've been working with my dad for some extra money; he showed me how it's done.' Her dad was a property manager for some of the rich summer people and got their homes ready for them. Pools were part of the service.

"'Wait a minute,' Cindy puffed. 'What about the people that own this place... when are they coming down?'

"Lizzie favored us with another of her smirks. 'Never,' she announced. 'My dad says the property is tied up in court over an inheritance squabble. He said it could be years before things get straightened out. In the meantime, the estate pays him to check on the place from time to time and make sure there's no burst pipes... that kind of thing.'

"Then I chimed in, 'Isn't he going to notice that the pool has been filled?'

"'Only if we forget to put the cover back on,' Lizzie assured me. 'He only comes up here once a month, and that's always on a Monday—we just stay clear then so if he does notice he won't know it was us.'

"Sasha started to say something, but we were already racing for the back of the house. The pool lay like an opal shimmering in the sun. We all shrieked and started dancing around like idiots on the warm flagstones. Then, after a few nervous glances at the shuttered windows, we kicked off our sandals and sneakers, stripped out of our tops, shorts, and panties, and jumped in… all except Sasha. She stood uncertainly at the edge of the pool.

"The water was warmed by the sun, but cooler down by your waist and feet; it felt marvelous. We were hidden from the world up there, with the house and the sky as our only witnesses. The nearest neighbor was several hundred yards away through the dense maritime forest.

"'Come in!' Lizzie demanded. 'Don't be such a little prude!' she yelled to Sasha.

"With a sigh and a last suspicious glance at the house, Sasha did as she was bidden and began to peel off her sundress. It drifted to her feet in a whisper of fabric and she stepped out of her sandals. All the while she tried to keep one slender arm over her breasts. At last, she had to give this up in order to remove her underwear, and once done, stood revealed beneath the high summer sun. I think we had all gone silent.

"Overhead, I was dimly aware of gulls shrieking. She was breathtaking… exquisite, I guess would be the best word."

The woman turned to Father Gregory, "I know how this must sound, but in spite of how I look, it's not like that. I don't…" she seemed to consider his sensibilities and chose her words. "I don't *desire* other women, Father. But she was like a little goddess… as white and smooth as porcelain, her limbs as long and perfectly formed as anything in nature. She looked at us all staring at her and blushed, her hands returning to her breasts.

"'They're too small,' she said, then shook her dark curls in despair at her imperfection and was only the more lovely for it—Diana hesitating at the edge of the sacred pool.

"I heard myself answering, 'No Sasha, you're just fine. Get in the pool now.'

"Without another word, she slid over the rounded edge and into the water. Within moments she was swimming around the shallow end, sleek as a seal, her large, dark eyes glistening, her cheeks flushed with pleasure, while the rest of us hooted and splashed water at each other like the children we really were. We all swore never to reveal our secret place. It was the first of many days we would spend there."

Helen paused as outside the open window the wind suddenly stilled and the shrubs and branches ceased their rustlings; silence spread over the churchyard. Moments later came the tap and rattle of large, heavy raindrops striking car tops and the dry, dusty leaves, growing in volume until it became a restless, insistent murmur.

"We began to bring towels and lunches with us so that we could spend the whole day when we went," Helen continued. "We told our parents that we were going to the beach and they never questioned it; after all, we were all turning brown—even Cindy's complexion was clearing up and she must have lost twenty pounds that season. The mysterious cuts and scratches on Lizzie began to disappear too. And miracle upon miracle, I stopped growing. I was still half a head taller than all the boys I knew, but with any luck, I hoped that some of them might catch up with me soon. Sasha's swimming never got any better though, no matter how much I worked with her. She was terrified of the deep end and wouldn't go there on any account.

"Lizzie had found a key in her father's desk for the pool house and had a copy made at the hardware store. They never questioned it—they were used to her running those kinds of errands for her dad. So now we even had a place to get out of the weather when we wanted. Not that there was much need for it that summer—it seemed like every day was a gift—the perfect summer day, day after day. Even when it did rain it never seemed to last for long, and we would sit it out on the patio furniture stored in the pool house and drink sodas. We wanted it never to end.

"It did, of course. After Labor Day we had to return to high school. To everyone but Sasha it was like a prison sentence. Tenth grade was not much better for us—the witches I mean—than the ninth had been. It wasn't long before Cindy began to pack on weight again, and before October Lizzie's cuts began to reappear. It wasn't quite as bad for me—I think being so tall and large-boned actually intimidated some of the meaner kids so that they mostly left me alone… and that was how I felt—alone.

"I found myself mooning over some of the nicer boys and envying the 'happy' couples that were pairing off wherever I looked. At that age, life is so painful. I just wanted some boy—he didn't have to be good-looking—to just hold my hand and say that he liked me; that's all, just that he liked me. That's all I wanted. It seemed so little to ask.

"Maybe because of the pool that summer, I decided to try out for the swim team. I had a lot of time on my hands and basketball season hadn't started yet, so I thought, 'Why not?' I got on without a problem.

"We practiced at the special services school where they had an Olympic-size pool. I was a good swimmer and got even better. The boys' team went there too. That's where I first noticed Terry

Stafford. Not only was he cute, but he was taller than I was—the perfect boy for me, and he swam like a fish.

"The first time I saw him course from one end of the pool to other and then launch himself out all wet and dripping, I stopped breathing. And when he snatched off that silly cap we had to wear and shook out his curls, I knew that I was in love… and that 'like' would never again be good enough. I don't think I had another coherent thought for the rest of the day."

Helen paused and looked over at Father Gregory, then added hoarsely, "Hell, my heart still flips over when I remember that moment. Strange, isn't it?"

"No," the little priest answered, "not strange at all… it's impossible to get through this life without loving someone… perhaps many, if one is blessed." He had his own memories. The rain outside continued its soothing drone.

"I went home that day in a state—I don't think I knew my own name," Helen resumed. "But when I got there, my mother was very upset. She told me she had just got off the phone with Lizzie's mom—Lizzie was in the hospital. One of her cuttings had gone too deep.

"It was like a dream to me. After Terry… this. I felt like I couldn't wake up. 'Is she okay?' I asked my mom.

"She squeezed my arms and nodded, then said, 'Never, *ever*, do anything like that… do you hear me?' I bobbed my head. 'Never!' she repeated.

"When can I see her?" I asked.

"'We'll visit tomorrow,' mom promised.

"Tomorrow came and went and she couldn't seem to find the time to drive me over to the hospital—she didn't want me to have anything more to do with Lizzie. I called Sasha and Cindy, and we all agreed to ride our bikes out the causeway and over to the mainland hospital.

"When we tumbled into the room she was sitting up in bed like she had been expecting us.

"'Don't bother knocking,' she said.

"She looked awful… ghastly white… and the stitching!

"Sasha threw herself on Lizzie and began to cry like a baby. It was like she had known her all her life—that's what she was like.

"Lizzie patted her on the head like she would a puppy, then reached behind her pillow and pulled out a large book. 'I stole this from the county library about a week ago,' she said, 'and had mom bring it to me yesterday. I should have started reading it sooner, then maybe I wouldn't be in this damn place.'

"I leaned over Sasha's still heaving back to see the title—*The Golden Bough*, it read. I had never heard of it. Lizzie looked from one of us to the next, then added, 'There are *other* gods for people like us,' she tapped the cover of the book, 'and we should get to know them.' Then she slid the book back under her pillow and lay down. None of us knew what to make of it."

Father Gregory shook his head, saying, "There is only *God*… the poor girl was in a state of shock, and too young for such a book."

Outside, the rain began to climb the wall of the church as the wind rising off the ocean increased in power. Suddenly, bullets of water began to pepper both priest and penitent through the open window and Father Gregory, shielding his eyes against the sudden onslaught, slammed the window shut and latched it. The room returned to stillness but for the tapping of a dozen long fingers at the colored glass. He turned and smiled weakly at the room's other occupant. "I do fear what you will tell me next," he said.

"We were just girls," she offered.

The priest sat once more. "What did Lizzie require of you all?"

"She was released a few days later and we started meeting at the dune house in the evenings—sneaking out. She brought other books then and read to us from them. Mostly it was dry academic stuff on ceremonial magic and rituals in other cultures, but Lizzie had an active imagination, and where there weren't details, she filled in. We had a new respect for Lizzie, I think, because of her near-death experience—she was wiser now, more powerful. It sounded so easy, really, to have what your heart desired, all you had to do was ask for it—demand it, really, in just a certain way, a way that had been practiced by women down the centuries but kept largely secret.

"On Halloween night—Lizzie insisted on calling it *Samhain* after its pre-Christian origin—we met at the pool. Lizzie had gotten there before us and uncovered it. I'll never forget the reflection of the moon trapped within the dark waters, a slight breeze rippling the surface.

"She had us steal candles and bring them. And there, on the flagstones, she drew a pentagram and other symbols from the books and placed the lit candles at the five points. 'We have to be sky-clad,' she told us."

Father Gregory glanced up inquiringly.

"Naked, Father."

"Oh," he murmured.

"So we all stripped down and gathered around the pentagram. Even Sasha went along with it all… up to a point.

"Lizzie read some things that we all had to repeat in a chant, then picked up a small, sharp knife she must have stolen from her mom's kitchen. 'Each of us must make a sacrifice,' she said, 'an offering of blood.' In her other hand was a wine glass chased in gold leaf.

"'Where did you get that?' I asked.

"She cut her eyes at the dark house that loomed behind us, then back again.

"'The sacrifice must be freely given,' she went on.

"I heard Sasha and Cindy breathing through their mouths looking at that sharp, little knife.

"'Say aloud what your heart most desires,' Lizzie commanded, 'then give the blood offering—I will start.' Setting the glass at her feet, she threw her head back and cried, 'Give me power over all my enemies that I may destroy them!'

"Then, just like that, she cut the webbing between her thumb and forefinger, of course, she had had a lot of experience with cutting. She allowed the blood to dribble like black ink into the glass, then brought the chalice to Cindy. 'Now you,' she commanded, as a dark rivulet crawled toward her elbow. She didn't seem to notice.

"Cindy's face glistened with sour sweat, but she took the knife and made the cut almost without flinching. Lizzie held her hand over the glass. 'Say it.'

"'I just want to be thin,' she whispered, 'that's all… thin like the other girls.'

"The chalice was brought to Sasha. She looked like the ghost of some beautiful dead girl beneath the orange moon. 'I can't,' she whimpered. 'I can't…' she whimpered. 'I can't… I'm Orthodox Christian… my mother… I can't do this.' Then she began to sob in fear. I think she was afraid Lizzie might cut her anyway.

"Lizzie shoved her away from the rest of us and hissed, 'Get out of here then… you're screwin' everything up for the rest of us.'

"Sasha grabbed up her clothes and fled weeping toward the front of the house and our hidden bikes. From somewhere, like spirits in the air, I heard the laughter of small children.

"Lizzie stood in front of me; it was my turn. 'You're not gonna chicken out, are you?'

"I took the knife from her hand, tipped my head back, and said loudly, 'I want Terry Stafford to fall in love with me!' The cut hurt far worse than I anticipated, but I didn't let a single drop of blood go to waste.

"Lizzie took the goblet and returned to the pentagram, threw a glance back at Cindy and me, then raised it on high and shouted, 'For these boons our blood and souls we do offer!'

"Cindy and I were struck dumb as statues by the oath, frozen beneath a heaven that fell endlessly away into the stars. The shattering of the glass into the heart of the pentagram shocked us back to reality. We all scrambled to leave that place then, snatching up our clothes and even forgetting to cover the pool. I think we feared that there might be something else… something might be coming; something we didn't want to see.

"When I got home, I found that I had cuts on the bottom of my feet from the broken glass… but I never felt a thing."

The drumming on the window increased in intensity—a demand, a summoning. "Goodness," Father Gregory breathed, "the storm has found us."

Helen remained silent for several moments, then raising her shaggy head to regard the dark, foreign priest said, "The next afternoon, during my lunch period, Terry brought his tray over to my table and sat down."

Father Gregory replied simply, "Did he?"

Helen sighed and smiled with the memory. "I think I just held my breath… waiting for him to go away again… it couldn't be true… it couldn't be this simple. Sasha raised her eyebrows at me. She acted like Halloween night had never happened.

"I picked at my sandwich and didn't look up. 'Pass the salt?' he asked after a while. I think I jumped when he spoke but slid the shaker over to him without looking up. His fingers brushed mine and I imagined that they lingered just a fraction too long to be accidental. I glanced up and he was looking right into my eyes, smiling. 'Thanks,' he said. Sasha's eyebrows went up once more; she was trying not to grin. She didn't know anything about my demand. She hadn't been there for my offering.

"After a while, he finished his lunch and got up... I thought a little reluctantly, and said, 'See you later.'

"Sweeter words had never been spoken. The room felt like it was spinning around. 'See you later,' I replied.

"When he had left, Sasha seized my hand and I cried out; it was very sore and slightly infected. A shadow slipped across her face, then vanished. She said, 'I think he likes you.'

"He sat at our table several more times over the next few months, and we finally took to actually saying a few words to one another, hardly a conversation, really. But I was just happy to have him sit with us. It seemed enough... at first.

"That fall and winter passed away like a dream—Cindy *did* begin to lose weight and Lizzie suddenly found herself the matriarch of the school's hippies. I guess I shouldn't have been surprised; she was a natural leader and the whole alternate-lifestyle scene fit her like a glove. In her own way, she was becoming very popular and so, I guess, did vanquish her enemies. She certainly stirred up a lot of envy amongst her rivals, that's for sure.

"As for me, there was Terry...

"Sasha remained unchanged... she had asked for nothing. But she didn't need anything, did she?"

Father Gregory made no reply to this and Helen continued. "Terry hadn't asked me out yet, but he had taken to waving to me at swim meets. I always attended even when the girls weren't competing and felt a little shameless doing it. He would sometimes speak to me at practices. Nothing much, just things like, 'Mrs. Sampson is crushing me with homework… how about you?' Scintillating topics like that. When he smiled I would grin back like an idiot.

"That spring, just after Easter, it all came unraveled. With a simple exchange of harmless words I set everything in motion. It was one of those golden days when Terry favored me with an appearance at my regular lunch table. Sasha had called out sick that day with a stomachache—this was usually code for our periods.

The priest winced but remained silent.

"Terry looked around the room after he sat down. He appeared confused, or uncomfortable, I was unsure. 'Eating alone today?' he asked. I nodded and asked how he was making out with Mrs. Sampson's history assignments. He shrugged like it was a matter of little importance, then dove into his lunch. I felt uneasy and I couldn't say why.

"'Do you have a pool at home?' I dared. Terry stopped chewing and looked at me like I had just grown a second head.

"'You're joking, right?'

I blushed.

"'If only…' he finished around a mouthful of something.

"Then I did it. 'I know of one that you could use,' I said. 'It belongs to some people my folks are friends with, and they let us use it whenever we want, even when they're not there.'

"'Who's we?' he asked, suddenly interested.

"'Me and some girl friends of mine,' I answered, even in that moment knowing that I was making a big mistake.

"He seemed to mull this over. 'The girl you always eat lunch with?' he asked.

"'And others,' I added quickly. 'Cindy Heenan… Lizzie Ledbetter.'

"Terry rolled his eyes at Lizzie's name, 'Oh boy,' he said. 'Isn't she the one everybody calls the Witch?'

"I lied and answered, 'I have no idea. She's a close friend of mine.'

"He shrugged again, then asked, too casually, 'What about your girlfriend that's usually here with you… what's her name?'

"'Sasha,' I told him, a cold hand touching my heart.

"'Sasha,' he repeated, 'that's a pretty name. Does she swim with you and your other friends?' I nodded, all feeling draining away from me.

"Then, as if giving it some careful consideration, he added, 'Yeah, okay, I'd like to come and try your friend's pool. When?'

"Lizzie was 'officially' opening the pool for swimming that Saturday, if the warm weather held." Helen smiled tiredly at the priest. "Spring weather can be very iffy around here, Father."

The priest smiled back and pointed a long finger at the window in acknowledgment.

"Well, that spring the weather did hold and when he showed up in swim trunks and a towel we all stared—he really was very handsome. He even brought a cooler of soda and chips for us all to share. The only one not thrilled was Lizzie—I just hadn't drummed up the nerve to tell her—that was very foolish and cowardly of me, but I just couldn't risk her saying no. She was furious, of course.

"'You've broken the circle,' she hissed in my ear, then spent the rest of the afternoon glaring at us all as we mooned around Terry.

"It became obvious before the day was out that it was Sasha that he had come to see. He couldn't keep his eyes off her and before long he was playing silly games in the pool that always resulted in his having to chase, catch, or tag her, but even he couldn't coax her into the deep end. Cindy and I were forgotten little by little. Lizzie sat in the shade of the pool house porch and watched it all happen.

"Sasha was laughing and squealing the whole time and I had never seen her more beautiful than that day. I don't know how I hadn't seen it coming. When I look back now it was so obvious—of course, it could never have been me.

"I was hanging on to the side of the pool, looking out. I just couldn't bear to watch them a moment longer. Tears were burning my eyes, but I couldn't tell whether they were from sorrow or anger—I was being consumed by both. Lizzie's shadow fell across me as she knelt and placed a hand on my arm. Cindy was bobbing next to me, her pudgy face creased with concern, tears of sympathy standing in her small eyes.

"Lizzie whispered almost too loudly, 'She was never *really* one of us. She didn't make an offering, and you broke the circle by bringing him here. *This* is what happens.'

"She stood suddenly, hands on hips. 'Tomorrow night,' she commanded, 'all of us…' she pointed at Sasha, who was so busy being silly that she never even looked in our direction. 'Her too… here,' then added, 'He's not to come… ever again. Understood?' Cindy and I nodded in unison.

"The following night, as if by secret communication, Cindy and I arrived ahead of Sasha. I could hardly hold my head up and felt as if my limbs were weighted with lead. Cindy was quiet and anxious. Lizzie was already there, pacing.

"The pool was lit by four or five tiki torches Lizzie had 'liberated' from neighboring properties. The flames from them smoked the air with the taint of kerosene.

"She seized each of us by a hand, forming a closed circle. 'We have been betrayed,' she began, 'and one of us sorely hurt.' Cindy giggled at the 'sorely' part, but Lizzie snarled at her, 'Shut up… there's nothing funny here.' Cindy did as she was told. 'Now we must make things right again… restore the proper balance that the Goddess demands.' Cindy and I exchanged quick looks.

"Lizzie went on, '*She* demands a true and living sacrifice!' In answer there was the trilling of a bell from the other side of the house—Sasha's bike.

"Lizzie looked hard, first at me, then at Cindy. 'Tonight, sky-clad… the deep end—since her boyfriend's a swimmer, it's time she learned.'

"Sasha called for us as she came around from the front, 'Hello, I'm here everybody!' She was as happy as a lark. Even in the near darkness she beamed. I hated her far more than I could ever have imagined.

"We all began to strip and make for the pool. Sasha followed suit as she ran across the flagstones. She had overcome her previous shyness about skinny-dipping; now she seemed to love it. 'Wait up,' she called out.

"She looked perfect and wild beneath the flames of the torches as she slid like a nymph into the cool waters. I remember her smooth white skin pebbling. 'Oh, it's cold,' she complained as Lizzie swam up and took her hand.

"Sasha's face showed her surprise, Lizzie had never been the affectionate type, but when I took her other hand, she smiled with pleasure. I could almost hear her thinking, 'Everything is going to be okay.'

"But as soon as she realized where we were pulling her, she began to panic. Lizzie said, 'Don't be afraid, it's about time you got over this 'deep end' thing anyhow… especially now that you have a swimmer as your lover.'

"Sasha tried pulling her hands free. 'He's not my lover,' she said, then looked at me, her eyes widening. 'What are you doing?' We pulled harder for the deep end.

"She began to struggle, trying to pull her hands free of ours and kicking her legs, but I was much larger and stronger, and between the two of us she stood no chance. I could just make out Lizzie's face across from me in the flickering torch light; it was a rictus of malice, fury, and envy casting her sharp features into something foreign and frightening. I didn't know who she was and wondered, for just the briefest of moments, what my own face must look like.

"From the edge of the pool I heard Cindy crying out something to us… but I couldn't make out the words through the blood pounding in my ears. She was pleading with us, I think. Sasha's head went under and both Lizzie and I leaned onto her shoulders. Her dark beautiful hair floated up to us as shimmering blue tendrils.

"Suddenly, with a strength I would never have suspected, Sasha shoved hard off the floor of the pool and shot up to the surface, breaking loose of our grip. Lizzie was furious. I caught a glimpse of her teeth bared like an animal's in the frothing water. 'Bitch,' she hissed.

"Sasha, sobbing and gulping for air at the same time, stroked hard for the safety of the shallow end. Lizzie launched herself before she had covered three yards—a scarred, pallid monkey mounting the back of a fallen angel. Cindy's cries had turned to sobbing and an unintelligible string of words.

"Before my eyes I watched Lizzie literally climb onto Sasha's shoulders, clamping her thighs around her neck and squeezing.

It might have looked like some kind of roughhousing but for the fact that Sasha's head was beneath the water, her hands clawing upwards, flexing open and shut. Lizzie seized her wrists and held them fast.

"Then Lizzie began to howl in triumph from her perch like some naked baboon."

"Dear Lord," Father Gregory whispered.

"That's what did it," Helen said evenly, "her face; that sound.

"I swam over and gripped her around the waist, and with one hard pull, yanked her backwards. She was on me before I even knew it… clawing, biting, and shrieking. It was then I understood. I gripped her hard and spun her around… even with all that fury, she was no match for me. I shoved her under.

"I could feel her heart through my fingers, it's drumming and hammering, and even beneath the waters she screamed and cursed me, her life rushing out in gouts of air bursting through the surface. It seemed to go on a long time, but it was all over in just a few minutes, really. When she finally went limp and sank away from me, drifting down the slope into the deepest end of the pool, Sasha was just dragging herself out onto the concrete apron. Cindy was trying to help her, offering her a towel, but Sasha waved her off. 'Get away from me,' she managed between ragged breaths. It was all over… it was done."

Father Gregory shook himself as if waking from a dream. "Sasha…?" he breathed. "But I thought… yes, yes, I see now." He sat in thought for several moments, then asked, "Surely the police were involved in this matter?"

Helen nodded. "Yes… the investigation didn't take long. Sasha told them that I had saved her from drowning and that Lizzie died in the effort. The scratches on my arms were from trying to save her as well. Cindy agreed with our story; I think she was terrified to do otherwise. After all, she had seen me, hadn't she... what I was capable of?

"Sasha's family moved away shortly afterwards. She had become very nervous and withdrawn and I think they wanted to get her away from what had happened, from us, too. I think they suspected that there was more to it than what came out.

"When Lizzie's mom and dad thanked me for trying to save her, I turned to stone. They wanted to think that I was some kind of hero. They needed that. My silence was interpreted as grief, so that was all right. I skipped her funeral.

"Cindy died about fifteen years later." Helen turned her vacant gaze onto the priest for a moment. "I was told she weighed sixty-five pounds and suffered massive organ failure. She got her wish too, I suppose. She had become an anorexic."

The pounding of the sea was audible through the walls of the church, the storm scooping it up into great grey swells and carrying it forward to crash drunkenly onto the nearby beach.

"Me too," Helen added. "After Sasha left, Terry started showing up at my lunch table again. He seemed bewildered, and suddenly shy-natured. Almost reluctantly, maybe because I was all that he had left of Sasha, he asked me out. We dated off and on for the remainder of high school. When I came home for spring break during my sophomore year of college, he asked me to marry him. I couldn't seem to gather the energy to say no. You know the rest."

Father Gregory nodded his round head in agreement, then both confessor and penitent sat in silence. The storm outside swept over St. Brendan's Church with a sound like heavy wings thrashing the slate roof.

Helen spoke first. "Will my Olivia be spared?" she asked hoarsely, emotion finding its way, at last, into her voice. "Will God be merciful now?"

Father Gregory sat for a short while before saying, "God is always merciful, dear lady, though I cannot say if your granddaughter will live. This is unknowable by man. But if she does not, it will not be because of you… or anything you may have done or even thought. God would never punish a child for your sins."

Helen sagged forward, rocking herself. "Then what's the point? If I can't save her, what is the point of it all?" she asked.

Father Gregory mulled this over, then answered, "Through all of these things you have told me, and that you have lived through for all these years, you have kept a long-overdue appointment. We are always being called, and even through these terrifying events that you have both endured and participated in, you have glimpsed Him, if only in a dark manner. Perhaps it was your love for your little Olivia that has awakened you. If this is so, accept this gift from her and do not make the mistake of turning away."

Helen rose from her chair while shouldering her purse. "If I don't come back," she asked, "will you tell the police what I've told you?"

"I will not," he answered.

Father Gregory stood as well and made the Sign once more between them. "Tuesdays at seven p.m. in the parish hall," he said, then added, "You will meet many kind people." Helen regarded him in silence a moment, then went out.

Opening the small window, Father Gregory squinted through the driving rain to watch as she loped across the blacktop of the parking lot, her large feet throwing up crowns of water. As the headlamps of her car came on and it lurched into motion, he raised a hand in farewell, though it was unlikely that she could make him out. The vehicle crossed the lot and made its way into the street, the brake lights blinking once,; then she was gone.

Father Gregory closed the window and resumed his seat, turning off the light that indicated he was available for confessions. He had no wish to hear any more of sin and suffering, pain or loneliness, and sitting there in the semidarkness of the small room he murmured a hasty plea, "Dear Lord, if with the night weeping may enter in, then with the dawn, let there come rejoicing. Amen." And with that pushed himself to his feet and turned for the sacristy. It was his turn to officiate the Vigil Mass and the faithful waited.

Shadow Lane
(2020)

Emma was first off the school bus, leaving her younger siblings to follow as she hurried to her father's workshop behind the house. She had spotted his truck, with its chaotic load of copper tubing, tools, and PVC pipe, parked in the driveway. As it was early for him to be home from work, and due to the anniversary, the idea of him sitting alone inside the leaning weathered structure made her uneasy.

Entering without knocking the fourteen-year-old found him hanging by his neck from a rafter.

Rooted to the floor as if struck into stone, Emma, nonetheless, felt herself falling backwards through space, her vision collapsing to a narrow, grey tunnel. It took an act of will not to faint and she lacked the breath to scream.

With a great rushing noise in her ears she recovered enough to see that he had botched the job, misjudging the length of rope required. Balancing on the toes of his scuffed-up work boots, her father spun slowly around, digging with thick fingers at the cord that was killing him.

Tossing her backpack to the floor, she snatched up a rusty utility knife from the cluttered workbench, and righting the stool he had stepped off from, hopped onto it and cut him down. He collapsed with a thump onto the packed earth of the workshop floor.

Stepping down, she knelt and managed with some effort to loosen the knot. As he began to gasp and strain to fill his depleted lungs, she cried out to her siblings who were only just coming down the drive, "Michael! Get Grandma—Pop's had an accident! Wake her if she's sleeping!"

Michael seldom questioned Emma's authority, not only because he was the middle child at twelve, but because she had demonstrated her judgment and leadership on too many occasions to be casually challenged. He raced to the house and vanished within.

Her nine-year-old sister's thick shadow fell across Emma and her father, who had now begun to weep. Making small, grunting sounds, he covered his whiskered face with broad, grubby hands.

The girls were dressed identically in the pleated, blue plaid skirts, white blouses, and knee socks of Saint Elizabeth's School; otherwise, they bore little resemblance to one another. Emma was of average height for her age, thin and pale, with brown eyes showing shadows beneath them. Kaitlyn was large for her own, her face full and placid, the blue eyes still and untroubled.

"Why's Pop crying?" Kaitlyn asked, making no effort to come closer.

Glancing up at her, Emma answered, "He got something twisted around his neck and it nearly strangled him."

"Oh," Kaitlyn replied as she sucked on a piece of hard candy, the soggy paper stick it was mounted on making small circles. Her dark, untrimmed hair obscured one eye.

Shoving past Kaitlyn and rushing into the workshop, Grandma Tyndall fell to her knees beside her son. "Oh dear God," she cried, taking in the rope, the raw, bleeding circle around his neck, the bloody starbursts in his eyes, "Oh my dear God! What have you done to yourself, Jimmy?" Her body odor, fruity with alcohol filled the dank space.

As he turned away from her, the older woman began to stab at her cell phone to summon help.

"Give that to me," Emma demanded, taking it from her grandmother's ineffective fingers. After hitting 9-1-1, she returned the phone, and rising, went back to the work bench as Grandma Tyndall began to screech at the operator.

Placing the knife back where she had found it, Emma noticed the piece of lined paper. She recognized it as being ripped from her father's writing journal. He often wrote poetry within its pages in a lovely longhand. Emma remembered him saying that he owed the nuns for that, and knew it was his greatest wish to be a published poet.

Holding it beneath a shaft of late autumn sun angling through a dusty window, she read:

SYLVIA
Your love was not worth having, yet I held it fast.
Your touch drew blood.
With your death came a moment's joy, exultation… then only night remained.

Emma folded the page with trembling fingers, then slid it into her sweater pocket. Turning back to the others she found Michael, his eyes brimming with unshed tears, helping their father into a sitting position. This appeared to ease his breathing. In the distance a siren arose.

"I'll get Pop some water," she said, hurrying past Kaitlyn who still blocked the doorway.

Entering the house, she went straight to the dresser in her parents' bedroom and opened the drawer where her mother kept her jewelry. Her father had changed nothing since her murder, so the rosary was exactly where Emma remembered it to be. Taking it out, she fed its length into the same pocket as the poem as if it might cancel out the words written there.

Filling a water glass in the kitchen she saw an ambulance and police car arriving, their sirens attracting curious neighbors into the yard. Watching as if in a dream, she observed the medics removing equipment packed in orange, nylon bags from the ambulance, then tossing them onto a gurney and hurrying down the drive, a tall police officer following.

With a slight start she realized that the water was overflowing from the glass, running over her hand like an icy glove, and turned off the tap. A moment later she poured it out, her offering made inconsequential by the arrival of these adults.

When she saw her father being wheeled from his workshop she stepped out onto the porch. Surrounded as he was by medics, Michael, and Grandma, she couldn't even see his face.

After a few minutes, the ambulance swallowed up her father and grandmother and sped away, leaving the children alone with the neighbors.

Noticing several of the local mothers eyeing them, Emma called from the steps, "Michael… bring Kaitlyn inside the house!"

Emma had learned over the past year that many of their neighbors on Shadow Lane suspected their father of their mother's murder, and now she would not tolerate their company nor accept their help.

Once they were inside, she surveyed the others. Michael's troubled face was crumpled with new grief, his school blazer forgotten on the patchy lawn, his collar pulled open, the knees of his grey trousers stained with dirt.

Like his younger sister, he seldom spoke unless called upon, but was always in motion when allowed, excelling at different sports at St. Elizabeth's. Since their mother's death, he had also been involved in numerous fistfights as well—ugly rumors about their mother, their father, and the motive for the murder being rife throughout Wessex Township.

Turning her gaze to Kaitlyn, Emma was unable to perceive any real effect on her bovine features.

"Do you know what today is?" Emma asked them.

Michael nodded, while Kaitlyn shook her head, then answered, "Thursday?"

"It's the anniversary of Mom's murder," Emma reminded them, "and the police are going to think Pop is guilty because of what he did today."

"His accident...?" Kaitlyn asked.

"He tried to kill himself," said Michael, his voice catching.

"You lied," Kaitlyn accused Emma. "That's a *vernal* sin!"

"Venial," Emma corrected her before continuing, "The police have stopped looking for anyone else, and Pop's having a harder time than ever getting work."

"How do we know Pop *didn't* do it?" Michael asked, wiping his eyes, desperate for assurance.

"Because he loved Mom," Emma replied, feeling the weight of the hidden poem—its potential meaning. "He loved her with all his heart. I know that. But we have to prove it."

"How?" Kaitlyn asked.

Retrieving the rosary from her pocket, she held it in both hands for the others to see.

Eyes glittering, Kaitlyn reached for the string of green glass beads with its silver crucifix.

"No," Emma warned her. "It's not to play with. This was Mom's rosary and we're going to swear an oath on it… then, I'll tell you."

She held out the rosary, cradled now in her palm. "Place your right hands on the crucifix."

The others did so, one on the other.

"Repeat after me: I believe in my father's innocence."

"I believe in my father's innocence," they intoned.

"I will do everything in my power to prove his innocence."

"I will do everything in my power to prove his innocence," they parroted. Kaitlyn giggled.

"Stop that," Emma snapped, then went on, "I invoke the protection of St. Michael the Archangel."

This was repeated, though Kaitlyn giggled again, elbowing her brother at the mention of his name.

"And I pray for the intercession of the Blessed Virgin Mary, Mother of God."

This too was recited.

"And I swear by Almighty God, that I will never reveal this secret pact. Amen."

"What's that?" Kaitlyn asked.

"A promise," Michael whispered from the corner of his mouth.

When they were done, Emma said, "Follow me."

Leading them to the room she shared with Kaitlyn, she reached under her bed and pulled out a dusty cardboard shoebox. Opening it, she dumped the contents onto her carefully made bed, littering the coverlet with dozens of newspaper clippings and printed copies of online reports of their mother's murder. "This is everything that's been printed about the case," she announced.

Kaitlyn leaned in to scrutinize the scattered papers. "Do they say who killed Mom?" she asked.

"That's what *we* have to find out. I've read all the newspaper reports and anything else I could about the investigation. There's not much."

Michael's face took on a set, hardened expression. "So what do we do?"

"We investigate."

"How?"

For the first time Emma hesitated. "We start with this man." She pointed out a grainy photo in one of the yellowing clippings, an old mugshot taken years before according to the caption. "Sheldon Hand—he's the tramp that was seen near where Mom was found in the woods. I think he was the main suspect for the police. He was picked up for questioning several times."

"Why'd they let him go?" Michael asked.

"Not enough evidence, I guess… but that doesn't mean he didn't do it."

"Where is he?"

"If he's still around he'll probably be at the homeless camp behind the shopping plaza."

"When do we go?"

Emma gave this some thought. "This weekend when we'll have some time."

"If he killed Mom, we should stab him," Kaitlyn suggested.

"That's a *mortal* sin," Emma informed her, putting her research back into its box and sliding it under the bed. "I'm not sure what we'll do… but first, I want to make sure he's there."

When she stood up again, she found her siblings still waiting. "I'm going to microwave some chicken fingers for dinner. You two do your homework and I'll call you when it's ready."

As they left to find their bookbags, Emma sat down on the bed, her heart full and heavy. On her dresser was a photo of her mother taken years before at a family picnic. She was smiling and happy, hugging both her daughters to her. In the background, Michael and her father had their shirts off, striking bodybuilder poses. Emma couldn't remember who had taken the picture. It was before Grandma Tyndall had to come.

Taking a deep, shuddering breath, she felt a tear slide down her cheek. Wiping her eyes on a sleeve, she rose and headed for the kitchen, her mourning, though not her fears and doubts, over for the moment.

ೞ

The following afternoon Emma was summoned to the school office by Sister Joseph.

"Sit down, Emma," the principal nodded at an empty chair positioned in front of her austere desk. "You're not in any trouble," she added, "but as I've been unable to get through to your grandmother, I thought I should speak to you before the dismissal bell."

"Grandma Tyndall wasn't feeling well last night, Sister."

Her grandmother had come in sometime after nine o'clock and had been unsteady on her feet. Assuring her granddaughter that her father should be home in a few days, she had staggered off to bed trailing alcohol fumes.

Emma hadn't bothered awakening her that morning, pouring cereal and making toast for her siblings, which she often did in any event.

"I'm sorry to hear that," Sister Joseph replied, her white blouse and grey veil crisp and fresh in contrast to her worn, crumpled features. "You've had a lot to deal with recently, haven't you?"

By this, Emma understood that Sister Joseph meant her father's suicide attempt.

"Yes," she answered.

"I'm afraid I have to add something else. It seems your brother has been in another fight. This time it was in the locker room of the gym, and he split the other boy's lip pretty badly."

When Emma failed to respond, the senior nun added, "I know that it's been a difficult year for him, too. Ordinarily, three fights in two months would draw a suspension, but I'm going to waive that for mandatory counseling on Thursdays during gym class. I think he needs some help right now, wouldn't you agree?"

Emma nodded, then asked, "Was he hurt?"

"A few bumps and bruises… but that's it. He's quite the scrapper, your brother—the other boy was three years his senior." Sister Joseph smiled at the tired-looking girl. "You'll talk to him about all this, won't you? About all this fighting? He'll listen to you, I think."

"Yes, Sister," Emma agreed, "I will."

"Tell your dad, too, when he's back home and feeling better. He'll want to know."

"What was the fight about, Sister Joseph?"

Sighing, the nun replied, "I was so hoping you wouldn't ask that." She studied Emma for several moments before answering. "Aidan Fischer made an unkind remark about your mother."

"What did he say?" Emma inquired, though she was certain she already knew. It was what all the fights were about.

"It's not important…"

"Is he being punished?"

"Of course, he is."

"Not enough, I bet."

"*That* is enough," Sister Joseph halted her with an upraised hand. "I'm certain your brother will fill in the details for you, if pressed."

"Did you know my mother, Sister Joseph?"

"Yes, of course… but not well. I only knew her as our school nurse, and she left shortly after I took the helm here."

"Did you fire her?"

The old nun folded her large, veiny hands together on her desktop. "Why do you ask that?"

"Because she said that you did… *and* because everyone in town says that Mom slept around. Was that why she was fired, Sister Joseph?" Emma felt the pressure of hot tears behind her eyes. "Could that be why she was killed?"

A bloodied Christ looked down on them from his crucifix on the wall.

"My dear child… how you all must suffer. No, I didn't fire your mother. She resigned." After a moment's hesitation, she added, "She led me to believe that in the near future she would no longer need to work."

"Not work…?" Emma repeated, dazed. "Mom and Pop were always fighting about how we could barely make ends meet—I don't understand, Sister."

"Your mother was not always… straightforward, Emma. She saw things in a different way than many of us."

"What do you mean? Are you saying Mom was a liar?"

"Nothing of the sort. I'm only telling you this because I know what you are trying to do—you want someone to answer for your mother's death. But justice can only be founded on truth, and neither of us knows what that is in this matter. Please leave these things to the police and look after your family, Emma—they need your strength. Pray to Our Blessed Mother to protect and guide you. She will, you know."

"I already have, Sister," Emma answered, rising, her face flushed with anger and shame. "I have prayed very, very hard."

☙

The three of them watched the small camp of ragged tents and lean-tos through a screen of low brush. Around them the woods, thick with oak, aspen, and sassafras, had begun to turn with the season.

"Is that him?" Kaitlyn asked.

Emma was studying the grainy photo from the old clipping, her eyes darting back and forth from man to picture. "No…" she answered, "… I don't think so."

The few men who had crawled and staggered out from their makeshift shelters appeared dazed and cold. Some walked about in circles slapping their biceps as if to restore circulation; others remained stationary, having found small patches of sun to stand in, swaying to and fro.

The children had waited the large part of Saturday morning for the camp's occupants to stir. Emma knew that Grandma Tyndall wouldn't miss them, as she was spending her time at the hospital, having informed the kids that their dad was too fragile yet to see them.

"That's him," Michael declared, pointing at one of the last men to emerge into the trash-strewn clearing.

Emma double-checked her photo. "Yes," she agreed.

Sheldon Hand was one of the walkers, moving about, hugging himself, and cursing loudly at the brisk morning. Like the rest, he was unshaven, his clothes ill-assorted and loose-fitting. Nothing about him appeared clean, and his movements were erratic and ceaseless.

"Venial… venial… venial…" Kaitlyn repeated after each new string of curses.

"Hush," Emma warned her.

Suddenly, Sheldon bore down on an older man, shoving him to the ground and going through his pockets. "Goddamnit… goddamnit," he kept saying, coming up empty time after time.

"Help… help!" the older man cried, while the scuffle was ignored by the rest of the indigents.

A corpulent woman in her sixties wearing a sequined leotard came out of one of the tents, her white, dimpled thighs and buttocks dotted with sores and insect bites. "Screw him!" she cackled at the fracas. "He's a sonofabitch!"

Rising, Sheldon kicked the other man in the ribs and began to walk away from the camp in the children's direction.

"Let's stab him!" Kaitlyn exclaimed, though no one had brought a knife.

"No… everyone stay still! He hasn't seen us," Emma ordered, wishing she could have left Kaitlyn at home. The "plan" she had come up with now seemed both foolish and dangerous.

Michael faded back into the bushes.

Sheldon almost passed them by, but the bright red of Kaitlyn's sweater caught his attention.

"Hey!" he cried, bending down to peer through the intervening brush with bleeding eyes. "Who're you girls? What are you doing here?" When they didn't answer, he demanded, "Do you have any money… or cigarettes? You better tell me!"

Before Emma could think what to say, he began to make his way toward them.

"Stop!" Emma commanded, standing up and placing herself in front of Kaitlyn. "If you don't, my brother will knock you in the head."

Sheldon paused to study the situation. "What brother? You ain't got no…"

He had already started to turn when Michael swung the oak branch he had found hard into his shoulder, knocking him off balance and onto one knee. Before he could rise the boy rushed at him, the makeshift cudgel held high.

"Don't!" Hand screamed.

"Stay down," Michael warned him.

"Who the hell *are* you kids?"

"You don't need to know that," Emma took control again, heart pounding. "All you need to do is answer my questions. If you do… and tell the truth… you'll get this." She revealed the bottle of Canadian Club she had taken from her father's workshop. It was three-quarters full.

"You didn't have to hit me," Sheldon whined, rubbing his sore arm. "Let me have a drink." He reached reflexively for the bottle and winced with pain. "I think it's broke."

"How did you know Sylvia Tyndall?" Emma asked.

"Who…?"

"The woman who was murdered near here."

"I didn't know her… I tol' the cops that over and over. She was nothin' to me."

Michael hoisted the branch higher, warning, "You better answer right, or I'm gonna bash your head in."

Even Emma could see that he meant it.

Cowering, Sheldon cried, "It's the goddamn truth! I just saw her by the tracks… like she was waiting for someone… just standing there."

"Did you speak to her?" Emma persisted.

"No… why should I speak to that bitch? I don't go lookin' for…"

Michael hit him hard in the arm again. "Don't call her that, you bastard!"

"Ow… goddamnit!" Sheldon screamed, clutching his bicep, but managing to scrabble a few feet away before Kaitlyn blocked his path, a large rock in her hand. "You're her kids… ain't cha?" he cried. "Well, I'm tellin' the truth! I just *ast* her for some money, that's all!"

"Like you asked us?" Emma countered.

"No! No! You kids just scared me, that's all. No, I ast her polite-like, but she tol' me to get away from her, so I did—end of story!"

"Venial," Kaitlyn pronounced, lofting the rock to shoulder height.

"*What the hell are you kids doin'?*" demanded a voice from behind them.

Startled, they turned as one to find the fat lady in the leotard scowling at them.

Taking advantage of this, Sheldon leapt to his feet, rushing past his captors and into the woods.

All Emma could think to say was, "Run!"

Watching them flee, the woman noticed the liquor bottle Emma had dropped in her panic. Picking it up with a grunt, she toasted their departure with the black and yellow smile of an old piano keyboard.

※

"You could have seriously hurt that man," the policeman told them, sitting across from the children who were side-by-side on the sofa.

Emma, Michael, and Kaitlyn had barely recovered their collective breath when Officer Douglass knocked on the door.

Still shocked at what had happened—what they were capable of—Emma had spun wild-eyed on her siblings. "I'll do the talking!" she had hissed before opening it.

"He could've pressed charges, you know," the officer continued, a troubled look on his kind features as he gazed from face to face.

Emma nodded primly, hands folded, as if she might begin to pray. Michael's face was closed, impassive, while Kaitlyn appeared bored and unconcerned.

"He came at us," Emma said, which had some truth to it.

"But why were you there in the first place? That's no place for you kids to be."

"We were collecting leaf samples for my science class."

"He said that you were questioning him about your mom's death," Officer Douglass countered. "Is that true?"

"It came up when I realized who he was." Emma could hardly believe how easy it was to lie.

"It came up…?"

"Yes, sir."

"He had an alibi, you know," Officer Douglass said after a moment. "Several people at the camp said that he was with them during the time of the…" he glanced at Michael and Kaitlyn, "…the incident."

"He's a big, fat liar," Kaitlyn declared.

"They're all afraid of him—they'll say anything he wants them to," Emma countered.

"How would you know that?"

When she remained silent, he added, "Be that as it may, you kids are to stay away from him, you understand?" He looked to each of them for acknowledgement.

Each nodded in their turn.

"Alright, then," the big man said, rising to his feet. "You tell your grandma to call me when she gets home, okay?"

Emma took the card with his number on it and nodded once more.

Standing in the doorway he looked back at the silent trio and added, "We're still working on the case, you know."

As he closed the door behind him, Emma shrugged.

✧

After Sunday Mass, Emma led her brother and sister into the cemetery behind the church. Father Rodrigo had allowed her to select flowers from the altar for the occasion.

When they arrived they found their mother's grave adorned with a fresh bouquet of long-stemmed roses.

Kneeling to examine the glass vase that contained them, Emma found a small envelope with the florist's name and address attached with a twist of wire. Snatching it off, she removed the card and read, "Love you, miss you always." There was no signature.

It was not her father's handwriting.

"What's it say?" Kaitlyn leaned over her trying to see.

"Who's it from?" Michael asked at the same time.

"Nothing... I don't know. It's not signed," Emma replied, feeling as if she had been slapped in the face. She shoved the envelope into her pocket remembering the poem that had recently been there, and now lay hidden in the "evidence" box beneath her bed.

Picking up the vase she flung the expensive flowers at the foot of her mother's grave, then placed their own lesser offering in it.

"That looks better," she pronounced.

Taking her brother and sister's hands in her own, they stood in silence, linked by their flesh and common purpose.

Kaitlyn broke the hush by saying, "We should be happy—Mom's in heaven. Right?"

Pulling them both to her in unconscious imitation of her bedside photo, Emma embraced her siblings, answering, "Yes… yes, of course she is."

***

Leaving her brother and sister at the library after school, Emma went to the florist shop. Situated in a white and green-trimmed building on Mercantile Street, her entry was announced by an old-fashioned bell over the door. She had remained in her school uniform for the task at hand.

"Hello there, young lady, what can I do for you?"

Standing behind the counter wearing a white jacket and gardening gloves, the thin, bespectacled florist was arranging his latest creation.

"Someone left a bouquet on my mother's grave but forgot to sign the card. My father and I want to thank them, but don't have a name or address. Could you help us, please?"

The request appeared to catch the florist off guard, his smooth face pursing in thought. "The arrangement was from this shop?"

"Yes," Emma confirmed with a smile, "the envelope said so. It was a beautiful arrangement of roses with baby's breath, in an emerald-green glass vase. My mom would have loved it."

"I'm so sorry for your loss," the shop owner replied. Then, as if having made his mind up, he smiled a little and said, "Well, we do sell quite a few roses here, of course. When was the funeral—Saturday?"

"No, sir," Emma answered. "We lost Mom a year ago. I'm sure they were left for the anniversary which was last Thursday… or maybe even this past weekend, as the flowers seemed very fresh."

"Oh…" he murmured, his face contracting once more with the unexpected answer. "Well… since they didn't go to the funeral home, or the church, the order will be in with the dailies." He tapped a key on his desktop computer and the screen glowed into life. "Thursday, you say?"

"Or Friday or Saturday…"

"A dozen…?"

"Yes, sir."

"Well… you're in luck… maybe. I have only four orders that match that time frame." He glanced over the screen at Emma. "Think you'd recognize the name? It's probably a relative or a neighbor, you know."

"I think so," Emma answered. "I sure hope so."

At the fourth, she nodded.

"Friends of the family, or relatives?" he asked, delighted at his handiwork.

"Friends," Emma confirmed, forcing herself to smile back. "Mr. Fischer and his family have been our neighbors for years and years, so I won't need the address. Thank you. My dad will be so happy to know."

Stepping out into the fresh air after the cloying aroma of the flower shop, Emma experienced the same sense of vertigo that she had upon finding her father dangling from the rafter—had it been just four days before? Aidan Fischer was the boy who had said something "unkind" about her mother, and whose lip Michael had split. The Fischers had not even attended her mother's funeral. They hardly knew them.

☙

On Tuesday, their father was released from the hospital and was home upon Emma and Kaitlyn's arrival from school. Michael was still at soccer practice.

"Don't get him talking," Grandma warned. "The doctor said the swelling will take some time and not to tire him."

Making no reply, Emma brushed past her into her father's bedroom followed by her sister. Seeing him sitting up in bed, the room dimmed to twilight by the drawn curtains, she flung her thin arms around him, squeezing tight. "I love you, Pop," she wept into his ear. "We all love you!"

"Love… you… too," he croaked, taking her by the shoulders to study her. "All… of… you."

Emma could see that he hadn't shaved in days, and his eyes were pouchy and swollen. The bandage around his neck concealed the rope burns.

Kaitlyn reached out and tugged on a lock of his long, greasy hair. "Your hair is dirty," she observed, then kissed his bristly cheek. "Ow… that stings," she added, wiping a sleeve across her lips.

"Why, Pop?" Emma asked in a whisper. "Why?"

Shaking his head a little he began to cry, then covering his face with his big hands turned away from the girls, saying only, "Miss… Mom…"

"Suicide is a mortal sin," Kaitlyn told him. "Sister Benedict told us that."

"Hush," Emma commanded her. Turning back to her father, she placed a hand on his quaking shoulder, stroking him. "You just rest, Pop, and don't worry. Everything will be okay. I promise. Now get some sleep."

Rising, she led Kaitlyn out of the room, closing the door behind her.

"Now look what you've done," Grandma Tyndall remarked, having monitored everything from the doorway.

"You don't know what you're…" Emma began as the front door flew open and Michael staggered in holding his hand to his head. Blood was leaking through his fingers and onto the shoulder of his grass-stained soccer jersey.

"Michael!" Emma cried, rushing to him.

Grandma swayed as if she might faint. "Oh dear God," she muttered, "what next?"

"I'm okay," Michael snapped, pushing Emma away. "Don't make a big thing about it." He headed for the bathroom with the girls and Grandma following.

Wrenching on the cold water at the sink, he leaned over splashing the side of his head, staining the water pink as it drained. He had a deep cut to his ear.

"What did you do?" Kaitlyn asked.

"Nothin'," he answered. "Someone threw a rock at me as I was coming home."

"Where… who…?" Emma demanded.

"I don't know who," Michael admitted. "They were hiding in the woods by the tracks and I didn't see them."

Michael often followed the tracks of the disused railway home from practices. It bisected Shadow Lane, and had well-worn paths either side left by pedestrians and dirt bikes.

Grandma supplied a worn washcloth to Michael, instructing him, "Press that against the cut while I get the hydrogen peroxide. I think it's in your dad's room."

"Dad's home?" Michael asked, wincing as he applied pressure.

Nodding, Emma asked, "Near the hobo camp?"

"Pretty close."

When Grandma Tyndall returned they went silent.

Later that evening, as her siblings did their homework, Emma joined Grandma Tyndall in the living room. She was watching *Wheel of Fortune* and coaching the players from her armchair.

When she noticed Emma staring at her, she stopped and muttered, "We should've called the police about Mikey."

"Why didn't you?" Emma replied.

The older woman turned back to the game. "Didn't want to upset your dad, I guess. He's been through too much already."

Emma had never informed her of the incident with Sheldon Hand, and when Officer Douglass had called the house and left a message, she had deleted it.

"Why didn't you like Mom?"

Grandma's reddened eyes slid onto Emma and held. "What makes you think I didn't?"

The television roared at one of the host's quips.

"You didn't though, did you?" Emma persisted.

Taking a careful sip of her "evening highball," the old lady replied, "I love my son… he's *my* child, ya know. I don't like seein' him hurt."

"And our mom loved *us*," Emma countered. "So why didn't you like her?"

Missing the coaster with the sweating glass, Grandma Tyndall set it on the side table, with a smear of red lipstick on its rim. "I know she did. But when she hurt Jimmy, I had a hard time with that."

"How… hurt?"

A groan arose from the audience as the wheel landed on bankrupt.

"I suspect you know how—you're not a little girl anymore."

"Did Pop do it, Grandma? Did he tell you that?"

The older woman spun around, eyes blazing. "Is that what *you* think? Is that why you think he tried to hang himself?"

"No…" Emma replied, hating herself for doubting, for allowing those few lines of verse to poison her faith, "… but I have to know the truth—Sister Joseph says you can't have justice without truth."

The old lady glared at Emma for several moments longer before answering, "I never asked him, and even if he had of done it, I wouldn't tell ya. What good would it do anybody now anyway?" She brushed her glass with trembling fingers, tipping it over onto the carpet. "Damnit all—look what you made me do! Get me some paper towels!"

Rising, Emma remarked, "They're in the kitchen," then walked through the puddle on the way to her room.

☙

"She didn't tell me nothin'," Emma heard her grandmother saying to someone at the door. "And I didn't get no messages neither."

She knew without hearing his voice that it must be Officer Douglass.

"Emma!" Grandma Tyndall shouted. "You get your little behind in here… and bring your brother and sister too!"

They had all just arrived home from school and were in the kitchen eating snacks.

"I warned you I'd have to speak with your pop or grandmother," Officer Douglass reminded her as they marched into the living room. He looked as if he were already regretting the action.

"Yes, sir," Emma replied, staring down at the stained, lumpy carpet. "I must have forgot."

"There's no police action required," he picked up where he had left off with the older woman. "It's just a matter of protocol that a parent or guardian be informed. I'm confident there won't be a repeat of the incident."

Grandma Tyndall looked unconvinced. "I wouldn't bet on that with these kids."

"Well…" the big policeman smiled. "I'll take the chance this time."

Setting his hat on his head, he turned to go.

"Wait…" Emma stopped him, "… I want to show you something."

She held out the florist shop envelope in a trembling hand.

"Don't, Sis," Michael pleaded under his breath.

"What's this?" the puzzled cop asked, taking it from her.

"Someone left it on Mom's grave—with a vase of roses."

Officer Douglass opened the small envelope. After reading the few words on it he looked up from beneath his eyebrows at the girl.

"What the hell does it say?" Grandma Tyndall asked.

Ignoring her, Douglass said, "Why are you giving me this?"

"I think it's from the man who killed our mom."

"Why would you think that, Emma? There's not even a signature here."

"I know who sent it—it was Mr. Stephen Fischer," she replied, the trembling now in her voice. "I think he and Mom…"

"Sis… be quiet!" Michael demanded. "You don't know anything! Don't say anything about Mom."

"What's she going to say?" Kaitlyn asked.

"Nothin'…"

"I'll take this to the detectives working your mom's case," Douglass interrupted them, thinking over the possible implications of what he had been given. Turning to Grandma, he added, "We may need for Emma to come down to the station later, Mrs. Tyndall."

The older woman nodded as he backed out the door. "I hope you're happy with all the trouble you're causing," she scolded the girl.

Michael stomped off to his room.

"Why's everybody mad?" Kaitlyn asked.

༄

After verifying her information with the surprised florist, the detectives brought Stephen Fischer in for questioning. Sitting in another room, separated from the interview by a cinderblock wall, all Emma could hear was the rumble of male voices, followed by lengthy silences. Officer Douglass had volunteered to keep her company as Grandma Tyndall was left in charge of Michael and Kaitlyn. Her dad was still recuperating in his dim bedroom, his knowledge of the current events kept just as dim by his mother.

It was almost eleven at night when the door to the tiny room opened. Detective Gavin Wolfe edged his heavy body into the room, closing the door behind him. Taking in the frail girl with his bulbous, bloodshot eyes, he announced, "He's admitted that he had... uh... that he knew your ma, Emma."

Emma felt her body tautening, her nerves beginning to sing.

"But when it comes to killing her... he says, no... he never would've done that... and that he *didn't* do it."

"He's lying," Emma breathed, leaning forward. "I bet Mom was going to break up with him. That's why he did it!"

Running a hand over his short, reddish hair, Detective Wolfe shook his head. "His story is that he broke up with her cause his wife got wind of it." Wolfe shrugged, his round face puckering. "We've got no witnesses, or physical evidence tying him to the scene, Emma... and his wife's alibiing him for the time of the murder. We're gonna have to let him go."

"No!" Emma cried. "He'll just run away now!"

"He wouldn't get far," the detective promised her. Nodding at Officer Douglass, he went out of the room leaving the door open.

"Let's get you home now, Emma. It's getting late."

As Officer Douglass escorted her through the lobby, she saw a woman and a boy, their faces red and puffed with crying. The boy sported a swollen lip. She shared two classes with Aidan Fischer and recognized his mother from school functions and Mass. Both turned away as Emma went by.

༒

In the small hours of the morning, after what seemed an eternity of tossing and turning, Emma felt herself, at last, drifting off to sleep. Across the room, Kaitlyn snored and mumbled in her bed.

Outside, the wind picked up, lashing the branches of the trees in the backyard.

Sinking by grey layers deeper into sleep, she became aware of a small noise—a sliding, slithering sound. She pictured Kaitlyn slipping out of her bed to go to the bathroom down the hall. The wail of the wind seemed to grow louder.

"Kaitlyn…?" Emma murmured in her drifting down.

There was no answer, and she sank several degrees deeper into unconsciousness.

A cold breeze played across her face, riffling her hair. Frowning, she pulled the blanket higher.

Then, like an alarm sounding, she remembered that the window had been closed.

As her eyes flew open something large and soft was pressed onto her face. The most she could manage was the beginning of a scream.

With arms and legs thrashing, she struggled to escape the suffocating pressure, but even this was hindered by blankets made taut and unyielding by the weight of her attacker who straddled her.

As she began to black out, Emma saw her father once more hanging in his workshop, her mother's casket at the foot of the altar surrounded by flowers, her brother with his bleeding ear leaning over the sink, heard Kaitlyn asking, "Do they say who killed Mom?"

Then suddenly, the pressure was gone, and air came flooding over Emma like a wave, cooling and filling her lungs with returning life. Sound followed like a thunderclap, startling and loud, full of confusion. Her eyes flew open to a brilliantly lit room.

"I hit him with my field hockey stick!" Kaitlyn crowed, grinning down at her sister's face while brandishing the makeshift weapon. "Cracked him in the head!" Behind her the window was wide open, the wind rushing through the room, Michael leaning out of it.

Grandma Tyndall was crying out from down the hall, "What is it now? What's going on?"

Pop stumbled in, his face a mask of confusion and fear. "What happened?" he rasped.

Turning, Michael cried, "Someone tried to kill Emma, but he got away. Call the cops, Dad!"

When his father hurried over to Emma instead, gathering her up into his arms, Michael swept past them to make the call himself.

"Are you alright?" he asked, peering down into her white face.

Still panting, her heart racing, all Emma could manage was a nod.

"The police are on the way!" Michael shouted from the kitchen.

"Who?" Emma demanded of Kaitlyn. "Who was it?"

"I dunno," she answered with a shrug. "It was too dark."

෴

For the second time within twenty-four hours Emma was in the police station. This time, however, the entire family had been asked to wait in the lobby with her. Officer Douglass came out to meet them.

Instead of asking them in he looked around the otherwise empty, four a.m. lobby, pulled a molded plastic chair out from the wall, and sat opposite them. He appeared to be thinking very hard about something.

"After we responded to your house," he began, leaning forward, "we brought in a K-9 unit from the sheriff's department. The dogs got a good scent from the pillow and picked it up again outside the bedroom window. You won't be surprised, I'm sure, that they led us straight to the Fischer home."

"I knew it," Emma exhaled, vindicated.

"You've arrested Stephen Fischer?" her dad asked, having been told of the flowers, the earlier interview.

"No, we haven't, Mr. Tyndall."

"Why not?" Emma cried, but Douglass held up a hand.

"Because we've arrested his son, Aidan, instead."

Emma and her family stared at the officer in silence.

"We found he had a sizable cut to his scalp when we arrived," he explained.

"Ha, ha!" Kaitlyn crowed, breaking the spell. "That was me!"

"That dick!" Michael erupted. "Is this because of our fight? Is that why he went after Sis? I'm gonna kill…"

"We're charging him with that," Officer Douglass stopped him.

Looking from one to the other of them, he took a breath, then added "… and with the murder of Mrs. Tyndall… your mother."

Emma felt as if she couldn't breathe. "What…? I… Mom?" she managed.

"I don't understand," her dad said. "Why would he do that? Why would that… that *boy* kill Sylvia?"

"He found out about the… about Mrs. Tyndall's relationship with his father," Officer Douglass went on, "heard his parents arguing over it numerous times, his mother threatening divorce. Apparently, when he discovered his dad hadn't broken things off like he promised—that, in fact he was planning to leave them—

Aidan decided to do something about it… something terrible. You all know what that is already."

Turning to Michael, he said, "And he was the one that hit you with the rock."

"But why Emma?" Mr. Tyndall asked.

"He saw her at the police station earlier and figured she had something to do with his dad being brought in about the murder. He had already killed for him once, I guess he thought it might work a second time, as well."

"And his parents…?"

"As far as we can determine, until tonight, they knew nothing of what he'd done."

"Dear God…" Mr. Tyndall whispered, "… dear God in heaven…"

Taking her father's trembling hand into her own, Emma said, "I knew you'd never hurt mom, Pop… I *always* knew it in my heart," and for the first time since her mother's funeral, she wept without restraint.

☙

As the sun rose over the October cemetery, Emma, Michael, and Kaitlyn stood once more at their mother's grave. With her jacket pulled tight against the chill, dawn breeze, Emma turned to the others and said, "Now that we have justice for Mama, there's still one more thing we have to do."

"What?" Kaitlyn inquired, plopping down onto the damp grass. "I'm tired."

"We have to forgive her," Emma answered, ignoring the complaint. "She hurt us, and now we have to forgive her so we can be happy again."

"I hate her," Michael muttered. "I'm glad she's dead."

"No, you don't," Emma corrected him. "You're just mad. We're all mad. We've been mad for a whole year… and sad, too. But you do love her, Michael. We all do."

Reaching over, she took her brother's hand in her own, and with the other pulled Kaitlyn to her feet. "Come on," she ordered them, dragging them along to the cross that bore their mother's name.

Retrieving the rosary they had sworn their oath on from her pocket, she draped it over the crucifix, saying, "Go on… tell her. You know you want to."

And one at a time, they did.